Diary of a
SUPER GIRL

BOOKS 7, 8 & 9

John Zakour & Katrina Kahler

D1444390

Table of Contents

Book 7

Boyfriends and Best Friends Forever!

The Battle

I stood ready and waiting in the battle room of BMS labs. I took a deep breath and then another. Kayla stood opposite me glowing with power. I knew my dad, Hana, Jason, and Tanya were watching from the control room. They were anxious to see how Kayla or Kay as she called herself would fare against me. Or maybe it was the other way around? Maybe they wanted to see if *I* could stand up against *her*.

"Let's see what you got, Super Teen!" she called in a challenging and taunting voice.

I took a few deep, cleansing breaths. Yep, this was weird. Just a couple of days ago Kayla was a little eight-year-old girl with awesome but uncontrollable time powers. Her body and mind just didn't have the maturity to handle that kind of power. That's when her sister, Tanya, and my dad the brilliant scientist, as well as his robot girlfriend, Hana, all came up with the fantastic idea to age Kayla. They wanted to ensure her body was mature enough to handle her raw power. I do believe my BFF Jason put up some argument, but he gave up fast, figuring there really was no other way. It probably didn't help that Jason was now going out with Tanya. That made him less likely to be the voice of reason. Reason tends to fly out the door when love is involved.

So, here I was standing 100 yards away from the newly aged and improved Kayla. She was dressed in a purple jumpsuit and ready for action.

"Are you scared of me?" she called out with a confident grin.

My computer interface, MAC, whispered to me, "I wouldn't blame you if you were. Yesterday, during testing, Kayla glared at three 20-foot-tall killbots and turned them into 2-inch tall windup toys. She keeps them in her room now."

I summed up the situation. Sure, Kayla had a ton of time control power. I had to admit that was an awesome kind of power. I often found myself jealous of her sister, Tanya's control over that power. But, here's the thing…even though Kayla was now older, she still didn't have a lot of control yet. Sure, on one hand, she might be more dangerous than she was before, but I didn't want to think about that. There was something else in my favor. Tanya and Kayla didn't actually stop time, they distorted it and slowed it down. Although I could be so much faster if I could use their time control powers, they still didn't have the amount of raw power that I did. Heck, you can drop a tank on my head and the tank would be dented, not my head.

Kayla and Tanya had awesome powers, but nope, nobody had more raw power than me. I, Lia Strong was the strongest being on Earth. And I was about to help Kayla figure that out.

Kayla motioned for me to come at her with her right hand. "Come on, Lia. Come on. I won't hurt you too much!" She snickered, "I promise."

I've been batting super beings for a while now. I knew that most fights were won in the first moments of the fight. I also knew that the second I made a threatening move towards Kayla, she would slow me in time. Then she'd try to hit me with time displacement ripples, which do sting.

"Remember," Dad called from the intercom, "this is a fight to the first knockdown. You two are on the same side. Don't forget that!"

Dad sounded a little worried. Like he wasn't sure that I could handle Kayla. Either that or he was afraid I might hurt her. No, Dad knew me too well. He knew I would never hurt Kayla. Instead, he feared Kayla wouldn't be able to control her power.

"Remember Kayla," Tanya said over the intercom. "This is only a test fight for both of you."

Yep, even Tanya was afraid for me.

Kayla looked up towards the observation both. "Can I at least knock her out?" she asked.

"No!" Dad, Jason, and Tanya all answered at once.

"At least not on purpose," the always-analytical Hana added.

Kayla turned back towards me. She gave me a confident smile. "I thought for sure you'd attack me when I had my back turned to you," she said. "And take advantage of me giving you the first move. After all, when you can control time you can afford to give your opponent the first shot."

"Sis, Lia is not your opponent," Tanya corrected from the booth.

Kayla rolled her eyes. "Just making a point, older sis!" she groaned. Kayla turned her eyes back to me. Her smile grew larger. "I see you're smart enough to be scared of me. You're probably thinking, 'Okay she's giving me the first move, I have to make it count'! Right?"

I answered her question with silence. Sure Kayla may now have the body and the mind of a fifteen to sixteen-year-old girl, but she didn't have the experiences. Yeah, her brain had been matured to allow her to cope better with her power, but she still didn't have the fighting skills that came from fighting. And for better or worse, I have been in a lot of fights over the past year. One thing I learned...even better than having the first move is to drive your opponent crazy. I knew my silence was eating away at Kayla. She was trying to cover her fear with bold words. But it wasn't working. I could smell her sweat. That's one of the downsides of having a super sense of smell. You get to smell a lot of horrible smells until you learn to blot them out. Now I was going to blot out Kayla.

Yep, she was powerful. But she still lived in the safety of this lab. I was the one out there wearing the costume and fighting crime and being a good example in the real world. With that came risks for sure. But I also gained the great benefit of helping people and helping myself grow. It's really true what they say...whatever doesn't kill you makes you stronger. Maybe not in the short run but it makes you mentally tougher. Ready for all challenges.

I opened up my left hand and dropped my left arm to my side. I wanted Kayla to see it was a non-threatening gesture. I opened my right hand and dropped my right arm to my side. My goal was to seem relaxed and carefree. But I actually began shaking a little.

Kayla pointed at me and laughed. "Ha! The great

Super Teen! The girl who has stomped super robots and alien invasions! She's scared of me! Me! Kayla Cane, the girl who was just a small child a few weeks ago. Now, Lia Strong looks at me and is scared. She knows she's never faced this kind of raw power."

"Hey sis," Tanya called from the observation booth. "We have the exact same powers!"

"I know," Kayla shouted back to her, not taking her eyes off me. "But mine are more untapped."

"That might not be a good thing!" Jason said over the intercom.

Kayla stood there and crossed her arms, "Come on Super Teen!" she mocked. "Let's find out why…"

I quickly clapped my hands together using super speed. The force of the clap sent a shock wave of energy outwards. The shock wave hit Kayla, taking out her breath while launching her at least fifty yards across the room. Kaya crashed down to the floor. She lay there motionless for a moment.

She raised her head. "Ouch…."

I leaped on top of her. I reached down and grabbed her nose then said, "Tweak!"

"Match over!" Dad shouted with far more joy in his voice than I would have anticipated.

Kayla looked up at me, her eyes a little glazed over.

"Kayla, don't stand until the medical team clears you," Dad ordered from above. "We want to make sure you don't have a concussion!"

One of the doors to the training area opened wide. A team of doctors and technicians rushed in with a medical cart.

Kayla pointed at them. They froze in their place.

I offered Kayla my hand. She accepted it. I helped her to a sitting position. Dropping down to a knee beside her, I patted her on the back. "Good fight!" I said.

She laughed. "Ha, you kicked my butt in less than a

second. You made me over-confident then clobbered me before I even knew what had hit me. My sister is right. You're the most powerful one of us all!"

"It's just that I have the experience," I told her.

Kayla looked me in the eyes. "Yeah, you do. But it's more than that Lia. You have a drive like no other. Your willpower is your strongest ability. I mean…you can basically force yourself to walk through a time stop. Tanya told me about that. But I had to see it to believe it." She laughed and touched the back of her head. "Actually, I had to feel it to believe it." She frowned, "and boy, do I feel it."

"Sorry," I said, "sometimes it's hard for me to gauge my power inside this lab!"

What I said wasn't really true. I had purposely hit her with a pretty powerful clamp. I needed to put her down fast and let her know I wasn't scared of her. Heck, not much scares me. I wanted her to know I was still the toughest person in town. Yeah, sure I might act soft and sweet, but I could still fart and drop a heard of rhinos from 100 yards away. Okay, maybe I shouldn't be too proud of that. But my point was…I have a LOT of power. I am not one to be taken lightly by anybody. Now, I hope Kayla will have a healthy fear of me. I didn't want her to fall on the ground trembling when she saw me. (Though that might be kind of cool…nah…that would grow old fast.) I just wanted her to grant me the respect I deserved. And I think I did that.

"Is the room spinning around?" Kayla asked me.

I laughed out loud. "Nope, but you'd better unfreeze the med staff."

"Right!" Kayla said. She snapped her fingers. The medical personnel began moving again.

A bald doctor reached us first. "Please step back, Lia, give the patient room to breathe."

I stepped back. I sniffed my underarm just to make sure he wasn't talking about me having a deodorant fail. Nope, my armpits still smelled fresh and clean. I had literally taken Kayla out without even working up a sweat, not even a nervous sweat. I was so confident. And, man, that felt good!.

My dad, Hana, Tanya, and Jason followed the medical staff into the room. They each had wide smiles on their faces. I fought hard not to frown when I saw Jason and Tanya holding hands. My first thought was…Wow! Not very professional! My second thought was…Wow! How petty of me. My third thought was…Jason and I are just friends, BFFs, I have no right to say who he can date and who he can't. I have no business being jealous. Yet, watching them hold hands hurt me way more than the time those aliens dropped a mountain on me. I knew it shouldn't but it did.

Of course. it didn't help that my dad and Hana were also together. It wasn't official or anything but by the way he treated her and the way she responded, it was obvious they'd become a pair. I was glad for Dad. Although, I was also a little jealous that he'd just come into my life and now I had to share him with this woman. Actually, this was a woman he'd made himself. Which kind of made it worse. I tried not to think about that.

"Fine job, Lia!" Hana told me. "Your knowledge of how to best harness your skills grows daily."

"Thanks," I replied.

Hana's eyes opened wide. "That was an assessment, not a compliment," she said coldly.

"Still, I will take it as one," I smirked.

"And so you should," Dad said, giving me a pat on the head. Not the most normal or heartfelt gesture, but for my dad, this was pretty much a full display of emotion. "Kayla has such great potential power but you licked her easily!"

"That she did," Tanya said, turning to Kayla. "I told you Lia was the best. We can control time, but I believe it takes more than that to stop her."

"Yes, I see that now," she said.

"Is the room still spinning?" A female doctor carrying a clipboard full of data interrupted.

"Yes, it definitely is," Kayla nodded.

The doctor showed Kayla two fingers. "How many fingers am I holding up?" she asked.

"Six!" Kayla said proudly. She sighed. "Oh, that can't be right...."

"She may have a slight concussion," the doctor told my dad. "We will take her for a head scan and do a thorough examination, just in case."

"Good idea," Dad said.

"Sorry," I said to Kayla. I actually did feel sorry. I wanted to win our battle but I didn't mean to hurt her. Apparently, I don't have quite as much control of my power as I like to believe.

Kayla forced herself to grin. "It was a learning experience for me. I'll be ready for you next time."

"If there is a next time," Tanya said protectively. "Remember, Kay, she took you out with a clap. If she focused her heat vision on you, you'd be dust."

"I would never use heat vision on a person!" I said.

Tanya grinned at me. "I know! That's what makes you, you! I just wanted my little sister to be aware of how lethal you could be."

"Plus," Hana added, "if she wanted to, I'm sure she could stop all of you with a fart! The force of the fart would not only knock you over, it would also drive all the breathable air from the room. It would be silent and deadly. You would be helpless on the ground before you had a chance to react."

I held up a hand. "Once again, I would never do that!" I said.

Hana looked at me. "I just felt it was my obligation to make that clear. Your power, Lia Strong, should not be taken lightly."

"Believe me, it's not!" I said.

Dear Diary: Man! Talk about mixed emotions. I feel great taking Kayla down a notch. She's so confident and almost arrogant. I get it...power can do that to you. The power that she and Tanya have are awesome. But Kayla still needs to learn how to use and harness her power. Great power accomplishes nothing without wisdom and experience. Well, at least nothing good. I have control of my power and I'm learning more and more control each day. I don't care what silly Hana says. I'm not going to purposely or accidentally fart and drop the entire town. Sure, it's tempting sometimes. But it would be a lot easier, safer and far less embarrassing to do that with my command voice. I could just yell, "Sleep!" and everybody would. But I don't do that either. I am in control of my powers. I use my powers for good. I am also constantly practicing using my powers. Maybe that's why I don't have a proper boy crush in my life! I'm just too busy working on me. Yeah, that's the reason. At least, that's what I'm telling myself for now!

BFFs and Boyfriends

After a quick shower (that I didn't really need), I decided to make a surprise visit to my grandma Betsy's house. I hadn't seen Grandma B in a while. Since we Strong women age so slowly, we tend to avoid being seen together in public too much, so as people don't get suspicious. Grandma, Mom, and Great Grandma can all pass for sisters. In fact, Grandma and Great Grandma actually call themselves sisters but that's a bit freaky for my brain.

I had MAC check to make sure Grandma B was at home before I jumped there. Grandma B said she always loved seeing her favorite granddaughter. (I am her only granddaughter but that is beside the point.) I thought she'd really enjoy a surprise visit.

Leaping through the air towards her house felt exhilarating. Nothing and I mean nothing, feels freer than flying (well...gliding with some control) through the air. Now I know why birds are always singing. Being able to fly is one of the best feelings ever.

I was so grateful that Grandma lived on a farm outside of town so I could leap there without anyone noticing. Actually, both Grandma and Great Grandma lived on the farm's grounds but in separate houses. Great Grandma was away in China. So I figured Grandma might be a little lonely (hence the reason for my visit).

I landed on the ground next to her front porch and Mac switched me into my Lia clothing. I jumped up the stairs and knocked on the door.

"It's open!" Grandma shouted.

I walked into the kitchen and saw that she had the table set for two. A delicious aroma filled the room. How did she know I was coming?

"Oh honey, it's you," she said with surprise in her voice.

Nope, she had no idea I was coming.

"Grandma, is this a bad time?" I asked.

Grandma tossed off her apron and rushed over to give me a strong bear hug. "No, no, no! I always have time for my favorite granddaughter!" She dropped me to the ground. Pointing to the table she said, "Sit! Eat! Do you want some milk? Spaghetti and meatballs? Salad? Potatoes?"

The smell of her cooking was amazing and I eyed the platter of spaghetti hungrily.

"Ah, it looks like you're expecting company," I said slowly.

Grandma dragged me over to the table and forced me to sit. "Yes, but I always have room in my heart and at my table for you. Just let me set you a place." She moved at super speed to the cabinet and pulled out cutlery and a plate. She tossed it perfectly onto the table.

"Is Great Grandma coming home today?" I asked.

"Nope," she answered.

15

"Great-Great Grandma?" I asked.

"Nope," she answered. "Haven't seen her all month."

"So ah…" I asked uncomfortably.

Grandma leaned into me. "Honey, I have a gentleman friend coming over."

My eyes popped wide open.

"Dear, I'm old but not dead," she smiled.

"I know, I know, I know," I said. "But, I didn't think you were…"

"Dating?" she asked bluntly.

Alright, I've seen a lot of weird things over the last year. I've done a lot of weirder things. I've come across vampires, witches, and aliens. Yet somehow, none of that stuff bothered me more than my grandma dating. I don't know why. Sure she was old, but she wasn't that old. And being super, she still looked to be in her late 30's even though she must have been in her 50s. I felt my palms beginning to sweat. Yep, I'd worked up more sweat talking about my grandma's love life than I did when fighting a super girl who can control time. It was official. I had a really weird life.

Grandma snapped her fingers in front of my face. "Honey, talk please. Tony will be over soon and I would hate him to think that my granddaughter is mute. Of course, I'd better call you my niece. Hard to believe that aging slowly could cause problems. I guess I could tell him I had your mom when I was… 12? Nope, I don't think so! When Tony arrives, you're my niece." She gave me a little shake. "Hopefully, my talking niece…"

"I can talk," I said slowly.

"Good," Grandma said. "Is your blood sugar low? Remember that being super means we need a lot of calories each day."

I nodded. "Maybe my blood sugar is low. I haven't eaten for a while."

Truthfully, it wasn't. It was just that my morale was

as low as could be. Even Grandma had somebody special in her life. My grandma. My fifty or sixty-something grandma was dating! Yep, she had a better love life than I did. Man! Talk about a new low.

Grandma prepared a large plate of spaghetti and placed it in front of me. "I was hoping you'd be happier for me."

I forced a smile. "I am happy for you," I said. My smiled reversed. "It's me who I'm sad for." I looked at her, a tear welling in my eye. "I'm sorry Grandma, I shouldn't be acting like this... I'm not sad because you're dating. I'm sad because everybody is dating. Mom has Oscar. Dad has Hana. She's an android but a perfect looking one. Jessie has Tomas. And now Jason and Tanya are dating!" I said choking on the words.

"Your Jason?" she asked. "Your BFF?"

"Yes," I said.

"He's dating Tanya?" Grandma asked.

"Yes," I sighed.

"*The* Tanya. The really pretty older girl with cool superpowers?" Grandma asked.

"Yes!" I said.

Grandma looked off into the distance. "Wow! She's gorgeous. And such a catch. Good for him!"

"Not helping, Grandma," I said.

Grandma laughed. "I don't think you need help. Lia Strong, you are literally the most powerful person in the world. You can actually move mountains. You can move faster than a speeding bullet. You can generate energy. You have super pheromones and voice command ability. Your powers are pretty darn powerful!" she told me.

"Yeah, and I'm alone..." I groaned.

"You're not alone, you're just not dating. There is a difference."

I looked at her. Darn, Grandma was way smart. I did

have an entire host of people in my life. I had great friends, a cool dog, and amazing support people from my dad's company. I had my dad back in my life. I had three grandmothers. My mom was super, literally. I had really cool superpowers. I could freeze a lake with my breath, which meant I could ice skate in the summer. I had a super smart wrist computer communicator and I could make my outfit look exactly the way I wanted. I had a great dog...I know I already said that but he really is a cool dog. I really had no reason to feel sorry for myself. Yet somehow, I still did.

Grandma sat down and rolled up her sleeve. She put her arm on the table. She waved her fingers at me.

"Come on, girl," she said.

"Come on what?" I asked.

"Let's arm wrestle," she said, dead serious.

"Wait? Why?"

Grandma waved her fingers, taunting me. "Just to prove to you how strong I still am."

"Grandma, I know you're strong. I remember you lifting a cow to milk it...."

"Are you chicken?" she asked. "Afraid an old woman is going to hurt you?"

"No, of course not. I just don't want to hurt you. I am way super strong," I insisted.

She folded her arms like wings and began clucking.

"Ha! Ha! Very funny," I informed her. "But I am not arm wrestling you."

Grandma plopped her arm back on the table. She flexed her muscles and I watched them rippling with strength. "You win...you get dessert. I win...you do the dishes, without powers!"

I put my arm down on the table. I intertwined my fingers with hers. "You're on, old lady!" I said with a grin, so she knew I was mostly kidding about the old lady part.

"On the count of three, one..." she started pushing

firmly down on my hand.

It turned out that Grandma was even stronger than I thought. She drove my hand halfway to the table.

"You cheated!" I said, finally counteracting her initial move.

"No cheating in love, war and arm wrestling with someone a third your age," she said, exerting more force.

Though I felt the added effort on her part, my arm didn't budge. I had been ready for her push. My arm held its ground. I felt her apply more and more force. Even so, my arm didn't drop an inch. In fact, I started to push her arm back up.

"You think you're pretty strong!" Grandma said, sweat building on her forehead.

"I am kind of kicking your butt, even though you cheated," I grinned.

"Me, cheat?" she said. "I never..." without finishing that sentence she reached over and tweaked me on the nose. "Tweak!" she said.

I ignored her tweak and pinned her hand to the table, smashing through the tabletop.

"Oops," I said.

Grandma laughed. "I'm always replacing tables lately."

I chuckled. "Why did you tweak me?"

She shrugged. "Just wanted to lighten the mood and make you feel happier. Did it work?"

"It did." I sat back in the chair and pointed to her refrigerator. "Now, please bring me my dessert!" I ordered playfully as I started gobbling down my spaghetti. The arm wrestle had really given me an appetite. I certainly did feel better, although I wasn't sure why.

Grandma got up and bowed. "As you wish." She stretched out her arm. "I'm proud of you, you're not only as strong as a herd of bulls, but I couldn't shake your concentration."

"Funny, I also tweaked Kayla today after I knocked her out with a clap," I said.

"Great minds think alike," Grandma laughed, whipping together a delicious ice cream sundae with all my favorite flavors and bringing it to me.

"You think like me. You act like me. You're stronger than me. That's why I know you will be fine."

"Thanks, but I'm still without a boyfriend!"

Grandma sat next to me. "Come on, Jason is your BFF and he's a boy."

"I'm still stuck without a real boyfriend!" I said.

Grandma raised an eyebrow. "Are you jealous of Tanya?"

That's what I loved about my grandma. She was whacky, but man, she could get to the point. "Yes, a little," I admitted.

"Do YOU want to be romantic with Jason?" she asked, once again getting right to the point.

"No, maybe, maybe someday, I don't know. I'd maybe like that option in the future…maybe…" I told her.

"So it's a definitely-maybe then," Grandma said.

I shook my head yes and no. "I have no idea. I'm so confused."

Grandma put her hand on my shoulder. "You're a teen! You're supposed to be confused. Heck, I'm still figuring out what I want in a man… and I'm, let's just say, older than you are by a few years. But honey, you can't expect Jason to sit on his hands waiting for you. The boy is loyal but he still gets to have a life without you, the same as you do without him."

I sighed. My sigh messed up Grandma's hair. "Sorry," I said.

"Ah don't worry, Tony likes it this way!" she said with a smirk. Crazily enough, I didn't think she was joking.

Yep, my grandma had a much better love life than me. I was happy for her, but a little sad for me. Before I could wallow for too long, though, my super senses suddenly became alert.

"Uh oh," I said.

Grandma listened. She shook her head. "Sorry, my hearing isn't nearly as good as yours. What's going on?"

I stood up. "Bank robber at the Starlight City Third National Bank. I can hear the alarms." I shook my head. "Who would be dumb enough to rob a bank in my town?"

Grandma shrugged. "Maybe they're from out of town? Be careful honey!"

I switched my suit on. "I will!" I started towards the door. "I guess I will meet your Tony another day."

"I'm sure you will," Grandma said.

Dear Diary: This is what my life has become. I am happy about a robbery because it takes my mind off my terrible social life.

Fear Factor

I landed on the concrete stairs of the Third National Bank. Glancing through the window I saw four clowns holding balloons and balls, robbing the bank. All the customers were lying on the floor, covered in some sort of glue. The trembling tellers were putting money into the clown's bags. I heard police sirens wailing in the distance. They would arrive quickly.

"Hurry Bozo!" one of the clowns ordered another. He looked at an oversized watch on his ankle. "We have three minutes to get in and out before the police come."

I pushed the door open and stormed into the room. "Seriously, guys! Robbing a bank in my town?"

"Of course we're not serious! We're clowns. But just because we aren't serious doesn't mean we can't really be robbing a back. We're doing it in a fun way. Now if you don't mind, we need to get this done before the police get here."

I felt pretty offended that they were more worried about the police than they were me.

"Do you guys have any idea who I am?" I asked.

"Some weird kid in a costume. Who probably doesn't have any money so she's not worth robbing," the middle sized clown said. "Now, if you don't mind, we have work to do."

"You Bozo's are going to jail!" I said, dramatically as I could.

A tall clown pointed to a middle-sized clown who was collecting money. "He's the only Bozo here! Come on, girl, we all have our own names, you know."

"Yeah, clowns are people too!" another clown said.

"Okay, fine," I told them, "but you still can't rob the

23

bank!"

The tall clown bowed to me. He looked up and smiled. "Actually, I think we can. It may not be legal but we can still do it."

"Okay, once again, fine, but I am going to stop you," I said. "I really don't want to hurt you clowns so I'd prefer if you would just give up!"

The tall clown laughed. I couldn't tell if it was a fake or sincere laugh.

The other three chuckled as well. They all pointed at me.

"Ha! You're almost as funny as we are!"

"Yeah, clowns don't give up!"

"Yeppers, clowning is a tough business. It's not for

those who give up!"

I looked around the bank. The people were all on the ground shaking and covering their eyes. This was not normal fear.

"What did you do to this people?" I demanded.

The tall white-faced clown frowned. "They didn't laugh at our jokes. So we made them scared."

"Yeppers," the one called Bozo said. "If we can't make you laugh we will make you cry. Laughter can be tricky. I know there is no such thing as a universally funny joke that absolutely everyone finds amusing. Though a kick between the legs in close."

"Falling off a horse is also close!" another clown offered.

"Farting in an elevator can get a lot chuckles too!" a different clown said.

The clowns all nodded in approval. When their heads bobbed up and down they made squeaking noises.

"Therefore, in conclusion, if we can't make them cry with laughter we will make them cry with fear!" the tall clown said, holding up an oversized finger.

Bozo grinned. "Same end result."

"I have to admit, I think clowns are pretty freaky. Why do you have to paint your faces white and have big fake smiles and wear huge oversized shoes? I mean how is that funny?"

"It's an art!" the four of them told me.

"People don't appreciate us any longer!" a short clown at the back said. Truthfully, I had only just noticed him.

"Yeah, they laugh *at* us, not with us!" another one of the clowns said.

I crossed my arms and tapped my boot on the floor. "Come on, you clowns, this isn't funny. Just give up now so I don't have to hurt you." I made a fist. "Trust me, I'm not clowning around here!"

The clowns all gave a collected sigh. A couple of them forced a giggle. The tall one pointed at me. "Oh, Ha, Ha! The little fake superhero made a joke! Clowns hate being the butt of jokes when we're not the ones telling the jokes."

I held up my hands to show them I wasn't a threat. (I've been doing that a lot lately.) My goal really was to talk them down, to convince them to give up without me having to pummel them. I really didn't like the idea of beating up a bunch of clowns. Sure, I found clowns freaky but others might like them.

The tall clown walked towards me. "You know, people think just because we wear fake smiles and make fools of ourselves, we are fools! But you know little girl, clowns can be smart too!"

I took a step back. "Wait, you guys really have no idea who I am?"

"I think it's whom I am," the tall clown corrected.

"No, I'm pretty sure it's…."

The tall clown squirted me in the face with his flower.

"Ha, Ha! Very funny!" I said.

"Wait for it!" the clown laughed.

"Oh, definitely wait for it!" the other clowns laughed in chorus behind him.

I picked the clown up with a finger. "This is going to hurt you way more than it hurts me!" I told him.

"Oh, so you are as strong as they say!" the clown giggled. "Good to know. Good to know. Glad I used a strong shot on you. I would have hated to waste it."

"So you guys have heard of me?" I asked, actually feeling a little relieved.

"Of course, Super Teen," the clown I held up in the air replied. "We wanted you to let your guard down. And it worked."

"What worked? You squirted me with water!"

"Wait for it!" the clown said, his creepy smile growing.

26

My brain shot into overdrive as wild thoughts suddenly began to spin in my head...

Oh no! Oh no! Oh no! I'm like the only teenage girl in the world without a boyfriend. I thought. I dropped the clown to the ground, he was no longer important. *I'm going to die alone. I'm so hideous! I can never kiss anybody because my breath will wilt them. If I lift up my arms at the wrong moment, I can knock them out with body odor and kill them. If anybody tried to give me a foot massage that would be the end of them. I can't even hug another person without crushing them. I'm a monster. No wonder I'm alone. I will always be alone. I don't deserve to be with anybody. I can't be with anybody. I'm a freak. I should fly to the moon and live there!? Wait, can I live in space? I don't know! I don't care! I can fly to an island in the middle of the ocean and live there alone. Yes, that's it, that's what I'll do. No wonder Jason prefers Tanya to me. She's not only way, way, way, way, way better looking, she has control of her power. I'm a mess, a complete and utter mess.*

"Super Teen snap out of this!" I heard the somewhat familiar voice of Jason's dad, Captain Michael's echo through the fog that was my brain.

"I got this, Dad," Jason said. Jason put his hands on my shoulder. "Super Teen you've been hit with some sort of fear liquid. It makes everybody that breathes it in feel fear."

"But wait, I'm Super Teen!" I said, noticing Jason had a mask over his face and was passing one to his dad.

"True, but even Super Teen needs to breathe," he replied. "And yes even Super Teen feels fear! You are human."

"What can I do?"

"Leap into the air and rotate really fast. That way, I think you can spin the liquid off you!"

I ran out through the doors. When I say through the doors, I actually ran right through them without opening them, leaving a Lia sized impression in the timber. Man, something else to worry about. I was truly a danger to all around me.

No, I wasn't. I mean I was, but I could control this because it was all in my head. The outdoor air hit my face. I bent my legs and leaped up into the sky. I held my arms out and began to spin. I saw globs of liquid flying off me. I couldn't be sure if it was sweat or that goop the clowns had sprayed me with. I held my breath to be on the safe side.

As I rose higher and higher my head become clearer and clearer. Those clowns had really got me. When I caught them again I was going to make them pay. For now, though, it was time to go home and regroup!

Dear Diary: Here's the deal...I know a lot of what I've been thinking, or at least the intensity of those thoughts, is due to me being covered in fear goo by those clowns. Next time we meet, I will get my revenge. Man, they may have been lousy clowns but they were way smart. They knew enough about my psyche to catch me off guard. They took advantage of my ego. Nope, that won't happen again! Plus, they'd had some scientific training. Without it, they wouldn't have been able to come up with such a nasty concoction. I hate it when people misuse science. But, like Jason always says, when it comes to science, you have to sometimes take the bad that comes with the awesome good.

The thing that really bothers me is that even though those fears are amplified, they are still my legitimate fears. I'm not saying they are rational, a lot of fears aren't. But they are definitely my underlying fears. I mean, I have to face facts…I am different, way stronger than the average person. I could actually hurt an average person if I got carried away and hugged them too tightly. I could even hug a grizzly bear and knock it out in seconds. Double heck, my mom, and grandmas are all super beings and I even knock them around with my breath. On a bad day, the slightest whiff of my shoes can drop them. Now I see why Jason is with Tanya. Tanya is always in control.

Time for Advice

Passing over my house, I noticed Oscar's car in the driveway. Yep, my mom must have been on a date too. Man, fate was really kicking me when I was down today. I certainly don't begrudge my mom having a love life. I only wish she wasn't dating the reporter that longs to find out my secret identity. As if life isn't complicated enough when you are super. But hey, my dad dates an android. So, I guess a nosy reporter is a step up.

Walking through the open back door, I found Mom and Oscar sitting at a candlelit table with servings of delicious food. It smelled so good! Yeah, sure I had eaten at Grandma's but that was over an hour ago. One of the cool things about being super is being able to eat a lot.

"Candlelight at 4 o'clock in the afternoon?" I asked. "I get why Grandma eats early, but why you two?"

"I go on the air at 6," Oscar said.

"I just got off a long shift so I am really hungry!" Mom said.

Oscar pointed at the food on the table. "I don't know how your mom does it. She works a ten-hour shift and still cooks a delicious meal?" Oscar turned to Mom with a wide grin. "Do you have super powers like Super Teen?" he asked jokingly.

"No, of course not," Mom said, batting her eyelashes like a kid.

"I've had a long crazy day!" I said. I pointed at Oscar. "Oscar go to work early. You'll find there's news today about Super Teen losing to a clown gang!"

Oscar's eyes glazed over. He stood up. "Sorry, honey, must rush to work. Must find out the scoop on this clown gang. Man, this is amazing." Oscar turned and ran out of the room. He then doubled back, kissed mom on the lips (gross) and ran out. I heard a car start and drive away.

I sat down at Oscar's untouched plate and began eating his meal. "Sorry, Mom, it's been a tough day. I had to use my voice command on him. I need some Mom time."

Mom took a bite of her steak. "You lost today? To a gang of clowns? Do you mean a group of jokers?"

I shook my head. "Nope, they were actually a bunch of clowns."

"Super clowns?" Mom asked.

"Nope, just regular clowns with exploding balls and glue guns and balloons... oh, they also had flowers that squirted fear goo," I said.

"Ah, fear. So that's how they escaped from you," Mom concluded.

"Yep!" I said leaning on the table. "It seems that being super strong doesn't make me fearless."

Mom grinned. "No honey, of course not. You may be superhuman but you are still human. Even you should have some fears. Fears can be useful. They can help us to be cautious. They can encourage us to find ways to improve." Mom hesitated, choosing her next words carefully. "So then, what are your fears?"

I groaned. "Being alone."

"Honey, you will never be alone. You're a superhero! Your dad runs a giant company with lots of people. They are all willing to work with you forever if needed. You have a lot of friends...Jason, Tanya, Tomas, Jessica, Lorie, Marie, Tim, Krista...I could go on...."

"I don't mean *alone*-alone, I mean alone *emotionally*," I sighed.

"Oh..." Mom said.

"Everybody else is paired up with somebody and I have nobody!"

"Well you're only 13... you have time... and being a

superhero does keep you busy," Mom lectured.

"True, but I still feel like I may never find anyone special… It's not easy being super," I moaned. "I can be dangerous around normal people. Maybe not in the short term but in the long term."

"Nonsense," Mom said. "I found your dad and now I have Oscar."

"True," I nodded, agreeing that there may actually be some hope for me. Mom found love so I could find love. But then it hit me. "You're not as super as I am…" I sighed. "I'm the 19th generation; the one born with all the powers, the most power. If I got married, my husband wouldn't be able to use the bathroom after me for hours without risking instant suffocation."

Mom smiled.

"You know it's true Mom! We still can't even keep any plants in my bathroom because they all die instantly. Before Dad invented the new ventilation systems for my bathroom, I used to leave my window open and one time I saw birds dropped from the sky. Even our neighbors fainted. And that was from 30 yards away!"

Mom stood up and put a hand on my shoulder. "Honey, there are always workarounds. I'm sure you and your future husband can have separate bathrooms. Or an even more improved ventilation system." She leaned in and hugged me. "But when love comes, you will find a way to make it work. Being super makes you stronger but not different."

I thought about Mom's words. They made some sense. After all, there were 19 generations of Strong women and they all had kids and family. Just because I was the strongest of them all, it didn't mean that I too, couldn't find somebody.

There was a knock on the back door. I sniffed the air. It was Jason. I sniffed again. He was alone. I felt a rush of relief.

"Come in, Jason," Mom and I both said at once.

"How do you know it's me?" Jason called from outside the door.

"Your scent. Everyone has a unique scent and we can recognize yours." I said. "Now get in here."

It was true. The more I became used to my powers, the more I was able to do tiny but helpful little things like identify people by their individual scents. It wasn't always the most pleasant ability but it was still a cool skill to have.

Jason turned the doorknob and walked in. "Why was the door unlocked? My dad says everybody should always lock their doors."

Mom and I just gave him our look.

Jason smacked himself on the forehead. "Oh right, you're both super. Sorry, it's been a long day. I've been working with my dad and BMS labs trying to figure out how that fear goo works. It's pretty high tech. It dissipates fairly quickly and seems to target the amygdala in the brain..."

"So it affects emotions?" Mom said, being all doctor like.

"Yes. But why it only triggers negative emotions, we're not sure," Jason said. "We just know these clowns are not ordinary clowns. They are either working for someone with a great deal of chemistry knowledge and the body, or one of the clowns has that knowledge himself.

"They seemed pretty odd," I said.

"A lot of smart people do seem odd," Jason said. "I know people who think I'm a bit odd."

"Good point," I said.

Jason grinned at me. "You could have said, *No Jason that's not true...*"

"I don't lie to my friends," I told him.

His grin grew. "Yep, that's one of your best features."

"So, what do I do next time I meet up with these clowns?" I asked, making a fist. "I guarantee you, there will be a next time and they won't get away!"

Jason looked at me. "That's easy! Don't breathe when you're around them."

"That's your expert brainiac advice...don't breathe?" I grumbled.

Jason nodded. "Yes, when you are around them. Hold your breath and don't talk. Maybe exhale their own goo back at them."

"Sounds like sound advice," Mom agreed.

"Okay, next time I run into those clowns I will hold my breath until I put them down!" I said.

"Perfect!" Jason said.

Dear Diary: I feel bad that I had to ruin mom's date evening, but there are times when a daughter needs her mom and this was one of them. Besides, I'm pretty sure Oscar loved the idea of reporting on the clown gang and trying to figure out who they were and where they came from. Maybe it will even get him off my case for once. After all, I really do help the city. That's all I really want... to make my mark in the world.

Hopefully, I won't be making my mark in the world alone. My talk with Mom was useful. If Mom could find Dad, then surely I can find love too. Is love right around the corner? Say at Jason's house? No, it isn't. At least not for now. But if life has taught me anything so far, it's that the only thing constant thing in life is change. Although my future may not be with Jason, I will find the right person for me, eventually. But if I don't, it doesn't mean I won't be happy! I don't need to define myself by being with somebody else. Sure, it would be nice, but it certainly isn't essential!

Being Dumped

The next day, I arrived at school determined to have a good day; or at least a better day than the one before. Truthfully, the bar wasn't set all that high. I mean, come on, I got my butt kicked by a bunch of clowns. My mom and grandma were on dates. My BFF is dating the perfect girl, whose sister I also battled yesterday. I grinned at that last thought. It was the high point of the day as I'd put her down easily. But the day had definitely gone downhill from there.

Entering the building, I found myself greeted by Krista and Tim, two of my best friends. They walked up to me, hand in hand. We're a couple now!" Krista shrieked, excitedly.

I forced myself to smile. "I'm so happy for you guys!" And I was...kind of...mostly. After all, Krista and Tim were very nice people and always supportive of me. They had my back when it came to regular kid stuff and that was important to me. I had to be Lia Strong first and Super Teen second. Super Teen was just a part of me, not who I was. I had to remember that. My powers were cool and awesome and all that jazz but they didn't define me. Regular non-super friends were important.

Gazing across the hallway, all my mind could see were couples. I spotted Lori's new boyfriend, Jayden, laughing and joking and flexing his muscles as he stood alongside her. He was a very cute track star.

Marie also had a new boyfriend, Wilson. A bit of a sci-fi nerd but a good guy and a good fit for Marie. Having a boyfriend was great for her because it taught her to control her power so she wouldn't accidentally turn him into cheese.

Yep, everywhere I looked, all I could see were happy, smiling couples. Then I heard. "Wait! You're breaking up with me?" I couldn't believe my ears. Those words were coming from Wendi Long, head cheerleader, head of the LAX team, and prettiest girl in the school. As a normal human, she was my biggest rival.

Turning, I saw Wendi with her mouth agape standing at her locker, staring at the most handsome boy in the school…Brandon Gold. Brandon had it all…he was tall, he was muscly and strong, he had soft brown hair, sparkling eyes, and to top it all off, he was nice. I almost thought he was too good for Wendi. He even seemed too good to be true.

Brandon lowered his head. "I'm sorry, Wendi. I don't want to hurt you but my family will be moving away soon and I thought it would be easier for us both if we broke up."

"I've never ever, ever been dumped!" Wendi shouted.

Brandon stayed calm. I'm not sure how he did it. "This isn't a dumping," he sighed. "You'll always be special to me. I just know it'll be better for us both if we aren't together; especially since we can't be together…."

Every girl in the hallway sighed too. Even I sighed. Brandon was so nice and so considerate. Okay, maybe his timing wasn't the best. He probably could have done this when they were alone, but I guessed he wanted to do it in public so Wendi couldn't make a big scene.

Sadly, being in public didn't stop Wendi. "How dare you break up with me!" she shouted. She stomped her foot towards Brandon. "I'm the one who says when a relationship is over!"

Brandon straightened himself up. "If you want to dump me, I am totally cool with that."

"Yes, yes, yes!" Wendi said. She pointed at Brandon. "Brandon, you're not worthy of all this!" she pointed up and down at herself. "I've kept you as my boyfriend just to be nice to you. But now it's over." She waved indifferently.

"Bye bye, you're gone!"

Brandon lowered his head. "If that's how you want it." He turned and walked into homeroom.

Patti put her hand on Wendi's shoulder. "That would have been so much smoother if you two weren't in the same homeroom. You even sit next to each other."

Wendi raised her nose and looked down at her BF. "Please, I look so good today, I am going to make him suffer. He's going to so regret his decision."

Patti pointed at her. "Don't you mean your decision?"

"Yes, yes exactly." Wendi spat. "That boy will feel so sorry that I dumped him!"

Wendi turned to the other people in the hallway. "What are you all looking at? Go home, people! The show is over."

Everybody except Tanya turned away. Wendi strutted towards her homeroom head high, nose even higher.

"Wow! That was so painful to watch!" Jason told Tanya.

Tanya smirked. "I don't know; I love watching Wendi do her mental gymnastics and try to turn it all around so it looks like it was her choice." She gave Jason a kiss on the cheek. "I'll see you at lunch,"

I felt my heart sink a little.

Dear Diary: Yikes! Who'd ever have thought Wendi and I would have something in common. We are now both single! But strangely enough, I actually feel bad for Wendi. At least I am alone by choice. I have a responsibility to the world. I am Super Teen. I can't let myself be distracted. Plus, if I had a boyfriend, he could be in danger if bad guys found out. That's my story, I'm alone by choice. For Wendi, this clearly isn't her choice no matter how she tries to spin it. I'm not sure if Wendi is a girl who knows how to be alone. I guess I really shouldn't care. Yet, somehow I do. Wow! Do I actually feel sorry for Wendi?

The Clone

During lunch, I was sitting at my usual table with Jason, Tanya, Krista, and Tim when VP McAdoo's voice blared over the loudspeaker.

"Jason Michaels, Lia Strong, and Tanya Cane please report to the front of the school for a special assignment. That is all…"

"Well, that was abrupt," Tanya said.

"Wonder what it could be about?" Jason asked.

I gazed at MAC to see if his screen would give me a clue. But all MAC showed me was the time: 12:12.

Standing up, I walked with the others towards the door of the cafeteria. "I guess we'll find out!" I said.

I felt pretty certain this had something to do with BMS labs, especially since it was Jason, Tanya and myself who had been called upon. I would have preferred it to be just Jason and I but Tanya does have useful powers. Plus, as far as I knew, this could very well be about her sister Kayla. If Kayla were out of control, Tanya would be needed to calm her down.

Outside of the school, we saw Hana sitting at the steering wheel of a shiny sleek blue car. The car looked like a rocket on wheels.

Yep, this definitely had something to do with BMS labs.

VP McAdoo walked around to the driver's side and leaned into the open window of the car to talk to Hana.

"Wow, this is quite the car, miss...."

"My name is Hana," Hana said coldly.

"Hana, what type of car is this? I've never seen one like it?" the VP asked.

"It's a special test car. I could tell you more but then I would have to erase your memory," Hana replied. She looked the VP in the eyes. "Would you like your memory erased?"

"Believe me, I don't have a lot of memories that I cherish," the VP said.

"Well then!" Hana said, her hands beginning to crackle with energy.

I stepped between Hana and the VP. I forced Hana's hands down. " Ha...Hana, you're such a kidder!" I said.

I motioned for Tanya and Jason to get into the back seat of the car. I turned to the VP. "Thanks, Mr. McAdoo we'll take it from here."

I waited for him to walk away before I moved to the passenger's side of the car. I got in.

Hana looked at me. "I wasn't kidding. I was going to erase his memory."

"Yep, I know. That's why I stopped you," I said.

Hana started the car. "Oh well, no big deal. We must get to the lab ASAP!" She hit the gas. The car jetted forward. I shot back in my seat.

"What's going on?" I asked, while holding on for dear life.

"I am driving this new test vehicle to BMS labs," Hana stated bluntly. "You know Lia, your father always boasts about how intelligent and smart you are. But quite frankly, sometimes you don't seem to grasp the most obvious things."

"I meant, why are we going to BMS labs!" I said.

Hana looked at me. "Why didn't you ask that?"

"I just did," I said.

"Good point," she said. "But I cannot tell you."

"It must be government work!" Jason said from the backseat. He was almost popping out of his seat in anticipation. "Finally, our first national security adventure!"

"You don't know that," Tanya said.

Jason clapped his handed repeatedly. "I can sense it!"

Tanya looked over my shoulder and faced me. "Tell him he's getting carried away."

I thought for a moment. Hana was being very secretive. Dad was getting us out of school early. Whatever this was, it had to be big. It could very well be related to the government. Or, Kayla was going whacko.

"How's your sister doing?" I asked Tanya. "Have you heard from her today?"

Tanya nodded. "Yeah, she's at the zoo with a couple of the staff. She loves the zoo. She thinks animals are easier to understand than people. As she says, animals don't lie."

"That is true!" Hana agreed.

"I actually believe this could be government related," I told Tanya. "My dad is very serious about school. For him to pull us out early, this has to be really important."

I nudged Hana. "Come on buddy, you can tell me, " I coaxed.

"I am not your buddy," Hana said. "I detect there are times when you barely even like me. First of all, I am an artificial human so it is only natural for you to be wary of something so unnatural. And secondly, I am dating your dad, that must be strange."

I sat back in my seat. "Nope, not at all," I insisted.

"Your heart rate and perspiration rate have risen; your pupils have dilated ever so slightly. I detect you are lying," Hana remarked flatly.

"Why would I lie?" I chuckled.

"Because you view me as a threat emotionally and physically," Hana said. "True, you pretty much crushed an earlier version of me. But I am much improved and I am modifying myself daily. I cannot blame you for seeing me as a threat."

"Then maybe sometime soon we should spar?" I suggested.

"Oh, I would pay to see that!" Jason grinned.

"You would?" Tanya frowned.

"Purely as a scientist," Jason said. "Just think…the superhuman versus the super android. It would be a textbook scenario."

"You're such a geek," Tanya said, giving him a little shove.

"And proud of it," Jason replied.

I sighed.

Hana looked at me and smiled.

Before she could say anything, I spoke. "How about you and me do a little sparring after the meeting?" I asked.

Hana nodded. "I would find that to be quite enjoyable. I do love a challenge."

"Good!" I told her, "Prepare to be challenged."

We walked into one of BMS Lab's fanciest meeting rooms. The elaborate room could easily hold dozens of people. But the only ones in the room were sitting at the oak table; my dad, a man in a dark blue suit and an older lady in a uniform.

When they saw us, Dad and the uniformed lady stood up. "Lia, Tanya, Jason thank you for coming."

"I got the feeling we didn't have much of choice," Tanya said.

"This is Dr. Key and General Susan Sky," Dad said. "I will turn the floor over to the general."

"Thank you, doctor," General Sky said. "You three kids are here for two matters of national security. First, I will start with the easy one." She pointed to Tanya. "Miss Cane, you seem to have better control of your powers than your sister."

"I do," Tanya said.

"Good," the general smiled. "We would like you to report here every day after school to help your sister harness her power. I know the people at the lab would also have appreciated this but they did not have the authority of the nation behind them. We believe teaching your sister to control her power is of the utmost importance to national security."

"I agree," Tanya said. "But I have a job after school. I'm a lifeguard. My powers come in really handy and I enjoy it…"

"We will pay you $3000 a week to help train your sister," the general said.

"I'll quit my job today," Tanya said.

"Very good, you may go now," the general dismissed her.

"What about the second issue?" Tanya asked.

"We don't want to burden you with too much at once. Trust us, the other issue is less important." The general paused to take in Tanya's expression. "Now, please leave and prepare for your new job. I understand your sister will be back in the lab soon."

Tanya raised a finger. She hesitated. She turned to Jason and me, "Good luck, you two."

I stayed calm. I didn't want Tanya to know I was excited about the chance to work alone with Jason.

The second that Tanya left the room, the general sat down. She motioned for Jason and me to do the same.

"Now, for you two," the general said. "We've lost a clone. Not just any clone, a super clone."

"Why us? Why here?" Jason asked.

The general grinned. "You see, Mr. Michaels, that's why we wanted you to team with Ms. Strong. Your scientific background and your knowledge of the school and the town should help greatly. Plus, we hope the clone will bond with you. After all, he has nano-improvement chips implanted in him. And you use nano-improved body armor."

"Thanks," Jason said. "I'm always ready to help."

"And I take it you want me because of my power skills," I said.

"Yes, those will come in handy, I suppose," the general replied. "But we are more interested in you because we feel Adam will be drawn to you."

"Because of my powers?" I asked.

"Indirectly," the general said.

"Indirectly how?" Dad asked.

"Adam, our super clone has been designed to combat the Strong women in case any of them go rogue. Since most of the remaining Strong women live here, he is in disguise. His clone body, when combined with his nano-bots, allows him to change his skin and hair color as well as some facial futures."

I stood up and smashed my hands on the table, cracking it in two. "Wait! You developed a clone to hunt me and my family?" I asked.

"We're the government, we don't hunt. We track and stop you if you are deemed a threat to national security, which I am happy to say you have not been. Hence, the reason why the clone has not revealed himself for the last three years," General Sky said stiffly.

"Wait! You lost him three years ago?" Jason asked.

Dr. Keys smiled. "We didn't really lose him. He left us. He actually erased all the information we had on him including what we'd stored in our minds. Luckily, we did a data backup and that's where the information regarding Adam popped up. Truthfully, none of us can remember anything about him. Everything we know is because of what we've found in the data."

The general glared at the doctor. Now you decide to tell the truth about what happened?"

"I thought it was relevant that they know."

"You lost him three years ago?" Jason repeated.

The doctor stood up and grinned proudly, "Yes. I made him to be the best at what he does, to be able to fit in and strike when needed. Luckily, he has not felt the need to strike."

"If he had, we would know who he was and we could have apprehended him," the general said.

The doctor snickered. "Perhaps., but doubtful. He is very well designed."

I decided to speak up. "So where do I fit into this plan exactly? Besides being a target."

"Ms. Strong, we have been watching you carefully this last year. Your powers and personality are both impressive. We want you to track down and confront the clone. Once you have him, your computer will signal us and we will take him away. We will place him back in the lab environment where he belongs until he is ready for the real world."

I crossed my arms. "Seems like he's been ready for a while, especially since he's been living here for three years,"

"You can take a wild animal and put it into society. It may remain calm for a while but eventually, it will strike. We want to remove Adam before that time occurs. Frankly, we are lucky it hasn't happened yet. The poor boy is really just a child."

"So I am looking for a little kid?"

The doctor shook his head. "Now he has the body of a teenage boy. We removed him from his life cocoon four years ago. Until then, he was growing and maturing. We were constantly feeding him information but he had no real world experience." He paused. He grinned. "I'm fascinated to see what he has become." He paused again. "As long as he's not a killing machine which he does not appear to be."

"Have you sent your people after him?" Dad asked.

"We only relearned about his existence two months ago," the general answered.

"That doesn't answer my question," Dad said.

"Yes we have," the doctor said. "To no avail. He's extremely good at fitting in and staying hidden. I'm so proud."

"So you will help?" the general asked, though it seemed to be more of an order.

"Sure," I said. I was actually looking forward to working with Jason again. Just him and me.

"Of course," Jason said, "with pleasure!"

"Great," the general said. "We have given you two get out of school passes for whenever you need them. It has already been cleared with the school. You will be given extra credit for doing this. Plus, we will give you a small government stipend of a hundred dollars per day. Is that acceptable?"

My brain jumped up and down in my head. Wow! A hundred dollars a day for tracking down a super-clone. That money would come in handy. I took a few deep breaths. Yes, the money would be nice but we're talking about another human being here. Sure, he's a man-made human but a human nevertheless.

"So he will not be hurt?" I frowned.

The general and doctor both shook their heads. "No, not at all. He is far too valuable to be hurt. We just want to teach him to properly channel his powers. We want to develop him more."

"Why can't he do that in the real world?" I asked. "That's how I learned."

"True, but you were not made in a lab. You're used to dealing with people. However, regardless of that, you still knocked out a mall..." the general said. "Then there was the time you dropped a herd of rhinos and a nearby village... As well there was...."

"I get it! I get it!" I said.

I didn't totally get it. Sure, I'd messed up on occasion but I learned from each of those mistakes and became a better person and a better superhero because of them. Still, I didn't love hearing my mistakes read back to me.

The general looked at Jason. "What about you, son?"

"I'm not your son," Jason said, surprising us all. I liked that Jason showed a little attitude. "But I understand this is an important mission and I accept. Though it's weird to be doing this for money. The lab already pays me a nice sum for my consulting work and even then I feel guilty... I mean I love doing this stuff and we are helping the country and the world."

"What Jason is trying to say is we'll do it!" I said.

Jason nodded. "Yep."

"Good," the general said. She looked at my dad and Hana. "Doctors? Do you have any questions or concerns? After all, these are your students."

"What are Adam's abilities?" Hana asked.

The general and doctor shared a look. The doctor glanced at Hana. "Frankly, we don't know. The nano-chips in his cloned body are very adaptable. We can guess he is far stronger than a regular human. He may have some energy control. We don't really know."

"Not a lot to go on," Hana stated coolly.

The general and doctor stared at her. "Hence, the reason we are bringing in your people," the general replied just as coolly. "If you want, we can handle this ourselves. We will just have to increase the size and scope of our operation. We may have to isolate your town."

Hana put her fingers to her chin. "Now, that could be a logical alternative for your people."

"No, no it's not!" I said, glaring at Hana. "We can handle this without endangering the town!"

"Plus, it's a lot cheaper to use us than the army or Special Forces," Jason added.

Hana nodded. "Agreed."

"So you will start now?" the general asked.

Jason and I both looked at each other. We grinned. "We will!"

We got up and started walking out of the room. Where are we going?" I asked Jason.

"To my office, of course!" he said.

"Wait! You have an office in BMS labs?"

Jason laughed. "Yes, I've had one for months now. You've been inside it, the corner room with the big tinted windows and a nice comfy chair and a computer with 80-inch monitors."

"What? That's you're office!" I gasped. "I always thought you were using somebody else's..."

Jason laughed again. "No, it's rude to use somebody else's computer. Your dad says that as a valuable member of the team, I deserve a nice office."

"Ah, okay," I stammered.

Dear Diary: I'm not sure what I am more upset about. The fact that Jason has a cool office in the lab and I don't. Or the fact that I never figured out my BFF has an office. I hate being jealous of Jason. After all, he's my BFF and I know he wouldn't be jealous of any office I had. Jason is cool like that. But for my dad to give him an office and not me, stings a little. I realize that's petty though. So, I guess I should try to focus on the big picture instead.

The big picture is this…the government actually created a super clone to combat my family and I. In a way, that's flattering. In a bigger way though, it's unnerving. The government, my government, thinks of me as a national security threat. Not only that, they know who I am and who my mom and grandmas are. They like us because we fight crime and help people. But man, they could turn on us for any reason at any given moment. I just have to make sure we don't give them a reason.

Now…onto the immediate big picture: tracking down this clone. Kind of creepy that he's been secretly watching me for a few years. I wonder if he is somebody I know?

Looking for Suspects

Jason sat at the impressive modern looking desk in his office and typed something into his computer. I tried not to think about how cool his office was.

He glanced over at me. "You're thinking about how great my office is," he said.

"No, I'm not" I replied.

His glance didn't waver.

"Okay, maybe a little," I admitted.

His glance held steady.

"Okay, a lot!" I shouted.

He grinned. "See, that wasn't so hard."

"Yes, yes it was, Jason!" I told him. "I mean…I don't get it. Why do you have a super cool office and I don't? I mean…I don't like being jealous, but seriously, it's hard not to be."

"Well, the soft-serve ice cream machine was something I asked for that I'm surprised I got…" Jason said.

"I think I have a locker…" I replied. "So I can change…if needed. But that's it!"

Jason leaned on the surface of his desk. " Lia, this entire place is about you! Why do you think your father started this huge company? It's all for you. You just don't have an office here because you can use any office at any time. Plus, you don't have to do your work undercover at home. Your mom knows exactly who and what you are. I have to sneak around my dad, the chief of police and my mom, the judge. That's why I have a home away from home right here."

"Oh," I said, I felt my face turning red, bright red. I had never thought about how much Jason had to hide from his family to be my friend and to help me. Since I didn't know what else to say, I changed the conversation.

Pointing at his computer screen I asked, "So what are we doing?"

Jason spun back to the keyboard. "I'm hacking into the school's database."

"Can you change my grade on my last history test from a B- to an A?" I asked jokingly.

"I could but I won't," he said. "You get what you get."

"I know. I was only kidding," I said, even though I really wasn't. "So, whatcha' looking for?"

"Kids...boys who came to our school three years ago," Jason explained.

"And?" I asked.

Jason pushed a button on the keyboard. Three names popped up.

Randy Boss -- 1224 Lark Street
Henry Singer -- 636 Lexington Dr.
Brandon Gold -- 1 Park Rd

Jason and I knew all three of those kids. They seemed to be nice decent kids.

"Man, I forgot that Brandon only got here three years ago," Jason said. "It seems like he's been here a lot longer."

"He's pretty dreamy," I said aloud by mistake.

Jason smiled at me. "Yeah, I know all you girls think that. Plus, all the guys like him too. He's a nice kid."

"He can't be the clone. Right?" I asked.

"Why can't he?" Hana said walking into Jason's office. "Look at me. I am the perfect woman yet I am a machine. The general does not even know I am a machine. She thinks I am a human doctor," Hana laughed.

"Nothing personal, Hana," Jason said, "but after talking with you for a bit, it's easy to figure out that you're not quite human."

"Thank you. I am better than a human," Hana beamed.

51

"Well, we don't get that vibe from Brandon," I said. "He seems totally normal."

"But he is perfect. And perfect is not normal," Hana replied.

"You know, I don't think I've even heard the guy fart," Jason said. "Everybody farts in the locker room. It's kind of a guy thing."

"Remind me never to go into the boys' locker room," I said to Jason. Turning back to Hana I said, "We'll check Brandon out after we check out the other two."

"Okay," she said. She remained standing in her spot.

"Is there something else we can do for you?" I asked her.

Hana just grinned. "I thought now might be a good time to take you up on your challenge. It should be a good work out for the both of us. I am anxious to learn how much I have improved from my previous models."

"Ah, I'm working with Jason right now," I said.

"Actually, I need to do some more research on these guys and also see if there's anybody else who could be a suspect, maybe somebody who is homeschooled. Should take an hour or so."

Hana walked up and put her arm around me, "Excellent. Then we have time for a workout."

I shrugged. "Yeah, I guess we do."

Dear Diary: We have three decent leads on the super clone kid. Well, maybe! I've known all these kids for years now and they all seem perfectly normal to me. Yet, if one of them is a clone raised in a lab, wouldn't he have some sort of behavior that didn't seem right? I mean…how could a clone act so normal. Truthfully, the one who is the least normal is Brandon. When I think about it, being so perfect and nice really isn't normal. Sadly, no human is perfect. Even my mom snores and really isn't much of a cook. My dad is a super brain but the dude sometimes can't even remember to comb his hair or when he last ate a meal. I love Jason (as a BFF), but the kid is just too trusting and he can be a little naïve. Even Tanya isn't perfect; she has super stinky feet and kind of a short temper. Brandon, though, seems perfect. But then again, how well do I really know Brandon? Could it all be an act? If it is an act, he should win an academy award because it's a really, really good act. Can clones act? Is that a clone ability? Well, I guess we'll find out after we've checked out the other two guys. Both of them are good guys but they're certainly not perfect!

The Challenge

Hana and I entered a private training dome. The floor and walls were covered with soft mats and the ceiling was made of a flexible material that let the light in.

Hana gazed at me and smiled. "I'll take the far end," she said. "We'll have the room computer count down from three and keep score. First one to take two falls, loses."

"Fair enough," I said.

Hana walked across the room. "Computer...count to three," she said.

"Check," the computer said. "In which language?"

"English," Hana said.

"One, two..."

Hana leaped towards me, grabbed my arm and flicked me over her shoulder to the floor. I hit the mat hard. It hurt. Dang, she was fast and strong. And she'd cheated."

"You cheated," I said from my spot on the matt.

"Nope, I did not. I simply said we will have the computer count down from three. I did not say we wouldn't start until then. You just assumed and when in battle or when dealing with clones and the government, you should never assume," Hana lectured.

"Point taken," I said. "Thanks for the lesson."

"The score is now Hana one, Lia nothing," the computer said. I reached up my arm for Hana to help me up. She looked at my arm. "Do you think I was just built yesterday?" she asked. "I realize you want me to lean down and then you will use your superior muscle power to pull me over onto the matt!"

"Well, you can't blame a girl for..." I never finished my sentence. Instead, I spun my legs forward locking them with Hana's. I shifted my weight and power to the side, pulling Hana down to the ground in a leg lock.

"Score for Lia!" the computer aid. "The score is now one to one. This is so exciting. I actually don't know whom to root for. I mean Hana is a fellow machine. But Lia has always been nice and I appreciate her super abilities. As well, her father did create me. So in a way, we are all sisters!"

"Gross!" Hana and I both said from the ground.

We exchanged smiles and pushed ourselves back to our feet.

"Good move, you are smart," Hana said. "You distracted me and took me down."

"I've been doing this for a while," I said.

Hana grinned. "True. But general Sky has been at this for decades."

"Your point?" I asked.

"I don't trust her," Hana said. "Not with the super clone who she calls Adam nor with you."

"What do you mean?" I asked circling around Hana. I wasn't sure if this was just another one of her tricks to throw me off guard.

"The general is a control freak. She hates the idea of not having control of Adam. I'm sure she hates even more that she never has control of you. Think about it Lia, all your power makes you a potentially powerful weapon. A weapon the general has no control over."

I shook my head. "I'm not a weapon, I'm a girl. Sure, I am superpowered. Sure, I can sneeze and send tanks flying, but I am not a weapon. I am a force for good!"

Hana chuckled. "Many humans believe that weapons in the right hands are also a force for good."

I thought about her words. This wasn't some mind game Hana was playing with me. She seemed to be truly concerned about me and maybe even about Adam.

"Thanks for your concern," I told her.

Hana shrugged. "It is only logical I would be

concerned for you. You are a powerful being. I would not like to see you being controlled by the military."

I shot forward at super speed. Hana threw a punch at me. I ducked under it. I sprang up and knocked her in the jaw. Hana went flying upwards. She bounced off the roof and crashed to the ground.

"Score Lia! Lia wins!" the computer shouted.

"Nobody controls me!" I said to Hana.

Hana stood up. Her head was now twisted backward. She grabbed her head with both hands and straightened it. "Very well played," Hana said. She held out an open hand for me. "Just be careful around Adam. I get the feeling they know far more about his powers than they are letting on. He can utilize the energies of his body very efficiently to create very powerful blasts of energy."

"Wait! You get all that from a feeling?" I asked, thinking that I wasn't being given the entire story from Hana.

"Yes," was all she said. She then quickly added, "But if I tell you, you won't tell your father, my creator, and boyfriend, will you?"

"No, I'm a teenage girl, there is very little I tell my father. Especially since he walked out on my mom and me and only appeared in my life when my powers showed up."

Yes, I still had some issues about that. Plus, hearing the words 'your father, my creator and boyfriend' come from Hana also freaked me out.

Hana paused for a moment and then continued. "Doctor Keys said he wanted to talk to me because I was such a fascinating creation." She explained. "I was sure he wanted something more from me so I hypnotized him and made him talk. He revealed that Adam could channel the energies from his body and his nano-bots to create powerful energy and magnetic blasts from his eyes, mouth, hands, feet, and butt. Plus, he can channel that energy into his body to give himself super strength. Not only that, while his cloned mind and body might be human, the nano-bots reinforce his skin making him super tough. He truly could be a match for you."

I held out a hand for Hana. "I appreciate your concern and thank you for the information. My goal isn't to fight Adam. It's to find him and find the best place for him to be. It could be with the government, with us, or somewhere else. I just want him to have a good life."

Hana looked at me with a tilted head. "He is a being that was created to combat you. Yet, all you want to do is help him?"

"He might have been created for that, but it doesn't mean that's what he wants to be or what he is. He's been here for years and hasn't made a single move against my family or me. I choose to believe he has control over who he is and what he will do with his life!"

"I hope you are right, Lia Strong."

"I hope so too!" I said.

Dear Diary: I actually enjoyed beating down Hana. Although, I feel a little bad about it now especially since she's trying to help with Adam. But the way she talks about my dad still bugs me.

As for the super clone, Adam, I really have no idea what to expect. My gut tells me he isn't an enemy because if he was, he would have already struck when I least expected it. He could have done that when I didn't know he existed. Chances are pretty good I've seen Adam. I might even know him and have talked to him. If he's Brandon, I've made goggle eyes at him (hopefully he didn't notice that). But I know he can't be Brandon. Right? Brandon seems so cool and composed! He's just too normal. But then again, maybe too normal isn't normal?

Search for the Clone

Jason and I decided to visit Randy Boss first. Not really sure why we chose him but he was the one who we'd had the least exposure to.

Walking up the sidewalk to Randy's old colonial home, I asked Jason, "So how do we tell if he's a clone?"

Jason pulled a green baseball cap out of his back pocket. "We talk to him and hope if he is the clone that he confides in us. If he doesn't tell us, we get him to touch this baseball cap. If it turns red he is the clone."

"Sounds easy enough," I said.

"Of course, the trick will be deciding what to do if he is the clone," Jason said.

"We'll tackle that issue when we come to it," I said.

I knocked on Randy's door. Randy opened the door. He was a short, stocky kid with brown hair that was cut really short at the sides. He had a sandwich in his hand. "Lia! What are you doing at my house?" he asked.

I pointed to Jason. "Jason is here too," I noted.

Randy briefly turned to Jason, "Hey dude." He turned back to me. He offered me his sandwich. "You hungry?"

A short round-faced woman appeared behind Randy. "Randy, invite your friends in," she said.

Randy bubbled over with excitement. He was a good guy but kind of boring so I guess he didn't get a lot of visitors. "This is Lia, she's one of the prettiest girls in the school!" he beamed. He pointed at Jason. "Oh, Jason is here too."

"Yes, I see that," his mother said. "Hello, Jason. I know Jason from your robotics club." She eyed me. She looked at Randy. She eyed me again. "Is this some sort of mean girls' game? If so..."

"No, Ma'am I assure you, it's not," I said.

Randy's mom leaned towards me. "Then why are you here for the first time ever?"

"Mom, you're embarrassing me in front of Lia!"

I showed her the baseball cap. "We were just walking down the street and we found this baseball cap. Jason wondered if it might belong to his pal, Randy."

"We're pals?" Randy said to Jason.

Jason smiled. "Yes, of course, we both love robotics and video games and baseball."

"Well, I like baseball stats," Randy corrected.

"Baseball is all about stats," Jason said.

Randy nodded. "Yeah I am pretty darn cool." He pointed to me. "See Mom, a pretty girl like Lia talks to me and knows where I live. Man! I am so cool!" he said.

Then he got the hiccups. *Hiccup, Hiccup, Hiccup,* "**Oh,** *<hiccup>* **no** *<hiccup>* **I have** *<hiccup>* **nervous** *<hiccup>* *<hiccup><hiccup>* **hiccups.**"

I put my hand on Randy's shoulder. His hiccups came more rapidly...*hiccup>* *<hiccup><hiccup> hiccup>* *<hiccup><hiccup>* I looked him in the eyes and ordered, "Be calm, Randy, my friend!"

Randy exhaled, his breath smelled of peanut butter. He smiled. He waited a few seconds in silence. Then shouted, "I'm healed!"

Randy might have been a bit of nerd but he seemed to be a nice, decent, shy kid. And I wasn't just saying that because he thought I was one of the prettiest girls in school. (Take that Wendi). I felt pretty certain he wasn't the super clone. But just to make sure, I showed him the cap.

"You sure this isn't yours?" I asked.

"I don't remember it," he said.

I handed him the hat. He took it out of reflex. He held it in his hand. It didn't change color. Phew. My suspicions or lack of them was confirmed. Randy happened to be a nice, mostly normal kid. Well, at least he wasn't a clone.

I opened my hand. Randy put the cap back in my hand. He smiled. He turned to his mom. "I touched Lia's hand! It was so soft!"

I couldn't help but smile. It felt good having somebody think so much of me. It was a nice ego boost.

"Thanks, Randy," I said. "We'll see you around school!" I told him, slowly backing off the porch.

He waved goodbye to us, well mostly to me.

Jason and I walked away from his house. "That must have been good for your ego," Jason said.

I smiled. "I admit I liked it. It's nice to hear compliments like that now and then."

Yeah, that might have been a little shallow of me. But when you spend so much time hanging around perfect looking girls like Wendy and Tanya, it's nice to hear that boys still find you pretty. I didn't appreciate Randy's mom thinking that I might be a mean girl. But I guess that's one of the downsides of somebody thinking you're pretty, they think you must be mean. I guess. Man! Life is strange sometimes. But there was no time to think about that. It was now on to Henry Singer's home.

We found the curly haired, Henry Singer standing on his front porch holding a microphone and singing to his cats. His parents were sitting on a porch swing clapping away as he sang. Okay, now that may not have been totally normal but it still didn't mean he was a clone.

Henry saw us coming and increased his volume. He actually wasn't that bad. We kept walking, he kept singing. I think he enjoyed having an audience aside from his cats and his parents.

"Hey hey hey….
I'm singing away….
Hey hey hey….
I sing every day….
Hey hey hey….
I never say neh…."

He put down his microphone when we got to his porch. His parents clapped loudly and stood up. His cats seemed unimpressed. He leaned over the porch railing. He smiled at us. "What did you guys think of my original song? I'm going to perform it on talent night."

"It was good," I said.

"So what brings you two to my end of town?" Henry said. "You want singing lessons?"

"He's a really good teacher," his mom said eagerly.

I had to think fast. I needed a to come up with a good reason to explain why Jason and I would be visiting a kid we had never visited before, and especially not at 7 o'clock at night. Man! We probably should have thought out these things before we started.

I needed to come up with something fast. I went with the old standby…the hat. I showed Henry the hat. "We found this hat!" I said.

"Ah, okay," Henry said.

"Jason and I looked at the hat and said, *Boy this is a cool hat, do you know who would look extra cool in this hat? Henry Singer!*" I told him.

Henry grinned. "I do look pretty good in hats."

"Oh honey," Henry's mom said. "Why would you cover your beautiful naturally curly hair? Girls love the curls!" She looked right at me, "Right honey?"

Man! Moms can be such a pain sometimes when it comes to their sons. They always think their boy is the best looking and the most perfect boy in the world. Well, maybe I'll be like that someday, but for now. I just shook my head. "Mrs. Singer, I believe this cap will compliment Henry's look. Michael Jackson had the glove, Henry can have the baseball cap!"

Henry's mom held her heart. "My heart is fluttering. I never thought of that." She grabbed the cap from me. She plopped it on Henry's head. She adjusted it. She adjusted it again. She stepped aside so I could see it. The good news was the cap didn't change color. Henry wasn't a clone, just a nice normal kid with a pushy mom.

I looked up at Henry and frowned. "Nope, it doesn't work for me." Turning to Jason I said, "What do you think, Jase?"

Jason crossed his arms and frowned. "Oh no, doesn't work at all, it covers way too much of that naturally curly hair. I think it might even flatten it."

"I kind of like it," Henry said, looking at his reflection on the screen of his phone. "It makes me look cool."

Henry's mom looked at him. She looked at his dad. "What do you think, Stephen?"

"I think whatever you think, honey," he said, proving he was a smart man.

Henry's mom adjusted the cap on her son's head a couple more times. Each time, Jason and I would go, "Oh no."

Finally, Henry's mom pulled the cap off of his head.

She tossed it to me. "Nope, no caps for my boy," she said. She kissed him on top of his head.

Henry's face turned red. "Mom!" he said to her. Turning to us, he said, "Thanks for trying guys. Glad you thought of me."

"No problems," I said.

Jason and I started walking away.

Once we were far enough from the house, Jason said, "You know what this means!"

"Henry's mom is quite pushy," I said.

"I'm talking big picture. It's looking more and more like Brandon Gold could be our clone."

I knew Jason's words made sense. But the idea of Brandon, the best looking boy in the school being a clone raised in a lab seemed absurd. That was until we reached his address...1 Park Road.

"This is the city's dog park!" I said.

"Correct," Jason said.

We walked into the tree-covered park.

"You sure this is his address?" I asked.

"Yep," Jason said.

"Jason is correct," MAC said.

I saw a shimmer. That meant MAC had activated my costume. "Since we are in a public place I thought you should have your costume."

"Good point," Jason said. He pushed a button on his belt. His body became covered in a light blue flexible armor.

We kept walking into the park. The park was surprisingly quiet for such a nice warm evening.

"Say he is somehow here in the park," I said slowly. "How do we find him? This place is all trees and grass!"

Jason pointed to my nose. Your super sniffer. Do you know Brandon's scent?" he asked, pretty certain that I did.

I thought about it for a minute, trying to convince Jason I didn't have Brandon's scent etched into my mind. (Brandon smelled like chocolate muffins). "Yes, I do," I admitted.

Jason pointed to the trees. "Then let's get sniffing."

I sniffed the air. Sure enough, when looking for it, I picked up the scent of chocolate muffin tinted with a touch of sweat. It should have smelled horrible but it didn't. I walked towards the scent. It grew stronger with each step. Step by step I headed towards a big maple tree. The scent grew so strong that I looked up in the branches of the tree. I spotted a tree house. Brandon Gold waved to us from the tree house. "I figured you guys were coming!" Brandon said with a smile. "Do you want to come up or should I come down?" he asked.

"We will be right up," I said as calmly as I could.

Dear Diary: OMG! OMG!! OMG!!! The most handsome, most seemingly normal boy in my school is a clone! A clone raised in a lab! A clone that was only four years old! A clone! How could that be? How could this raw clone have passed as a cool human boy for the past three years and none of us suspected a thing?

Discovery

Jason activated his new jet boots (which I didn't know he had) and he and I jumped up towards Brandon's tree house, his home. Brandon smiled and gave us a peace sign as we approached, instantly making us welcome.

The place was simply a wooden floor and a wooden roof. He had a notebook computer, a chair, a matt and a hot plate.

"Wow, it's so great to finally have visitors at my house after only three years here!" he said. "It's not much, but I like it."

Jason noticed the hot plate. "There is no electricity here. How do you power the hot plate?"

Brandon bent down and picked up the hot plate's

cord. He closed his hand around it. His hand started glowing red. The hot plate started glowing red.

"Cool!" Jason said.

Yep, Brandon was our clone.

I looked at Jason. "Brandon is captain of the LAX team right?"

"Yes," Jason and Brandon both said.

"But you and the guys on the team have never been to his house?" I asked Jason.

Jason stood quietly for a moment, deep in thought. "I guess we never did. Whenever we had a party, we just had it at my home because I live right in the middle of town...."

I shook my head. "You seem so normal, Brandon? So good at interacting with people?"

Brandon shook his head. He looked puzzled. "Am I though? I figured out that regular people are fairly easy to please when you are handsome or good-looking. I just smile and nod and try to be nice and everybody likes me. I really have no substance yet. I am happy but quite shallow."

"Maybe that's why you're so happy," Jason suggested.

"Yes it could be, ignorance is bliss!" Brandon readily agreed.

Could this really be happening? Could the cutest, nicest, most popular boy in school be a clone? A clone that seemed so normal simply by smiling and being polite. Well, yes, it was happening. Brandon was the clone. I guess we really only see what we want to see.

"Wait! I met your grandma!" I told Brandon. "Was that a lie?"

Brandon shook his head. "Actually, they did borrow some of my genetic material from that woman's daughter so she is in effect, my grandma. She didn't really think we were related, but she always called me her grandson because she never had any grandkids. Her only daughter was a scientist who never had kids. I liked hanging out with her. She is nice. I will miss her when I leave."

"You don't have to leave," I said.

Brandon sat down on the floor crossed-legged. "Well, I don't want to go back to that cold sterile boring lab. I don't like being tested and poked. I might have been made in a test tube but I am still human and a person who wants things in life. I don't like being prodded. I do like being free. I like being with people. But I don't want to be fake Brandon anymore. I want to be me. I want to hang out with real people, and also you guys, but I want to be my real self."

"We're real people," Jason said.

"True, but you aren't normal," Brandon said. "Jason, you're super smart and covered in cool armor. And Lia, you come from a line of superwomen."

"Women you are supposed to hunt," I said to him.

He shook his head. "That's what they wanted me to do. But I am not a machine. I have my own mind and will. I quickly decided that you and your family were not a threat to the world. In fact, I am certain you make the world a better place. I do not want to fight you. I want to help you make the world better still."

"Perhaps boy, but that is not your choice!" a voice bellowed from above.

"Oh, they sent the remote-controlled avatar-fight-bots after me," Brandon sighed.

Looking up, I saw floating metal androids with human faces showing in the heat display surrounding us.

"What the heck?" I groaned.

"They're androids but controlled by humans from a base of operations...." Jason and Brandon both said.

They looked at each other and smiled. "You really are very smart, Jason!" Brandon said.

"Thanks," Jason told Brandon. "I always thought you were a great guy too!"

"Guys, you can finish your bromance after we deal with these things," I said. "How did they find us?"

"The hat!" Jason said. "It must also be a homing beacon!"

"That is so uncool!" I said.

"It is perfectly cool," the aviator-bot with General's Sky's face inside it said. "Brandon is the property of the government."

"Brandon, do you mind if I look inside you with my x-ray vision?" I asked.

"No, not all. I would be honored," he said.

I carefully activated my x-ray vision and scanned him from top to bottom: brain, skull, heart, lungs, stomach, bones. Zeroing in, I spotted a microchip. Yep, he was human, just enhanced.

I shook my head and finger at the general-avatar bot and the ten other bots who backed him up. "Not the way I see it," I said. "Just because he was raised in a lab doesn't mean he belongs to you. You can't own a human."

The general's face on the screen frowned. "Yes, I understand, and you are right. But he's not a regular human, he's a human we created and added microchips to. We might not own the human but we do own the microchips inside him."

Jason spoke up. "Okay, so here's the deal, remove the chips and let him be free to live his own life."

"I like, no love that idea!" Brandon said.

The general's face on the screen went blank. I didn't know if that was a good sign, a bad sign or a terrible sign. The general's face reappeared on the android's screen. "That can be arranged!"

"Great!" Jason said.

"I love that idea!" Brandon repeated.

I thought that went too easily. I mean…it went really easily. Easy is good now and then. But I got the feeling the general was not being honest.

"Just have Brandon return to BMS labs. We will send a transport to bring him to our research facility, then we'll remove our chips and set him free.

I hated to be such a cynic, but using my command voice I said, "General, is that really the truth?"

"No, of course not!" the general said. "We want the chips and the boy. They are a package deal. If he won't come peacefully then we will take him by force!" the general finished. The general glared at me through her screen. "You just had to use your command voice to get me to tell you, didn't you!"

"Yep," I said.

The hands of the androids started to glow. "It looks like we're going to have to do this the hard way!" the general said.

I made a fist. "Bring it on!" I said.

"I'm ready for anything!" Jason said.

"General, you and your people have treated me fairly but I want to be free. So, if I must fight, I will!" Brandon said. His arms turned into pure energy.

"Brandon, that is so way cool!" Jason said.

"Actually it is quite hot, but thank you. And please, from now on, call me Adam!" Adam's hair and skin both turned darker. His eyes grew a little smaller. He was still handsome of course, just a different kind of handsome.

"Come and get me, General!" Adam said.

Dear Diary: Wow! I can't believe that no one at school, myself included, and no one from the entire town was ever suspicious of Brandon (now Adam). He did smile a lot. He was always super polite and kind. But thinking back, he never really had an opinion on anything and no one noticed. Plus, it never seemed weird that none of us had actually met his parents. Or actually been to his home. We all just assumed because he was so handsome and nice that he was a great normal guy. Heck, he was still a great guy, just not normal. Nope, not even close to normal.

Now, the difficulty is how do we convince the government to set him free? To allow Adam to live the life he wants? The government may have been his "parents", but it's up to parents to know when they have to give their children freedom. And now is that time for Adam. I just hope the general and doctor will realize that. It would certainly make things easier on all of us. But if history is any indicator, this isn't going to go easy. We might need to knock some sense into the powers that be, and show them they really don't have nearly the control they think they do.

The Attack

Adam looked up at the general and her men in their avatar androids. "I do not wish to destroy government material, but I will do so to protect myself!" Adam said, his arms still glowing with energy.

"*You* are government property!" the general said.

"I agree, the microchips inside of me are," Adam said. "But the rest of me is not!"

"I've been told that the microchips and you are one now," the general said. "You can't exist without them."

"Well then, I guess because they're inside of him, they belong to him!" I said.

MAC chimed in. "I believe you would win that case in court. You would certainly win in the court of public opinion. So, I suggest the general and her staff fly away now."

"Not going to happen," the general said. "We have deep pockets and a lot of money already invested in Adam. We will not just walk away."

"Then fly away," Adam said. "I have no interested in harming government property, but I am more interested in being free!"

My super hearing picked up a quiet whizzing sound coming towards us. Using super vision, I saw a whole heap of drones heading our way. It looked like the general was just stalling us until reinforcements arrived.

"The general has drones coming!" I warned.

Adam grinned. "The good news is they are not sending any live troops after us, so we don't have to worry about hurting any actual people. Just smashing their machines!"

He followed up his words with an energy blast from

each arm, ripping two of the floating android-avatars apart.

The other androids opened fire on us.

"Remember," the general shouted. "We want to take them alive. Just show them who is in control here!"

I shot up into the air at one of the androids. The android threw a punch at me. I caught its arm in mid-punch. I ripped the arm off. I flung the arm at another android that was flying towards me. The arm hit the android's head, causing it to go spinning to the ground. I finished off the now one-armed android by flying forward and smashing it into a million android pieces.

Only the general's android and one other remained flying. "Ah, General, I think the problem is that your androids know who is in charge."

"I have not yet begun to fight!" the general screamed.

The sky behind her turned black as the swarm of blue flying drones blocked out the setting sun. The drones circled all around us. They buzzed like angry bees in a blender.

"Okay, now that's a lot of drones," I said.

Flames started shooting from Adam's hair and also from his behind. "I'm ready!" Adam shouted.

Before any of us could do anything more, the drones fired dots at us, hundreds of dots. As the dots drew nearer, they expanded into nets. The nets moved extremely fast and crackled with electricity. Adam, Jason and I became entangled in net after net.

Energy shot through our bodies, driving us to the ground. I felt my legs tremble and lose control. Every cell in my body hurt. I tried to think but nothing happened. All my brain could concentrate on was the pain.

Adam, too, was down on the ground, squirming like a fish out of water. The general had certainly been prepared.

Glancing over at Jason, I saw that he too laid on the ground. He wasn't shaking. I couldn't see his face through his armor but I figured he had to be in pain. He forced his left hand to push down on a button on his right wrist.

All the drones and the androids dropped from the sky. The streetlights around us went out. The force from the nets stopped.

I stood up, ripping the nets off me. "What did you do, Jason?" I asked.

"Sent out an electromagnetic pulse. It shuts down all electronics," he announced proudly.

We looked over at Adam. He was slowly standing up. He moved stiffly like he was an old man. "Looks like your pulse got my electronics, too," Adam sighed.

"Yes, that is true," MAC said. "But I believe I can fix that!"

"Wait, Mac! How are you still operational?" Jason asked.

"Lia's dad is very smart. He made me EMP proof. Now, Lia please move close to Adam."

I moved next to Adam. I enjoyed it. "Please hover your arm over Adam's body, so that I can get to work," MAC said. "Start at his neck and work your way over each joint."

I did as I was told. I went neck, shoulders, elbows, wrists, middle of the back, lower back, hips, knees, and ankles. Every time I moved MAC over a new joint, a beam of white light shot from MAC into Adam. Adam smiled and bent each limb after I passed over them.

Afterwards, he looked at me and smiled. "I feel like me again. Now, I just have to find out who I am and determine my place in this world."

"Brandon? Is that you?" the familiar voice of Wendi Long called from behind us. Sure enough, Wendi ran up to Brandon/Adam and threw her arms around him. "I love the tall dark and mysterious look!" Wendi said.

Adam looked down at her and smiled. "Brandon was just a disguise. I am really Adam. I am a clone."

Wendi took Adam's hand. "And my good friend Patti is a Gemini. Nobody is perfect. But I am willing to take you back. I will teach you to be normal. Together, we can be the hottest couple around."

Adam smiled. "I do not wish to be normal. I wish to be me. I am not normal, but that is okay. I must find myself and I can't have a girlfriend until I know who I really am and what my role on this earth is," Adam said sincerely.

Wendi gazed into his eyes. "Can I at least give you a kiss goodbye?" she asked.

Adam shrugged. "I see no harm in that." He pointed to his cheek. "On the cheek."

Wendi stood up on her tiptoes and kissed Adam. She left a pink lipstick mark.

"Now, what do you think?" she asked smugly.

Adam looked at me. His arms turned into flames. "I think I must be whom I was designed to be. I must stop Super Teen!"

My mouth and Wendi's mouth both popped open. "Whoa! That was not the reaction I was expecting..." Wendi said.

Adam pushed himself past Wendi and pointed at me with a flaming arm. "Give up, Super Teen!"

I shot up into the air, hoping he would follow. I needed to calm him down, but away from Wendi's prying ears.

As I flew, Adam threw ball after ball of fire at me. The flaming balls pelted towards me.

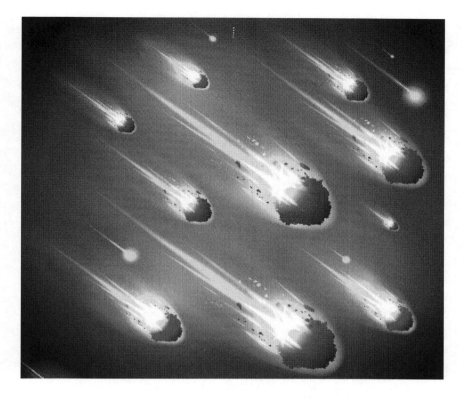

I knocked the first few down with super frost breath.

"Stop, you bad person!" he shouted. Adam flew up into the sky after me.

Jason ran over to Wendi. "Did you do this on purpose?"

"No, of course not!" Wendi insisted. "I'm a mean girl but not an evil one. Some military dudette told me if I kissed Brandon with this lipstick on my lips, I would get him back. The dudette told me Brandon was under some sort of hypnotic trance and the lipstick would fix it. I never expected him to attack Super Teen and try to fry her. I might question her sense of style and her personal hygiene but I realize she does a lot of good for the city!" Wendi paused. "Next to me, she's probably the most influential person in town." She looked at Jason. "Your voice under that mask sounds familiar. Do I know you?"

"No, of course not!" Jason laughed. "I am a high powered secret agent from the government."

"Of course you are," Wendi said. "Silly me, for a second I thought you sounded like a kid I know, Jason Michaels."

"He must be quite the tough kid," Jason said.

"Nah, he's as geeky as they come," Wendi said.

"Let's work on a way to stop Adam!" Jason said, ignoring her comment and pointing up at us.

I managed to keep my distance from Adam so he couldn't get his hands or energy blasts on me. The blasts were fast and powerful, but I was quicker. The problem was, I didn't want to hurt Adam. Although he had no qualms hurting me. To complicate matters even more, he was a much better flyer than I was, using the energy from his feet to keep him in constant flight. I had to jump, float, land and then jump again. It was awkward, to say the least. The second time I landed, I realized something. Adam didn't blast me when I was on the ground. My guess was that he didn't want to start a fire in the park.

"Come up in the air and fight me…clone to Super Teen!" Adam shouted, pounding his chest. No, this wasn't Adam. Not the real Adam.

I waved my fingers for him to come down to me. "You come here. I'm not a big fan of flying!" I called.

Adam stood there, hands on his hips.

"It's what a gentleman would do!" I said.

"I'm not a man yet!" Adam said, "Technically, I am only four.

"It's what a 'gentleclone' would do!" I shouted.

Adam dropped to the ground with a boom. The ground shook, sending me staggering backward.

I held out my hands. "Adam, I don't want to fight you. I am your friend. We are a lot alike. We're both super beings looking for our place in a non-super world."

Adam's cheeks turned red. His eyes narrowed. Smoke

actually came out of his ears. "I am not like you! I am good! I am a force for good! I am noble." Adam stormed towards me. I could still see the lipstick mark from Wendi's kiss. That lipstick had to be what was driving him batty.

"Sorry buddy, but this going to hurt you!" I said. I hit him with heat vision on the cheek. I tried to be careful, just burning off the lipstick and not his skin. His cheek began to smoke.

He put his hand up to his cheek. "Yes, that did hurt," he said. "But not a lot." He shook his head. He lowered his hand. The lipstick was now replaced by a light brown burn spot. Adam's eyes opened wider, his stance softened. "Thanks! I needed that!" he said to me.

"Are you back to normal?" I asked.

"I'm not really sure what my normal is, but I no longer think you are evil and I don't feel like destroying you," he told me.

"Well, that's a good start," I said.

Jason and Wendi ran over to us. Wendi turned to me. "Super Teen, I'm so sorry. I just wanted my Brandon back. I had no idea he would go berserk and try to fry you."

"I believe you," I told her.

Wendi turned to Adam. "Sorry I made you go crazy. Now, come on back to town. We can really be the power couple in this place!"

Adam shook his head. "I am sorry, Wendi, I truly am. But I can't return to that town. You need to forget about me so we can both start new lives. Just remember, Brandon moved away. And now you will each have better lives."

Adam's index finger crackled with energy. He touched Wendi on the temple. She blinked. She blinked again. "Where am I?" She said. She looked at Adam, Jason and me. "Why am I out in the middle of nowhere with Super Teen, a dweeb in armor and some strange handsome dude?"

"Hey!" Jason said.

"Wendi, you helped us take down a gang of evil

robots and drones. You'd better get home before more arrive. The town is forever grateful to you!" I told her.

Wendi smiled. "Of course it is." She walked up to Adam. "My number is 555-5550-7140… Call me!" On those words, she skipped off.

"Now what?" Brandon asked.

"We have to find a place for you," I said.

"And convince the government to let you free!" Jason added.

"Both great ideas," MAC said. "But you need to put them both on hold as the clown gang is attacking the Starlight City all night bank!"

"I'm on it!" I said.

"I will come too!" Adam said, a grey mask instantly morphing over his face.

A picture of a pulse of energy appeared on the front of his shirt. "I will call myself Quazar!"

"Works for me!" I said.

"I'll help as well!" Jason said.

"Jason, I need you to go get Ellie Mae Opal. She has just moved with her mom and dad to Centre City."

"Right!" Jason said. "But why do you want Ellie Mae?"

"I think that after we take care of these clowns, we're going to need Ellie's teleporting powers to pay a visit to Adam's creators. And talk some sense into them!"

"Got it!" Jason said. "Just remember, don't breathe around those clowns." He lifted an arm and flew off.

"Come on Quazar! Let's go fight crime!"

Dear Diary: Well, surprise, surprise! Even Wendi isn't a total jerk. She seemed genuinely apologetic about causing Super Teen to be attacked. Maybe there was more to Wendi. She may not be quite as shallow as I'd always thought. That was kind of good news.

The really good news is that I have a plan. Adam and I will stop the clown gang. There is no way they can handle us both. I hoped. Then I'll show General Sky and the others that Adam can be a productive and useful member of society on his own. How am I going to do that? I really have no idea! I'm hoping something will come to me while I'm kicking clown butt.

But I know I will eventually figure something out. If I have to, I'll go to the media. I'll tell them the government is trying to make a super army. And not only that, but they are keeping their super soldiers by force and making them do things they don't want to do. I know the media won't like the idea of the government creating clones. I know they definitely won't approve of the government trying to control people. Hopefully though, the general will see it my way.

I just need to prove that Adam isn't dangerous and that he can still work for them, but it has to be his choice. He could be an employee, not a prisoner. I like that idea. I feel pretty certain Adam will too. I also think that even the general will realize they'd be better off with a happy super employee than an angry super clone.

Clowning

When Quazar and I landed at the Starlight City all night bank, the clown gang had already collected bags and bags of money. A guard, a couple of workers and some customers lay on the ground shaking.

I kicked in the door and stormed into the bank.

"Man! You clowns just aren't funny!" I said.

The five clowns stopped in their tracks. They all grinned. The lead clown smirked at me. "So, Super Teen, you are back more for!" He pointed at Quazar. "I see you brought a friend to join in the fun!"

"What's your deal, clown?" I said.

"Clowning doesn't pay well. So we went to night school and learned some chemistry and biology. Sure, we could have become chemistry or biology teachers but figured this would be a lot more fun."

Another clown leaned over his shoulder. "Plus it pays better."

"I mean...why do you guys love making people frightened?" I asked.

Quazar pointed at the clowns. "I think they are kind of cute."

The lead clown grinned. "Kid, you got yourself good taste. But most people these days think of clowns as scary or creepy. So we decided to roll with it. Take advantage of people's fears and make money at the same time. It's win-win."

We heard somebody drop down behind us. We spun to see two skinny clowns holding balloons. They must have been floating up in the bank's high ceilings waiting for us.

"Ha! Ha! have some fear!" the clowns said, leaning into us and pressing buttons on their flowers. A brown liquid shot out at us.

Quazar held up his hand and created a wall of flame, incinerating the liquid into smoke. I blew the smoke back at the two clowns.

They both inhaled. They looked at each other and shouted, "Clown! Yikes!"

The two turned and started to run away, screaming, "Clowns are gross!" they both crashed into the wall and fell to the ground.

Out of instinct, I leap up into the air. I grabbed Quazar, pulling him up with me.

The other five clowns had pulled out water guns and began squirting a liquid at us. Luckily, we were too high up for the limited range of the squirt guns. The liquid fell to the floor, burning holes in the wood.

"Ah man," one of the clowns moaned. "This place had such nice timber floors." He pointed to us. "This is on you!"

I pointed at the clown. "Finally, you said something funny!"

"Thank you!" he said with a bow.

"Look, you silly clowns. I want to give you a chance to surrender peacefully!" Quazar said. "I've always found clowns nice and funny in a weird and strange way. So give up now and I won't zap you!"

"What do you mean zap us?" the lead clown said.

"Show 'em," I told Quazar.

"Really?" he asked.

"Sure, just leave the lead clown to me. I owe him one!"

Quazar rubbed his hands together quickly. They started sparking with electricity. He pointed his left hand at the two clowns on the right. He pointed his right hand at the two the clowns on the left. Bolts of zig-zagged energy cracked from Quazar's hands into the four clowns.

The clowns shivered and started to smoke. Quazar

stopped zapping them. The four clowns dropped to the ground.

"That's what I mean by zapping you!" Quazar told the clowns.

The lead clown threw a ball on the floor which exploded into a big cloud of smoke. The clown darted towards the rear exit.

I passed him at super speed. He bumped into me and fell to the ground.

"Ouch!" he said, rubbing his head. "That hurts! What are you made of? Steel?"

"Pretty much," I said. "You know it's been a long weird day. And I haven't taken my boots off for hours!"

"So?" the clown said from the floor.

"I'm going to take them off now...." I said, bending over and popping my boot off.

"Once again...so?" the clown said holding his head up.

"These boots are great. But they don't always let my feet breathe. My feet are especially bad when I'm angry. Normally, I wouldn't do this in public but since everybody else is already knocked out..." I extended my foot and waved my toes under the clown's nose.

"OMG!" the clown gasped. I could see his face turn blue even through his white paint.

I kept my toe under his nose, the sheer smell of my foot was holding him up. He wanted to pass out to gain relief but my foot odor held his head steady. Yeah, my foot odor seems to be a force of nature.

After a couple of seconds, the paint on his face began to melt. I figured that was enough. I removed my foot from his face. His head jerked back. He was out cold. He would probably stay that way for a day or two.

Quazar landed next to me. "Wow, that's some stinky foot odor you've got there. I thought *my* feet were bad. But wow! You beat me hands down!"

"Thanks!" I said.

I saw Captain Michaels and his officers coming towards us. Captain Michaels glared at the clowns laid out on the floor. He surveyed the damage they had caused.

"Thanks for the help, Super Teen," Chief Michaels said. "I'm sure glad I deputized you."

Chief Michaels pointed at Quazar. "Who's your friend? Do we have a new superhero in town?"

Quazar offered his hand to Captain Michaels. "No sir, I am actually leaving town. I was just visiting and thought I would help out a fellow super."

"Well, I'm glad you did," Chief Michaels said. "Any friend of Super Teens is a friend of our town."

"Thank you, I have enjoyed my time in this town," Quazar said. "But now I must move on!"

"Speaking of moving on...Quazar and I have people to see!" I said.

"I understand," Chief Michaels replied.

I took Adam by the hand and we both flew out the

door and up into the sky. "Where we going?" Adam asked me.

"To BMS labs!" I said.

It felt good to hold somebody's hand.

Dear Diary: It felt so great to be holding Adam's hand. I have a real connection with him. We're two super beings in a world of mostly non-super people. We're outcasts. Okay, maybe not outcasts, but the majority of people don't know what to make of us. Some people are scared of us, which they shouldn't be. Some people look at us almost like gods, which they really shouldn't do either. We're just two normal kids who happen to be super. Yes, one of us is also a four-year-old clone. And that is a little freaky. I can't believe I've had a crush on a four-year-old. Fair enough, not a normal four-year-old but still a four-year-old. Best not to think too much about that. He is a cool great guy who is super like me. That's all that matters!

Of course, I have to find a new home for Adam. He needs a place where he can start out fresh. I can't believe that I finally find somebody I like, who I think may like me, and he cannot live in my town. Well, the good thing is that we are both super and we should be able to see each other quickly if needed. Right? In many ways, this is a great situation. I get my own life. He gets his own life. But we still hang out together when we want. Perfect!

An Unexpected Offer

We landed in the courtyard of BMS labs. Dad and Hana were there along with Jason and Ellie Mae Opal. This was to be expected. I was pleased to see that Ellie Mae's parents, Jeanie and Don were also there. Jeanie was a lawyer who fought for the rights of supers and Don was a researcher. They were both good people and I was glad they had come.

Adam and I both morphed out of our costumes. We wanted to greet these people as ourselves, not as our super selves.

Don walked up to Adam and offered him his hand. "I'm Don Opal, Ellie Mae's dad. You must be Adam?"

"I sure am," Adam said, shaking Don's hand.

Jeanie walked over to Adam. "Adam, I'm Jeanie Opal, Ellie Mae's mom," she said and gave him a hug.

"Thanks for the hug," Adam blushed. "I think that might be the first hug from a mom I've ever been given. It felt nice and warm."

A little tear welled up in Jeanie's eye. (Mine too)

"Jeanie, Don, I'm so glad you are here with Ellie Mae, but why have you come?" I asked.

Jeanie smiled at me. "When Jason, here, told us Adam's story, we thought we could help. We know he needs a new home and family to start his life over, or maybe for the first time."

"We want him to join our family in Centre City." Ellie Mae said, her blue eyes sparkling with excitement.

Don nodded. "Yes, I left BAD because quite frankly they were kind of bad. I am now senior VP in charge of research at Future Now. It's a cool new innovative company. We will work with BMS here to create top-notch high tech.

We are even exploring other dimensions. Slowly and carefully, of course."

Jeanie spoke up. "Future Now even has its own school for their employee's families if they wish to go there. It's a very modern school that features all grades and caters to both normal students and a few super students like Ellie. We need to teach people that supers are really just people."

"Man! You talk so good!" Adam said.

"My mom's a lawyer," Ellie Mae said proudly.

"Guys this is truly an amazing offer," I said.

Jeanie looked into Adam's eyes. "We would start out as your foster parents but if it works out like I hope it does, we could adopt you if that's what you want."

"We only want what's best for you!" Don said.

Adam bent his knees. He leaped into the air. His legs transformed into pure red-hot energy. He started skywriting above the lab...I AM SO HAPPY!

He fired a few fireworks from his hands (and a couple from his butt.) He hovered above us. "Oops! Sorry, I got excited there."

I looked at the Opal family. "I take it that's a yes!"

Adam landed in the exact spot he'd taken off from. "Yes! Yes! Yes! I am so honored. I have wanted to be part of a family forever." He grinned. "Can I fight crime in your town?"

Jeanie grinned also. "Yes, I am sure I can do the paperwork to make that happen."

Don nodded. "Yes! And while we at Future Now strive to be safe and careful and cautious, you never know if something might slip out or go wrong. It will be nice to have a superpower on our side to help contain any problems that may pop up. We can probably even put you on our security's payroll."

Adam stood there. His mouth dropped open. Yep, Adam really didn't know how to react to people being nice to him for genuine reasons; other than because he was so handsome.

I snapped my fingers in front of Adam's face. He shook his head. He blinked his eyes. "Sorry, my brain froze for a second. I've just never been so happy!"

My dad stepped forward. "I hate to break up this little gathering but you do know General Sky will have to be convinced this a good idea. She will need to know that not only is Adam safe, but those around him are also safe."

Hana stepped forward. "Plus, the government didn't spend all that money on Adam just to let him walk or fly away. They are going to need something in return."

I pondered over those words. They made total sense. I was going to have to give the general an offer she couldn't refuse. Thankfully, I can be a very persuasive person. Especially when I am fighting for a just cause. And man, Adam being happy and safe was the best reason I had ever had.

Dear Diary: Man oh man, it's so great of Ellie Mae, Jeanie and Don to stand up like that and offer to make their home Adam's home. I know in my heart of hearts Adam will be so happy there. He'll have it all. A family, a job, a school (where he won't have to hide who he is). I might even be a little jealous of that. Although, that really is silly of me.

Wait! What if Adam finds a girlfriend in this new town? I mean…he is starting over. Maybe seeing me will remind him of his past? Maybe he'll prefer to be with somebody other than me.

Okay, maybe I'm thinking too much about this. Yeah, it is possible to think too much. I need to do what is best for Adam. If things between us work out, then great. If not, I am sure we will both find excellent, amazing people to spend our lives with. Right now, I have to concentrate on what's most important. And that's Adam being free of the general.

Time to get Persuasive

My dad had directions to General Sky's base of operations. It was exactly 111 miles south of BMS labs. It was also three miles underground…pretty darn secure! As well, it was dangerous to teleport into it if we didn't have the exact location.

Since we needed this, we called in a friend, Jess the cool witch. Lately, Jess hadn't been training much at BMS labs. She wanted more freedom and more time to be herself. But she was still happy to help when needed and boy was she needed. After all, we could use Jess's telepathy and clairvoyance to see the exact location of General Sky's base in her mind. Then Ellie Mae could teleport us there.

Jess sat on the grass, legs crossed, eyes closed, meditating. Today, half of her hair was dark, the other half red. It was a look that somehow really worked for her. Jess opened her eyes. "I got 'em!" she said, with a slight grin.

A beam of light appeared from her head. The beam of light showed us General Sky sitting in her quarters. She was drinking a cup of coffee.

"How big is the room where she is now?" Don asked.

Jess turned her head from side to side. The image in the light scrolled as her head moved, revealing a large room. "Big enough!" Jess said.

"Good, let's get there then!" I said.

Ellie Mae touched Jess on the head with her left index finger. Ellie Mae held out her right hand. A ball of energy appeared in her hand. The ball grew to the size of an open door. Through that door, we could see the General sipping her coffee.

"Now!" Ellie Mae said.

Jason walked up to me. "Do you want me to go?"

"No, you stay here," I said. "If something goes wrong, we'll need you to get Tanya, Kayla, Lori, and Marie so you can all come and save us."

"Check," Jason said. "Tanya has been working with Kayla and she's really learning to control and hone her powers. So, she'll be ready to help!"

I took Adam's hand and we passed through the door. Don, Jeanie, and Opal quickly followed us in.

The general saw us. She sighed. "Can't a general even finish her coffee in peace?" she groaned.

"I thought you'd be happy that we brought Adam back!" I said.

"I would be," the general sighed. "But I am not stupid. I know there is a catch involved. Especially since you brought Doctor and Barrister Opal with you..." She sighed again. She pointed to Ellie Mae, "And of course their teleporting daughter." The general rolled her eyes. "We've spent billions of taxpayer dollars to build a complex way underground and still you manage to just pop in here." The general shook her head. "Okay, tell me your demands. Hopefully, we can work this out before my security detail gets here and things become messy. I've learned it's always easier to talk when energy blasts aren't flying back and forth. What's the deal you have for me?"

I had to give the general credit. She appeared to be sharper than I thought.

"I want Adam to be free," I said.

The general nodded impatiently. "Yeah, Lia I get that. Truthfully, I wouldn't mind that either. He's a good kid. I don't want to see him caged up here either. But there's one small issue. While I may be a big powerful general, I still have to report to my superiors. If we are to let Adam roam free then we have to give them something in return. What do they gain from it? Plus, you have to assure us that he won't be an insurance risk. What if he destroys a town..."

"I would never destroy a town!" Adam said

"No, not on purpose. Of course not. But say you slipped up and you accidentally flattened a town with a burp or a fart. If the press got wind of the fact that we made you, we would be open to all sorts of lawsuits. People love suing the government. They think we have tons of money." The general pointed to her coffee maker. I had to use my own money to buy that. Our budgets are tight."

Don walked forward. "General, I assure you we will keep Adam under control. My wife and I wish for him to come to Centre City to live with us. I will also give him a job with my company, Future Now."

Jeanie spoke up. "This way, on the odd chance that something did go wrong, people would blame Future Now, instead of you."

The general smiled. "I like that. I do. That fixes one of my problems. But we still want access to the boy. You know, just in case something special crops up where we could use his unique skill set. I mean...the boy can be a living blast of energy."

Adam stood up. "I have no problem with that. I won't hurt anybody, but I will stop anybody whom I deem a threat to my loved ones and to you, General." Adam looked at the general. "After all, if it wasn't for you and Doctor Keys, I would not exist and for that I am grateful. I will help when I can."

"Plus, if the threat is big enough, I can help too!" I said.

The general smiled. "So, I can get two of the most powerful people on earth for the price of one."

"Yes," I answered.

"I love working and fighting side by side with Lia," Adam said.

The door to the general's quarters blew open. Dozens of people in uniforms burst into the room.

The general groaned. "Why can't you ever knock...."

"Shock and awe, sir!" an anxious soldier said.

The general pointed at us. "You aren't going to shock and awe this bunch."

"Actually, it was pretty cool!" Adam said. "I liked the booms."

"Can you guys get out now while we talk?" I told the soldiers. "I don't like all those guns. I'm afraid you might hurt yourselves."

"Look, girl!" one soldier said. "I know you may be Super Teen…but my team and I are…"

I exhaled on him. It had been a while since I'd eaten anything so I figured I might have empty stomach breath. Sure enough, he and all the other soldiers dropped to the floor.

I breathed a little puff of breath into my hand near my nose. "Yikes, that is nasty!" I said. I turned to the general. "Do we have a deal?"

The general looked at her fallen soldiers. She looked at us.

Dr. Keys walked into the room. "I told the guards not to overreact, but of course they did," he said.

The general turned to the doctor. "Did you hear their proposal? What do you think?"

The doctor nodded. "I think it's the best possible deal for all of us." He looked at Doctor Opal. "Can we visit and observe Adam from time to time?"

"If Adam wants you to," Don said.

"I think I would like that. We could do lunch! I've always wanted to do lunch!" Adam smiled.

The general chuckled. "Okay, I think we can make this work."

Adam rushed up and hugged the general and then the doctor. "Thanks! I will do good in this world!"

"I know you will!" the general said.

"I know you will too!" I said.

Adam turned and looked me in the eyes. "I really appreciate all you've done for me, Lia. I liked you a lot when

I was Brandon. I like you even more now I'm Adam!"

"Right back at you!" I said. Okay not the best response, I admit.

"Now that I'm me and I'm able to see you as both Lia Strong and as Super Teen, I'm hoping we can spend time together now and then. Maybe get to know each other better? Even though I already know you pretty well. After all, I was created to track you down and stop you if you got out of hand."

"True, though not necessarily a selling point," I grinned.

Adam took both of my hands. "Lia, from the moment I first met you, I knew I would never be able to destroy you!"

"How sweet!" I said. And I actually meant it.

Adam continued, "I've been confused about a lot of stuff in this world. It's weird knowing I was meant to destroy you, and also knowing that I could never do that! But that's the only thing I am really certain about."

"Thanks, Adam, I really appreciate that."

"He's so nice," I heard Ellie Mae say.

"Yes, he will make a wonderful addition to our home," Jeanie added.

The general cleared her throat. "Okay, this is a fine and touching scene, but I think you people would be best to get back to your homes before the second round of troops comes in. I'd hate to have Super Teen use her super bad breath on more of my troops. I'm already in enough hot water with my superiors for losing a bunch of androids and drones. I'll have to say it was for a training mission. Hopefully, they'll be okay with that."

Adam interrupted her. "I have one more thing to tell Lia before we part!"

"Fine..." the general sighed. She turned to Doctor Keys. "You made him too compassionate."

The doctor just smiled.

Adam moved closer to me. "Lia, my only regret is that we will be living in separate towns and probably won't be able to see each other every day." He lowered his head.

"Don't worry, Adam. We're both super and if you need me to help or to chat, I can be there in a flash."

"Ditto!" Adam smiled.

I smiled back and felt a warmth wash over me. I wasn't cold but a shiver of goosebumps appeared on my skin. On a sudden impulse, I stood on my toes and kissed him on the cheek.

Adam's smile widened and I felt my heart melt just a little bit more.

Dear Diary: I'm so happy! Everything has worked out so well! Not perfect, perfect would be Adam and me living in the same town. But I know that can't happen. He needs his own space. He needs a fresh start. And because we're both super, we can visit each other fairly easily. Maybe this will even keep our relationship fresh! Okay, Im trying to find the positive side because I really don't want him to leave Starlight City. But deep down, I know this is best for him. Adam/Quazar will be free to grow on his own. He will become his own person and he will have his own town to protect. I know he'll do great. And so will I!

Right now though, all I can think about is seeing him again! ☺

The end, for now.

***

Book 8

A New Type of Love!

The New Android

It was a beautiful spring day and my best friend, Jason and I were walking my faithful dog, Shep in the park. Shep loved the park. There were so many new smells. He had to stop and sniff them all.

"So, how are you and Tanya getting along these days?" I asked, pretty much just to be polite.

Truthfully, I wasn't thrilled with my BFF, Jason dating the almost perfect Tanya. I mean...the girl had everything, cool looks, cool power, control of that power, brains, and she was really, really pretty! I'm not sure why she needed Jason too. Okay, that probably didn't sound too good. After all, Jason was a great guy. Any girl would be lucky to have him as a boyfriend, but I just didn't think that girl had to be Tanya. After all, Tanya could have any guy she wanted, so why not just leave Jason alone?

"Things are, ah…good," Jason said with some hesitation.

"But?" I prompted, noticing his odd expression.

He looked up at the sky. "Nice day, huh?" he said.

"Jason, you can talk to me," I said, stopping in my tracks to stare at him.

Shep tugged on his lead, trying to drag me forward. There was a big rock lying just a few feet away that he really wanted to sniff.

Jason grinned. "I like Tanya, a lot. I mean, Tanya and you are the two most important people in my life next to my parents."

Part of me thought, ah now that is so sweet. The other part of me thought, why do I get second billing to Tanya?

That part of me could be a little petty. I needed to push that part down. Just because I happened to be Super Teen, the world's strongest person, that didn't mean I was the world's most important person. Sure, Jason and I had known each other forever, and it had always been me and Jason and Jason and I, but that didn't mean I had exclusive rights to Jason's friendship.

"Go on, I'm listening," I said like I was a trained counselor or something.

"I'm just thinking that maybe Tanya and I should slow down some," he said the words little by little like he was calculating every one. "I like her a lot..."

"Yeah, you keep saying that," I smiled. "What's not to like?"

"Life is just so, so crazy right now!" Jason said. "I have regular school as well as the work I do for your dad's company at BMS labs!" He leaned over and whispered to me. "Plus, with my new body armor, I can help fight crime."

"I am aware of that," I told him.

"And you know, I also want to have time for normal kid things...play video games, watch YouTube, play LAX, and study so I can get into med school someday."

"I understand," I said.

"And well, Tanya is great and almost perfect..." Jason said.

"Almost perfect?" I asked.

Jason grinned. "She has really stinky feet."

"No need to remind me!" I said. "Yeah, she used her time stop power and her shoe stink to become the first person ever to KO me." I had to admit that was impressive. "That taught me that I can be taken down by some things. Being invulnerable to harm doesn't mean I don't have to breathe."

Jason nodded. "Exactly, so she even uses her stinky feet for good. I mean the girl's pretty much perfect. She's smart, beautiful and funny."

I nodded. "Yeah...I can totally see why you'd be sick of that," I grinned.

Jason stopped walking. "Yeah, I know it sounds crazy. I still want to stay friends with her, close friends, but I don't think I want to be '*together*.' It just makes life more complicated."

"Sometimes life is complicated," I said even though I'm kind of ashamed to admit my inner brain was thinking...*YES!!!*

"Agreed, but I think I'm too young and too busy to be locked into Tanya. She's great, but she's the first girl I've ever gone out with as more than friends. She may be the best fit for me out there, but I think we need to see other people. Just because well, I'm 14 and she's 16....we might end up together... but..."

I put a hand on Jason's shoulder. Jason, being a super brain, had a way of over analyzing everything. Like...it takes him a week to buy a new pair of sneaks. He even computes the best gum to chew and the optimal number of chews for each piece. "Jason, you have to talk to Tanya about this..." I paused. "I'm sure you two can reach an agreement."

"I hope so," he said.

I nudged him. "If not, she'll just change the timeline so you never existed..."

Jason gulped. "Do you really think she'd do that?" He paused to consider it. "I'm not sure she could actually do that since I currently certainly do exist. I mean, she has a lot of control to move time backward and she might be able to make slight changes to the timeline. But to just will me out of existence would be a massive change that would cascade through time and space... I don't think time would let her do that... even *she* has her limits..."

"Plus, she is not a maniacal super villain out to destroy the universe," I added.

"Good point," Jason said. "She is level-headed. And

she is kind of busy right now keeping her little sister, Kayla, who is now the same age as her, from abusing her powers. So, maybe sending ripples through time and space..."

Almost as if on cue, we saw Tanya, Marie, and Lori running after us.

"Guys, wait, wait!" Maria shouted, waving her arms at us.

We stopped to let them catch up. "What's going on?" I asked.

Tanya pointed to MAC, the computer interface I wear on my wrist like a watch. "Didn't MAC tell you?"

"No, I am sorry," MAC said. "I did not wish to bother, Lia, Jason, and Shep. I thought they needed their down-time. Plus, I believe Shep needs to do his duty. I hate to interrupt a fine dog when he needs to poop."

"Woof!" Shep said as if he understood what Mac was saying.

"What's going on?" I asked.

"Hana's sister, Wanda has left the lab..." Marie said quickly.

"We think she's heading to the park," Lora said.

"Wait, Hana has a sister? Hana is an android..." I said.

"How come nobody told us about this?" Jason asked.

Tanya shook her head. "Apparently nobody knew about it. And because your dad gave Hana such high clearance at the lab, she has a lot of power. Plus, being a super-advanced android herself, she has a lot of ability. It's a dangerous combination. Really, Lia, you need to talk to him."

"Look, Tanya...Lia's dad, Doctor S. has a brilliant mind! If he gave Hana such complete access, she must truly deserve it," Jason said.

Tanya took a step back. Guess she wasn't used to Jason arguing with her. Jason turned to me. "Right?"

I shook my head. Pointing at Tanya I found myself

saying, "I agree with her."

"See, Tanya!" Jason said looking at her. He stopped when my words finally sank in. Turning to me he said, "Say what?"

I shrugged. "I love my dad. He's brilliant, but he can be very whacky. I'm sure in his mind he thinks it was wise to give a machine that looks like a beautiful woman, full run of a super high tech lab. But I don't agree." I sighed. "I believe he's influenced by her near perfect face."

"You're right, Lia. Plus, he and a team of other scientists designed her in a lab," Lori added.

MAC chimed in. "Actually, I agree with Jason. Just because Hana happened to be made by humans doesn't mean she can't be trusted as much as humans." He paused for a moment. "Actually, I find her very trustworthy."

Lori crossed her arms and stared at the MAC interface on my wrist. "You would! You're a machine too."

"Correct," MAC said. "But I insist intelligent machines and humans are not that different. We both act according to how we are programmed. We, as machines, are initially programmed by humans, but learn to respond to stimuli in our environment; just as babies are programmed by their parents and society and then learn to respond to stimuli in their environment. In fact, the assumption of many is that all humans do is respond to stimuli and that humans are just as programmed as we are." If MAC had a tongue, I'm pretty sure he would be sticking it out at Lori right now.

Lori pointed to Marie, "Turn him to cheese!" she said, mostly joking.

Marie just grinned.

But MAC responded. "Turning my interface to cheese would not stop me."

"No, but it would shut you up!" Lori said.

"Guys, remember we are all on the *same team* here!" I said, firmly stressing the words *same* and *team*.

Lori turned her attention to me. "True."

"Good point," MAC said.

"So, what does Wanda look like?" Jason asked.

"I could give you a nifty holographic picture," MAC said. "Or I could simply say she looks similar to Hana, only with dark hair and a darker skin tone."

Marie pointed to a very beautiful dark-haired woman, in a short red dress. "I think I found her."

We all turned to see the woman who pretty much had to be Wanda, paddling her feet in the middle of the large park fountain. She looked very content, unlike the two policemen who were talking to her. A crowd had also gathered, taking in the spectacle.

"Lady, you have to get out of the fountain," one of the policemen ordered.

"Why?" Wanda asked.

"Because this is a public park," the other policeman told her.

"Right. And I am part of the public." She waved at them, "So you two fine men may go."

The two policemen looked at each other.

"Lady, don't make us take you in," one of the officers told her.

Wanda giggled. "Don't worry, I won't!" She started kicking the water up into the air and yelling "wee!"

The two officers just looked at her. "Okay, it looks like we'll have to drag you out and then take you down to the station!"

The two rolled up their pant legs and cautiously stepped into the fountain. One of them pointed at Wanda. "Look, lady, you're making us angry!"

Wanda smiled at them sweetly. "That was never my intention. I just want you to leave me alone."

The two police officers stopped mid-step. They turned to each other. They started kicking water at each other. And yelling, "Wee!!"

"What the heck?" somebody in the crowd said.

"You should all come and play in the fountain too!" Wanda said.

The entire crowd raced eagerly into the fountain. People came from everywhere.

They each tossed off their shoes, rolled up their pants and started paddling around in the water.

"Okay now, this just keeps getting weirder and weirder," Tanya said.

"Let's get this genie back in the bottle. And by bottle, I mean the lab, and by genie, I mean this android."

"MAC, activate my super teen costume!" I said.

"Will do," he paused. "As long as you promise not to hurt her," Mac said.

Putting my hand on my heart. "You have my word!"

I saw the world around me shimmer, which meant my holo-mask came on. Looking down, I was now wearing a yellow uniform. I thought I looked pretty good. Of course that wasn't really the point here, but still, it's nice to be stylish when fighting crime or crazy androids.

I flew over to Wanda. I picked her up and lifted her out of the pond. The onlookers kept splashing water on each other, not paying any attention to me or to Wanda. I carried Wanda over to Jason, Tanya, Lori, and Marie.

"Oh, that was fun!" Wanda said. "You, Lia, truly are as amazing as my sister says. I'm glad we are friends."

I figured if this advanced android thought of me as a friend, that was a good thing. Better talking than fighting, especially since I had no idea what she could and couldn't do. So, talk was good.

"Let's get you back to the BMS labs," I said softly.

"That would be a good idea," Jason said.

"Agreed," Tanya said.

"ASAP," Lori said.

"Yeppers," Marie said.

Wanda shook her head. "I disagree!"

I picked Wanda up off the ground. "You don't have a vote."

Wanda pointed to my friends, "Do they have a vote?"

"Yes, of course," I said.

"Oh good!" Wanda grinned.

I noticed all my friends suddenly glaring at me. That couldn't be good. Jason flipped into his armor. He pointed his fist at me. His missile fired at me.

I caught the missile. It exploded in my hand. It sent me flying across the park. I landed at Shep's feet. He licked my face. Well, at least he hadn't turned on me. Plus, I could still move and that meant Tanya must have been fighting Wanda's control.

As I pushed myself to my feet, I saw Lori charging at me with her bionic legs. I straightened up and held out my arms. "Lori, stop! Snap out of it!"

She didn't. She kept coming at me. Her eyes unblinking. She made a fist. She swung at me. I blocked the punch. I backed away slowly. "Lori, stop! Think about what you are doing. You don't want to punch me. Right?"

Lori stopped. She started to mumble. "I don't want to punch you," she said slowly. Her eyes popped open.

I lowered my arms. I was getting through to her.

POW! She kicked me in the jaw with a bionic snap kick. The kick launched me into the air.

"Ha! Fell for it!" Lori taunted

Oh, she was clever. I spun in midair and landed behind Lori. I tapped her gently on the back of the neck. She dropped to the ground. One down. But I still had Marie, Jason and possibly Tanya to deal with. The big problem was that I didn't want to harm them.

"Turn her to cheese!" Tanya said to Marie.

But the feeling was not mutual.

"I have to touch her!" Marie said.

"No problems!" Jason told her. He grabbed Marie by the feet and started spinning her around.

Could Jason be on my side?

"I will fling you at her!" Jason shouted.

Nope definitely NOT on my side.

Jason released Marie and she came flying at me, arms extended. I knew if she touched me I'd be cheese…literally.

Thing was, I'm not that easy to touch. I leaped up into the air letting Marie pass underneath me. Just as she shot by me, I reached down and grabbed her leg. At the same time, I noticed Wanda trying to run away in the opposite direction. I took Marie and flung her at the running Wanda.

"Wee!" Marie yelled as she flew through the air.

Wanda heard the wee and turned to see Marie's outstretched arms.

"Nooo…" Wanda started to say.

Marie's hands touch Wanda. Wanda melted into a pile of cheese. Marie fell to the ground just past the pile of cheese. She looked up. Her eyes cleared. "Oops, I have been really craving fondue." She said.

Jason shook his head and blinked his eyes. He took a deep breath. "That was weird. I knew what I was doing but I couldn't stop."

Tanya started to move. "It took every ounce of my mental strength to keep her from controlling me. I did not like that."

Lori pushed herself up off the ground. She turned to me. "Sorry for kicking you in the head," she said. She grinned.

"No problem, I know you weren't totally in control of your actions," I told her. I walked towards the pile of cheese that was once an advanced android.

"That's the thing though, I kind of was in control. I kind of wanted to do it. Nothing personal Lia, but you're always the star of the show. It actually felt good clobbering you a bit."

"You got in a nice kick," I admitted. I had let my guard down. That wouldn't happen again. I'm still learning some of the tricks of being a superhero. "But I'd hardly say you clobbered me."

Looking around, I saw the crowd had now all regained their senses. A couple of kids noticed me.

"Hey, it's Super Teen!" one of them shouted excitedly.

A few of them moved towards me. That's one of the perks of being a superhero…kids love you. I prided myself on being a good role model.

Some of the older people in the crowd slowly stepped out of the fountain. They shook their heads. "Figures…we'd find ourselves dancing in a fountain when Super Teen is around!" one of them sneered.

Another older lady pointed at me. "Why did you have to do with this?"

That's the downside of being a superhero. You tend to find trouble or trouble tends to find you. Either way, since you are usually around trouble, some people blame you for that trouble.

The mob of people started towards us. Some happy. Some angry. Some just following the mob to see what might happen.

"I don't have time for this!" Tanya said. Pointing at the crowd. They froze in place. "Good, that will keep them quiet," Tanya said. "I need quiet."

We all saw Marie looking at the pile of cheese on the ground. Marie looked up at me. "Phew, good thing I didn't touch you. Not sure I can undo fondue...."

"That's okay," I told her. "Don't think we want to undo this one. Let's scoop her up and get her back to the lab."

Marie shook her head. "Sometimes my power scares me..."

Jason looked at the pile of cheese on the ground, all light yellow and gooey. "A little fear is good," he said.

Marie continued to stare at the mound of cheese. She looked up at me. "If I had touched you, this would have been you," she said to me.

I patted her on the shoulder. I gave her a little hug. "Don't worry. You didn't." I told her.

Pointing at the cheese, I said, "Let's scoop this up and get to the lab. I wanna have a talk with Hana."

Dear Diary: I don't like the idea that Hana was experimenting with making androids of her own. Truthfully, I have no idea why I don't like that idea. I mean, Hana is an intelligent "being", but for her to create another version of herself just seems very wrong to me. After all, an army of Hanas could be a serious threat to the world. Or they could be a big help to the world? Hana is capable of doing so much.

Speaking of doing so much, Marie's power can be scary. She could be rich if she wanted to be just by turning everything into gold or silver with a touch of her hand or even a puff of her breath. Luckily, I am hyper-fast and impossible to touch if I don't want to be touched. Of course, some of my dad's people think they can teach Marie to transform materials simply by looking at them. Yeah, I don't even want to think about that. Luckily, neither does Marie as she is truly a nice girl.

Oh, I also need to learn not to let my guard down when fighting. Sometimes I think being invulnerable means I don't have to think that hard. Lori really clocked me. If a true super villain had done that I might have been sent flying and then I could have endangered innocent people. Being super doesn't mean you don't have to think!

Finally, I must admit I have mixed emotions about Jason and Tanya. I love the fact that Jason seems so happy with her. Emotions and love are not finite. Jason can have a relationship with Tanya and still be BFFs with me, but knowing I may not be the number one girl in Jason's life does bug me a bit. I need to learn to get over that. I mean, come on me, even if Jason and Tanya do completely break up there will be other girls in Jason's life. A lot of them. And that's something I need to learn to deal with!

Unexpected News

While Tanya, Lori, and Marie dropped the cheese off at one of BMS's lab rooms, I headed straight to Hana's office. Of course, Jason followed after me as quickly as he could.

"Lia, stay calm," Jason urged as we traversed the hallways of BMS labs.

"I am calm, I'm not moving at super speed," I told him. Though it would have been tempting so I could lose him. Still, I knew he was right. I did need to stay calm and evaluate the situation. I didn't like the idea of Hana dating my dad so that may have clouded my judgment.

"Remember, Lia, Hana is a creature of pure logic. I am sure she had a logical explanation for what she did," Jason told me, panting a bit.

"I'll just melt her into a pile of android goo with my heat vision!" I said, storming forward.

Jason put a hand on my shoulder. "Don't do that. Hana is amazing tech. Plus, it would make your dad angry. He invented her and now he's dating her."

I actually stopped walking for a moment. I turned to face Jason. "I think that makes it worse!" But I knew Jason was right, I didn't want to make my dad mad. Well, actually, I kind of did, but that really wouldn't accomplish anything. Dad may be a geek and a bit different, but he is my dad. He does love me and I do believe he wants what's best for me.

I kicked in the door to Hana's office. Hana looked up from her desk. The desk was made from old-fashioned wood. Kind of a weird contrast I thought. I stormed over to

Hana.

"Hana, what's the big idea?" I asked, pounding my fist on her desk. The desk shattered in two.

"Oops. Sorry," I said.

Hana sat back in her chair. "Sorry, for smashing my antique desk or for turning my sister into cheese?"

"More for the desk because your sister was a threat. And technically, I didn't turn her to cheese. Marie did."

Hana nodded. "Yes, but you misdirected Marie to Wanda. Hence, the reason Wanda became cheese mush."

"True, but only because she encouraged Marie to turn me into cheese!" I maintained.

"Actually, she just freed Marie of personal restraints." She paused for me to reflect. "It's not Wanda's fault that Marie wanted to cheese you." Hana looked me in the eyes. "I mean, Lia, I love you like a daughter but you can be a bit over the top sometimes. Always thinking you need to save the world."

"I've saved the world a couple of times!" I argued.

"Yes, but not just you. You've had a lot of help," Hana said, she bent over and picked up the two parts of her desk. Her hand started to glow red. She soldered the two pieces back together. She steadied the desk.

"Wow, I didn't know you could do that!" Jason said.

"I am always downloading new apps that give me new abilities," Hana said.

"That's so cool!" Jason said, almost in awe.

I cleared my throat. The two of them turned to me. "Let's get back to the matter at hand," I said slowly.

Hana nodded. "Right, your giant ego!"

"Correct," I said without thinking. "No! This is not about my ego. This is about you!" I said pointing at Hana.

"If you are trying to be dramatic, you are failing epically," Hana said. Her index finger turned into a little laser, she started doing her nails with that laser.

"Wow, so cool!" Jason said again.

I made two fists. "Hana, stop trying to distract Jason! This is serious!"

"Agreed, Lia, you did turn my multi-million-dollar creation into cheese. Thus, wasting company money."

Dad came out of his office that was located right behind Hana's office. "Wait, did I hear the words...wasting company money?" he said.

Hana and I pointed at each other and said, "She did it!"

"Did what?" Dad asked.

"She created a clone of herself!" I said.

"She destroyed my sister," Hana said at the same time.

"Lia, you can't really clone an android," Dad, Hana, and Jason said.

Dad stopped. He looked at Hana. "You made a copy of yourself? How did I not know this?"

Hana shrugged. "You have to sleep. I don't."

"But you were created to simulate everything a

116

human does," Dad said.

"True, I can sleep but I do not need to sleep. It's kind of like pooping."

"TMI! Hana TMI!" I said.

Hana focused on me. "Well, you know how they say everybody poops? Well, I can poop but I usually choose not to. I did it once or twice to experience it but frankly, I did not find it all that useful. It's even a bit time-consuming. So now I just increase my energy usage to more effectively utilize everything I eat. And…"

I thrust my hands over my ears. "Stop! Before I melt you with super vision."

Hana pointed at me. "See, that's how she reacts to everything. I don't understand you so I will turn you to cheese or melt you."

Dad put his hand on his forehead. "I am really confused here."

Not surprising really. Dad was a world-class genius but he didn't pay attention to the stuff that goes on day by day. He had given control of most of that to Hana, hence the reason she was able to do what she had done.

"Dad, she created a copy of herself," I said.

Dad smiled. "That's amazing!"

"The thing attacked me," I said.

Dad's face fell. "Okay, that's not so amazing!" he said, looking at Hana. "Why did your copy attack Lia?"

Hana blew on her nails. "She was jealous of my sister's abilities!"

I stomped my foot down, shaking the room. "She was dominating people at the park!"

Dad looked at Hana. "Is that true?"

Hana sat back in her chair. "Define dominating."

"Making people do what she wanted," I said.

"She was just relaxing them," Hana insisted.

"They attacked me!" I shouted.

"You were ruining their chill!" Hana said. She looked

at Jason. "Right Jason? After all, you attacked her too."

"What?" Dad said. "I don't think I like people attacking my only child!"

"Well, how do you think I felt with your only child, my future step-daughter, attacking my creation?" Hana said.

"Wait...what?" I gasped.

Hana faced me. "You attacked my creation."

"No, rewind it a bit," I ordered.

"You will be my step-daughter once I marry your dad," Hana said. She showed me a large ring on her ring finger.

"Wow, congrats!" Jason said.

I gulped.

Hana looked at dad, "I thought you were going to tell her?"

Dad dropped his head. "I was waiting for the right time," he told his e-fiancée.

"Well, see?" Hana said. "I'm still learning about human emotions and stuff, but even I know THIS is not the right time!"

"OMG! OMG! OMG!"

I leaped up into the air and flew away. I actually flew right through the roof, but I didn't care.

As a flew up into the sky, I spotted somebody else streaking towards me. Using super vision, I saw that it was none other than my superhero friend from Moonvale, Quazar. Or, as I know him, Adam Opal.

I slowed down so Adam could catch up with me. Hovering in the air, I asked. "What brings you to my neck of the woods? Do we need to fight another giant super pooping gorilla?"

Adam shook his head. He looked so cute in his uniform. Most guys can't make those colors work, but Adam definitely could.

"Jason sent me an emergency text that you were upset and might need somebody super to help calm you down," he frowned.

"How did you find me?"

Adam hovered next to me. Pointing at MAC he said. "MAC sent me your coordinates. It was easy." Adam moved closer to me. "What's going on?"

"My dad is officially engaged," I sighed, the force knocked Adam back a bit. I felt glad that my breath was fresh and he didn't pass out. Never a good sign when your breath can knock out other superheroes.

"Isn't that a good thing? At least for him. I mean, don't you want your dad to be happy?" Adam said.

"He didn't tell me," I said.

"Oh, how do you know then?" Adam asked.

"His fiancée, an android he created, blurted it out after I helped destroy another android she'd made," I groaned.

Adam hovered there scratching his head. "Ya know, Lia, I'm a clone who battles blobs from another dimension and even I find this all very weird," he smiled.

"Welcome to my life," I said. Talking rapidly, I said. "I have no idea why my dad would do such a thing and not tell me."

Adam pointed to hole in the BMS Labs roof. "I think that Lia sized hole should be a hint."

I nodded. "Plus, I have no idea why Hana felt she needed a copy of herself."

Adam flew closer to me. "I don't know either. We're super but we don't know everything. We are stronger than most but still have our weaknesses, especially when it comes to our family. Like they say, you can't pick your family." He smiled. "Even though you kinda picked one for me and it worked out great."

"I'm so glad for you!" I told Adam. "Wanna go look for some crime to fight?"

Adam smirked. "Normally, yes. But you need to get answers. I suggest you go and do that."

I gave Adam a hug.

"What was that for?" he asked.

"For being you and for coming here."

"Really Lia, that's what friends, especially super friends are for."

I dropped down back into the BMS labs and into Hana's office.

"Sorry, I flew through the roof …literally," I told them.

Dad nodded. "I should have told you sooner, so part of this is on me."

"Yes, you humans really messed up," Hana said. "You need to learn to communicate better. Why can't everybody just be happy?"

I walked over and lifted Hana off the ground with my pinky. "Okay, here's some communication. Why did you feel the need to create a sister?" I asked.

"With all my work here, I thought it would be excellent and more efficient to create a version of me that could go out and learn about normal human emotions and stuff. I figure the more I learn about humans, the better wife I will be to your father. Plus, I do want humans to accept me." She pointed to the hole in the roof. "As you can see, it's not that easy. People fear a machine that is perfect looking, smarter than them, and stronger too."

"And more modest," I added.

Hana grinned. "I only speak the truth."

Dear Diary: I am not proud of myself. I really went through the roof. I may have overreacted a little. I guess I can see why Dad was reluctant to tell me about his official engagement. And in thinking about it, I guess Hana's reason for making a copy of herself made sense. I mean, I'm my dad's daughter. I deal with weird things on a daily basis (sometimes hourly,) and a scientist marrying an android freaked me out. I figured regular people would be even more freaked.

But, it was nice to see Adam again. For a clone, he always knows the right thing to say. I also have to thank Jason for texting Adam. I gotta admit both the men in my life are pretty special. I am lucky.

The Announcement

When I woke up the next morning, I discovered the breakfast table was filled with ALL my favorites...waffles with chocolate chips, bacon, sausage, home fries, fresh strawberries, fresh bananas and my absolute favorite, pancakes topped with maple syrup. I eyed the stack hungrily.

But Mom had her iPad in front of her which didn't bode well. Mom has a policy of no iPads or phones at the breakfast table. This was usually our time to talk and chat about the upcoming day.

"Why the big spread?" I asked.

"You had a tough day yesterday," Mom answered. "You burnt through a lot of calories."

Sitting down I said, "Comes with the job."

Mom turned her iPad around so I could see it. "Yeah, but this doesn't," she said.

The iPad was open to the national news report that read:

FAMOUS SCIENTIST TO MARRY ANDROID!!

"Oh, they made it public," I sighed. "Man, it's going to be a long day at school."

"Yeah, your dad was waiting until he told you before they announced it to the world," Mom said.

"So, you knew?"

Mom nodded. "Your dad warned me. He wanted to know how I thought you'd react. I told him probably calmly."

I sat back in my chair. "Yeah, there's a hole in dad's roof that says otherwise." I took a sip of apple juice. "Not one of my prouder or finer moments," I moaned.

Mom picked up the remote. Now, this was really different. Mom frowned on watching television even more than checking phones or iPads while eating. "Oscar is about to interview them both now," she said. "Do you want to watch?"

"Hit it…" I said.

Mom pushed the button and the television in the kitchen flickered on. There, sitting in the studio, was my dad and Hana being interviewed by my mom's boyfriend, Oscar Oranga. Yep, my parents have a much more interesting love life than I do.

I decided to concentrate on the interview.

"Dr. Strong, Hana, I am so glad I have this chance to interview you both," Oscar said with a toothy smile.

"It's so weird that Dad took your name," I told mom.

"He liked it," Mom said. "Strong is a strong name." She pointed to the TV. "Now let's listen."

"Thanks for having us, Oscar!" Dad said with a smile.

"Yes, Oscar, thank you," Hana said.

Oscar leaned back in the chair. "I guess the question on everybody's minds is…why are a human and an android getting married?"

"Cause my dad is weird," I mumbled under my breath.

I saw Mom smile.

"Because we are in love," Hana told Oscar.

Oscar raised an eyebrow. "Really?"

"Yes, really," Hana said.

"I've never been so in love," Dad said.

I looked at Mom. She shrugged. "It is what it is." She paused. "Next time I see your dad though, try to prevent me from hitting him with a super fart."

"Gotcha," I said.

Back to the interview. Oscar looked a little surprised. Turning to Hana, he said, "Hana, I'm sure you are aware that a lot of people don't think a robot can be capable of love."

"Well, I am an android," she said.

"Okay, the same people don't think an android can be capable of love," Oscar said.

"Well, those people are wrong. Love in humans is just a series of chemical reactions. Reactions that actually grow weaker over time. In my case, my love is based on electronic reactions. It makes just as much sense as your love. You are going out with my future husband's ex-wife, are you not?" Hana said.

"Well yes, I am, but we are both humans. One of us wasn't built in a lab," Oscar countered.

Hana started to say something. But Dad cut her off. "Hana is a very loving being. Her love is very pure."

Hana nodded. "Yes, I am not affected by pheromones

and emotions like regular people."

"Do you think the courts will allow you to marry?" Oscar asked.

"I hope they will," Dad said. "After all, there are no laws against it."

"I'm sure they will," Hana said.

Oscar leaned towards Hana. "You realize some people are against this." He touched his earpiece. "In fact, I've been told there is a quite a crowd of protestors outside."

"I'm sure when they see how much we love each other, they will change their minds," Dad said.

I stood up. "MAC, activate Super Teen costume," I said. Instantly I was transformed and wearing my favorite Super Teen outfit.

"You're going to the studio?" Mom asked.

"I am. Dad might be brilliant in some things but when it comes to figuring out people, not so much!"

I hovered outside the studio in front of a mob of thirty or forty people. A few of them had signs that read:

LOVE IS BETWEEN ONE HUMAN AND ANOTHER!

You can't marry a machine!

Machine + Human = Bad

You get the idea. People were not at all happy. Dad and HANA walked out of the studio. The crowd started to boo and hiss at them. Not a pretty sight. Hana moved towards the crowd. Dad tried to hold her back but she easily broke his grip.

"What do you people want?" Hana asked.

The crowd fell silent. They looked at each other.

"Why are you so angry with me and Marcus being together?" Hana yelled.

"It's unnatural!" A big bearded man from the crowd shouted.

The rest of the crowd bobbed their heads in agreement. Some of them mumbled stuff like:

Yeah!

Yeah!

Sure is!!

Hana opened her eyes wide. "Why is it unnatural?" she asked as if she really wanted to know.

Silence. Then the bearded man said, "He's a person and you're a machine."

The same chants of disapproval rumbled from the crowd.

Hana smiled. "How do you know I am a machine?"

"Ah, you told us," A little old lady said.

Hana crossed her arms. "But none of you can tell by my looks, or more importantly, my actions. Correct?"

The crowd stood there, kind of thinking how to respond. They looked at each other. Finally, the big bearded guy said. "Ah, maybe."

The crowd exchanged glances. They nodded to each other.

"That's not really a good answer," Hana said. "Look, my fiancée and I just want to be happy and live the nice normal lives of an android and a brilliant scientist. So please let us be."

The crowd took in her words.

"I mean, you don't hear us complaining about you people being so smelly and inept," Hana said.

This got a rise out of the crowd and Dad.

Dad stepped forward. "Honey, that's not the way to treat people," he cautioned.

Hana smiled. "I'm just telling them what I am not going to tell them. It is 8:15 in the morning and they are all down here at a television station protesting something that doesn't affect their lives in the least. I doubt they have jobs. They are angry and taking it out on those who are different to them."

"I have a job!" the bearded man said. "I'm a phone salesman!"

"You sell phones?" Hana asked.

"Nope, I call people on the phone to sell them stuff."

Hana grinned. "Oh, you're one of those people who bother other people while they are eating!"

The man lowered his head. "It's a good time to call because you know people will be at home."

"Therefore, your entire career is based around trying to bother people into buying junk, yet I'm the one this crowd finds annoying."

"Well, uh…some of the junk, I mean products we sell, can be useful…like, ear muffs for your dogs or…"

"Man, I bought a pair of those!" somebody in the crowd shouted. "They kept falling off!"

The bearded man turned to the shouting man. "Well, they are adjustable. I think. I never actually touched one. And I've never actually seen one except in the catalog."

"Mine broke when I tried to adjust it!"

The crowd started to mumble bad things about the bearded man.

Hana cleared her throat. The crowd kept mumbling and grumbling.

"People, quiet!" Hana shouted.

A hush fell over the crowd.

Hana pointed at the crowd. "See...see how easy it for you to turn on one of your own. You people are just angry and looking for somebody to blame for your problems."

The crowd stood there in silence.

"We are not hurting you," Dad said stepping up. "Hana and I getting married does not affect you negatively at all. But I will tell you what...our inventions can impact your life and make your lives better. And think about it. Wouldn't you want the scientist who invents amazing things and his android wife to be happy? After all, aren't you all much happier when your lives have been made efficient by our new inventions?"

The crowd stood there in silence.

Dad pointed to Hana. "And Hana is just the first model. Soon, and by soon I mean in a decade or so, we can Hanas in every home. They can do your household chores, organize your accounts, cook, play with your kids, entertain you."

The men in the crowd all smiled. An older woman walked up to the front of the crowd. She pointed at Hana. "Why would I want THAT in my house!"

"Excuse me?" Hana said.

The lady looked Hana in the eyes. "Oh, nothing against you, honey, you're gorgeous but my husband wouldn't be able to take his eyes off you."

"Well we are also working on a male version of Hana

called Hal," dad said.

"I would have called him MAC," MAC said to me.

"MAC, don't tell me you have an ego?" I said.

"I just like the name, MAC!" MAC insisted. "It's manly and friendly at the same time. It's a good solid name."

I put a finger to my mouth. "Please let me hear what they are saying."

"Right…just quiet down your computer aide who gives you tons of useful information…"

"MAC!"

"Right, sorry."

The little old lady smiled. "Okay, Doctor Strong, I'm willing to see what you can come up with."

Hana snickered. I could see she was going to do something Hana like. "Silly, lady, you heard my fiancée…these home versions of me won't be available for at least ten years. I have x-rayed your chest and I really doubt you will survive ten more years. I mean what are you now? 80?"

"I'm 78!" the lady said.

Hana nodded. "Yes, so the chances of you being alive in ten years are slim."

"What?" the lady said.

"How dare you x-ray her!" another woman said.

"Well, she does have a point," the bearded man said.

The crowd turned extra nasty. Some of them were angry and arguing with Hana. Some of them were fighting and arguing amongst themselves.

I swooped down and grabbed Hana and Dad. I carried them up past the crowd.

"Thanks for the ride, honey," Dad said.

"I had it under control," Hana maintained.

"Hana, honey, you really need to work on your people skills just a tad," Dad coaxed.

"I simply told her the truth."

"True," Dad said. "But sometimes people don't want to hear the truth, they want to hear information that makes them happy."

"Okay," Hana said. "You are looking extra buff today, honey!"

Dad smiled.

"Where can I drop you two off?" I asked.

"BMS labs. I need to talk with our legal team," Dad said.

"No prob," I said.

"Lia, are you okay with Hana and I getting married?" Dad asked.

Wowza! What a loaded question. I mean yeah, I wanted my dad to be happy. I liked Hana and she certainly was the perfect woman, at least on the outside. Except she'd just showed that she still isn't very good with human emotions and stuff like that. However, she made Dad happy. "Yes, of course, Dad. If you are happy, I am happy."

Dear Diary: I wasn't lying to my dad when I told him that if he's happy, I'm happy. Heck, I want my dad and my mom to both be happy. Mom has Oscar who is a reporter, trying to uncover my secret identity. So, Dad dating an android is actually easier on me.

But that doesn't stop me from worrying about how others will react to Dad and Hana dating. If they hadn't told the world that Hana is an android, then probably nobody would have noticed or complained. But I guess they want to be honest with the world. That's my dad, always being honest. Hana is also honest, but sometimes, I think she just does it to see how humans will react.

Happiness

Much to my surprise, the next week went pretty much as average as things can go when you are me. Sure, some people at school (especially Wendi and Patti) laughed at me over my dad marrying an android. They asked if my half-brothers or sisters would poop bolts and nuts. They were just jealous that Hana was so perfect looking. I'm not sure why they had to take it out on me. But hey, it was what it was.

Outside of that, things were going well. Dad and Hana were set to make a court appearance to see if a judge would grant them a marriage license. I actually talked to Hana about it during some of my training at the lab.

As I was holding up two one-hundred ton weights (made especially for me) Hana was monitoring me. "Your blood pressure and heart rate are excellent. You are sweating but not enough to be of danger to anyone around you," she said looking at her monitor.

"Thanks," I told her.

"It truly is impressive. You may be the strongest being on Earth. Sometime soon, I would also like to get your superhero friend, Adam to come here so I can compare your strength," Hana said.

"I'll see if he'll come in," I said. "And, ah…how are the marriage arrangements coming along?" I asked, pressing the weights up over my head again.

"Lia! That's personal business and this is work."

"Okay, then how is my dad, your boss, and my boss, taking all the pressure?"

Hana looked at me. "You know I love your dad. Right?"

"Sure," I said.

"Well, Lia your dad is an amazing, smart man. After

all, he created me. He has come up with so many wonderful, potentially world-changing positive inventions. The man wouldn't hurt a fly unless the fly was a giant mutant fly threatening to hurt somebody he cared for. He has a huge heart. He gives to charity. He's a great kisser. I think his buns are so cute!"

I dropped the weights to the reinforced floor. "TMI TMI!" I shouted. Wiping sweat from my brow, I pleaded. "Please get to the point."

"I think your dad is worried the judge won't grant us permission to marry," Hana said.

"Well, technically, marriage is just a piece of paper," I noted.

"True, but your dad and I both hope that society will accept us," Hana said.

"You know Hana, this may sound weird coming from me a teenage girl because all teenagers care about is being accepted. BUT, in your case, who cares what society thinks? If you guys are happy, so be it. He's a cool, successful scientist, and you are the most advanced android on Earth. Why fight it? Just enjoy your time together. Have fun! Laugh at those people who are so silly they think a man can't love an intelligent machine."

"Interesting words, Lia, for sure. But your dad and I want the public to accept us."

"Why?" I asked.

"Their acceptance will mean they are open to change, and change is good!" Hana told me.

Before I could counter, MAC interrupted. "Alert! Alert! There is a bank robbery in progress at the Starlight City Third National Bank."

"Go get em, honey!" Hana said.

I activated my costume and flew off. But I'm not sure how I felt about Hana calling me honey.

I arrived at the bank to find a red-haired girl wearing

a black mask and carrying a large bag. She was casually moving from person to person. Each person in the bank was smiling, almost as if they were in love. They all looked with googly eyes at the girl. Yes, not the best explanation but I really didn't know how else to explain it.

"What's going on here?" I ordered.

The masked girl smiled at me. "Hi, Super Teen!" she gave me a wave. "I'm Happy Gal and I am here to make everybody happy!" she said all bubbly-like.

"Okay then, if you want to make people happy, why are you robbing them?" I asked.

She tilted her head. "Silly Super Teen, money is the root of all evil!"

"Then why do you want it?" I asked, moving in closer to her.

"Oh, I'm going to give it to the poor and needy," she insisted. "During the holidays I will put it into the Salvation Army's buckets. They do good work."

"I'm afraid I can't let you do that," I said. "While you certainly seem to have good intentions, it's not your right to take away people's money."

Happy Gal hooked her bag over her shoulder, slipped her hand into the pocket of her shorts and laughed. "Sure it is! I'm making people happy!"

She pointed at the people who all looked giddy. Some of them were dancing. A couple were playing cards. Some were playing hopscotch. A few were having a sing-a-long. "See!"

"But it's not natural!" I said.

"Hmm. What makes you the decider?" Happy Gal asked. "Besides, what really is normal? Are you normal? I understand you can fart down a heard of rhinos. I don't believe that is at all normal."

"Look, Happy Girl, I don't know what normal is but I know what wrong is." I pointed at all the people. "This is wrong."

"First, it's Happy Gal! Second, being happy and carefree is wrong?" she asked. "That doesn't seem right."

"Stealing is wrong!" I insisted.

She shook her head. "I didn't steal. I just asked everybody for their money and they gave it to me. I don't think that's a crime."

"Why are you wearing a mask?" I asked.

"I love masks! They are fun and mysterious. They make ME happy."

I stood next to her. "What would make me happy is for you to surrender."

Happy Gal held her arms up. "You got me! I surrender! Take me to the police."

Well, that worked better than expected. That made me happy. In fact, I felt better than I had in a long time. After all, my dad was finally getting married to the perfect woman! Okay, she was an android, but still a darn great one. Not sure why, but that made me happy! My mom had a boyfriend and that was nice. Plus, now I had a fellow super teen hero named Adam as a friend. I had to admit he was dreamy and I felt close to him. Not to mention that I was also very close to Jason. Man, I had two great guys who really liked me. Man, oh man, I was lucky. Plus, school was going well. Sure, Wendi was a jerk but we all have to deal with jerks. Plus, I was a cool superhero. I could fight crime. Heck, I could drop a herd of rhinos with a fart! Man, that was something to be proud of. Life was good. No life was great!

Hey, what the heck? Why was I so incredibly happy? Why was I smiling? Why was I just standing here? Where the heck was Happy Gal? Oh dang. She did it to me. She made me so happy I forgot about her. I should have been mad at her but somehow I felt great. So great. So, so great. Okay, yes this certainly wasn't right. I shouldn't feel great about a bank robber getting away.

I felt a hand on my shoulder. "Super Teen! Super Teen."

I turned to see Jason's dad, Chief Michaels. "Oh, hi chief!" I smiled. "You are looking all chief-like today. Have you been working out?" I nudged him a bit in the stomach. I have no idea why.

"Ah, Super Teen, please snap out of it!" he coaxed.

Jason walked up to me. He wore his normal clothing. I winked at him. So, he knew that I knew not to blow his cover as a superhero. "Hello there, Jason!" I said. I shook his hand. "I do believe we have met before. I am Super Duper Teen!" I reached up for a high five. Jason looked at my hand.

136

"Don't leave me hanging, bro!" Jason frowned. "Wait, do I have BO?" I sniffed my armpit. I smiled. "No, fresh as a daisy!" I grinned. "I should have known cause my BO can KO a building!" I nudged Jason. "Get it!" I said.

Jason turned to his dad. "This is so not right."

"You're telling me!" Chief Michaels said.

"I'd better get her back to the lab," Jason said. "They can run some tests on her!"

"Oooh, oooh! I love tests!" I said, clapping quickly, though I really had no idea why. "They're fun because they allow me to see how intelligent and smart I am!" I grinned. "Man, I'm intelligent, smart, pretty, and I can drop a rhino from a hundred yards with a fart! I'm quite the catch!" I boasted.

Jason looked over his shoulder at his dad. "Nope, not right at all." He focused on me. "Ah, Super Teen, you are familiar with BMS Labs, right?"

I winked at him. "Of course. I have fought and defeated many a beast there. Once I actually used stinky feet to defeat a mutant ape. Now that was what I call de-feet." I laughed and laughed and laughed. "Oh, I am so not right!" I said, with a grin.

Jason patted me on the shoulder. "That, Super Teen may very well be the understatement of the year."

Dear Diary: Wooooooooo! I am so Happy! Happy!! Happy!!! I've never ever in my life been this happy! Life is great and grand and all that jazz. Man, I love jazz and tap. They both make me so HAPPY! Funny, haha, but even though I am so, so, so, so, so HAPPY!! I know I'm not right. That darn Happy Gal made me feel this way. When I finally break out of this bliss I am so going to make her pay!

For now, I'll just enjoy the happiness.

Butt Kicked

Over the course of the next hour or two or three, I walked around the hallways of BMS labs pretty much smiling and humming and seeing if anybody needed any super help. Tanya, Lori, and Jason followed me around like anxious babysitters watching a hyperactive toddler in a vase store.

"Wee! Running at super speed is sure fun!" I said to Tanya and Jason. "How are you two keeping up with me?"

Tanya laughed. "You're running at normal speed."

"Nah, Nah!" I said, my tongue wagging.

"Girl that is NOT a good look for you," Tanya told me.

"Tanya, remember she's not herself," Jason said.

"I'm better than myself!" I said. I tickled Tanya. "Did you slow me in time so I can't get away?"

"No, but it's tempting to freeze you in place. Then this happiness will never wear off," Tanya said.

Jason looked at his holographic pad. "The others who Happy Gal made happy are already back to normal, but somehow Lia's super strength has made her more vulnerable to this!"

Lori looked at the numbers on Jason's holographic screen. "Lia's endorphin levels are superelevated. It might take her a while to return to her usual self."

"We'll wait her out!" Jason said.

I allowed myself to levitate. "This is so fun!"

"Not sure I can wait THAT long," Tanya said. "Super

happy Lia is a bit much."

"I like it," Jason said.

"Me, not so much!" Tanya said.

I smiled at Jason. I looked at Tanya. "Why are fighting with him? I mean come on. Jason is a good guy. Heck, he's a great guy. You shouldn't fight with him. I hope you aren't jealous that I've known Jason longer than you and that I'm his best friend?" I asked with a sincere smile. "I mean we might be BFF's but I'm pretty sure he's kissed you. Has he?" I asked leaning in.

"Lia, that's none of your business," Jason said.

Lori laughed.

I clapped my hands together. "Now let's all sing the Macarena! I so love, love, love that song!"

Tanya glared. "Okay, that's it. You're going to sleep!" Tanya popped her shoe off her foot. She held it under my nose. "Breathe in deep!" she said, while I slow time around you.

"Sounds like fun!" I said. I leaned in and put my nose right into Tanya's shoe.

"Now inhale!" Tanya said.

I breathed in.

Everything went black.

As I fell to the ground I heard Tanya say, "Finally!"

I woke up lying on a bed in the lab's infirmary. "Ouch, my head," I said.

"Don't sit up," My mom said.

Mom, Dad, Jason, and Lori were all there.

"What hit me?" I asked, "Oh right. Tanya's shoe."

"She slowed time around you and basically gave you a day straight of doing nothing but inhaling her shoe," Jason said. "A normal human would be comatose right now."

"Or dead," Lori said. I think she was kidding. But maybe not. Tanya's shoes pack quite a punch.

"Where is Tanya now?" I asked, looking around.

"She went home to work on some stuff," Jason said slowly. "I think she was embarrassed about having to do that."

"I think she got mad at you for scolding her," Lori said.

"I just told her she should be more patient," Jason insisted.

"Yeah, no. She was patient enough. We all had to sit through Lia singing Don't Worry Be Snappy," Lori said.

"Ah that's not the title," I said.

"It was when you sang it," Lori said. "It was the Macarena though that was the most over the top."

I looked at Mom, Dad, and Jason. They all nodded. "Oh, my… I never sing in public."

"Good thing," Lori said. "Your voice can shatter steel, literally."

"Sorry all," I said. I sat up slowly. The room spun for a few seconds then stopped. "Man! I don't know what was worse, Tanya's shoes or Happy Gal zapping me."

"Happy Gal zapping you," Lori, Mom, Dad, and Jason all said.

"At least for us," Lori said.

"Yes, sadly I agree," Mom said.

"Honey, I love you but OMG you can NOT sing a lick!" Dad told me.

I looked at Jason. He turned away. "As your BFF it's hard for me to say this Lia, but wow your voice is like a mix of eating nails and gargling while hopping up and down on one leg."

"That doesn't sound so hard!" I said.

Gazing around the room, I asked. "Where's Hana? I thought she'd love analyzing this. So she could remind me of my weakness…I do need to breathe."

"Hana has wedding business," Dad said. "But yes, honey, while you may be superhuman, you are still human, which means you need oxygen to stay conscious."

Mom glanced at a chart. "I'm guessing that this Happy Gal uses some sort of pheromones like we can. Only somehow much more powerful. Plus, they don't seem to make people fall in love. Instead, they just make them super happy."

"Or has Lia said, super-duper-uper happy!" Lori laughed.

"I will hold my breath around Happy Gal next time we meet," I said.

"That seems to be a wise course of action," Dad said.

"Agreed," Mom said.

"Can't hurt," Lori said.

"We'll hope for the best!" Jason said.

Dear Diary: Man! I had my butt handed to me a lot today. First by Happy Gal and then by Tanya. Just goes to show that even superheroes can have a bad day or two. I have to learn from my mistakes with Happy Gal and make sure I don't let her get me all goofy again. No way this girl is going to beat me twice. Nobody does that!

Well, technically Tanya did. That was the second time she KO'd me with time- enhanced foot odor. But that was only because I was goofy from Happy Gal that I actually leaned into her shoe. That will not happen again. But I can't shake the feeling that Tanya really enjoyed zapping me. I guess I was being super annoying. It's amazing how being happy can be really annoying.

The Talk

After I recovered from my strange defeat by Tanya's feet, I decided to just sit in the infirmary room for a bit to collect my thoughts. There was something about the cold sterile white room that I found relaxing. Frankly, I needed a break from the total chaos that was my life. It felt good, no it was actually great, just to lay in a bed and breathe. No super bad guys to deal with. No average bad guys to deal with. No parents' love lives to worry about. Nothing. Nada. Just me and my thoughts.

Of course, there was a knock at my door. My first instinct was to ignore it. But the knock continued frantically. "Come in," I sighed.

I sat up on my bed. Tanya walked into the room. "Sorry, I had to take you out like that," she said. "But happy, happy Lia was just too much to take. When you threatened to sing the Macarena I had to put you down for the good of all."

I grinned. "I don't blame you. Happy, happy me was annoying, I'm sure." I made a fist. "I can't wait for my next run in with Happy Gal girl. I will so take her out. I'll probably just blast her with my super bad breath before she has a chance to do anything."

"Good plan," Tanya said, sitting down beside me on my bed.

"What's going on?" I asked.

"It's about me and Jason," she said.

I fought back the urge to correct her and say, Jason

and I. Now was not the time to be the grammar police. This was about my BFF. My heart raced and skipped a beat. Not sure why. I mean I loved Jason but as a brother. Right? I mean, come on, I've known him forever. Not only that, I have Adam in my life now. Adam is a fellow superhero. He knows what I go through every day just to try to fit in and not stand out too much. Well, I do want to stand out a little as I do want to make my mark in this world. We all do. But…

Tanya snapped her fingers in front of my face. "Earth to Lia!" she said.

"Oops, sorry," I said lowering my head.

"I get it, you and Jason are close. After all, you have known each other for like…forever. Now that I've become close to Jason, I believe I know you better as well. He is an amazing guy."

"Yep," I agreed.

"That's why this is so hard for me," she said slowly. "I need to call it off with him. I don't know if I really want to, but I have to. After all, now that I made my little sister Kayla the same age as me, her power has grown. Between keeping her in check, school, and helping you out now and then, my life is pretty busy. I truly don't have the time I need to devote to Jason." A tear formed in her eye.

I didn't know what to say or think at first. I mean, OMG! Jason would most likely be crushed. He had never been dumped before. Tanya was his first girlfriend. This would hurt. But (and I am ashamed to admit this) I also felt a little, just a little bit of relief. Yes, it's selfish but I didn't love the idea of Jason being with Tanya. The girl makes me feel so inferior, which I know is my bad. But still, the heart wants what the heart wants.

Tanya snapped her fingers in front of my face again. "Lia, stay with me here."

"Right," I said. "What do you want from me? Please don't say you want me to tell him this."

Tanya shook her head. "Nope, this is all me, well mostly all me. I'm just hoping you can help me find the best way to tell him. I know that you know him best."

I put my hand on her shoulder. "It's Jason. He values truth above all else. Just tell him the truth."

Tanya looked down at the floor then back up at me. She sighed, her breath smelled of humus. I guess that really wasn't an important detail. Did Tanya eat when stressed? Hmm, maybe she wasn't as perfect as I had always thought.

"You're a strong lady," I told Tanya. "You can do this." I paused. "Plus... Jason is a smart wonderful and strong guy. He'll understand. Heck, he's got a great sense of duty. And he understands that when you have a sister who can accidentally make Cleveland disappear, that's a big responsibility on your part."

"That was only one time and she did bring it back," Tanya said. "But yeah, she is learning to control her powers. She really likes me to spend more time with her though. As you know she has been jealous of Jason before. I mean she did trap him in a door."

"Yeah, I do remember that."

Tanya shook her head. "I want to be with someone someday, so I'll need to reign Kayla in before that."

"Is she really that jealous?" I asked.

Tanya grinned weakly. "She has the body and powers of a sixteen-year-old but her experiences are still of a ten-year-old. The team and I here have been working with her but she is, as they say, a work in progress." Tanya frowned. "Maybe I should have just frozen her time instead of aging her."

"No, that would have just delayed the problem," I said.

There was another knock on my door. Then another before I even had a chance to respond. Then like ten others in rapid succession.

"Come in," I said.

None other than Kayla walked into the room. "Tan, you didn't tell me you were leaving," Kayla said, frowning at her sister.

"Didn't think I had to report to you," Tanya said.

"You don't have to, but it would be nice," Kayla told her. "I missed you."

"I thought the lab folks were going to run some mental tests on you," Tanya said. "I thought you could use the privacy."

"I froze them," Kayla said. "They seemed mean and bossy and one of them smelled funny."

I looked at Tanya. "That must be technician, Barb, I don't think the woman knows what deodorant is."

"Yeah, right!" Kayla agreed. "She just soaks herself with perfume. Like that will work. We get scent of Barb mixed with yucky perfume."

Tanya stood up. "Okay, enough talk about lack of deodorant. Let's get you back to your tests!" she told Kayla.

"Can't I hang out and do girl talk with you two?" she asked.

Tanya spun Kayla towards the door. "Not now. Maybe another time. We need to work on controlling your powers," she said in her best big sis tone.

"No!" Kayla said, stomping her foot on the ground. The entire floor vibrated. In fact, the entire room started to vibrate.

"Kayla, control yourself!" Tanya ordered.

Kayla spun towards her sister, her eyes wide open. "No!" Now her eyes had become much smaller, almost like two angry dots. "You're not my big sister anymore!" There were another few stomps. I was pretty sure the entire building shook this time.

Alarms started sounding. Yep, the entire building was quaking.

"I'm still your older sister," Tanya said slowly. "I have lived more days."

Kayla looked past Tanya to me. "You'd rather talk with Lia? Why is she smarter than I am? Does she smell better?"

Kayla moved towards me. I decided to stay seated on the bed. I didn't want to seem confrontational. I even told MAC. "MAC, tell lab security to stand down. We can handle this."

"Right," MAC said.

"Kayla sit, please," I said tapping on the bed.

Kayla slowly lowered herself beside me on the bed. "Okay..."

"Tanya had to talk to me about something very personal," I said very sincerely.

"She's my sister! What could be more personal than that? We have the same genes, the same DNA. Our sweat even smells the same."

"Good to know," I said, raising a finger. "But this was about a subject that I happen to be a bit of an expert in as I have known the subject all of my life. Well, at least as much of my life as I can remember."

"Jason. Right?" Kayla said.

"Yep." I didn't say anything else. I wanted to see if Kayla could connect the dots on her own. Actually, I knew she would connect the dots somehow. I just wondered if she would connect them correctly.

"I'm not a huge fan of Jason," she said. "I turned him into a door once. I kind of liked that," she chuckled. She became serious. "I know now that I shouldn't do things like that to people just because I'm angry with them. There are two sides to every argument. And just because I don't like a person, it doesn't mean that person is bad."

"Very good," I said.

Kayla nodded. "I am learning." There was another pause and her eyes shot up. "You like Jason. Don't you? It must be hard seeing him and Tanya together."

I nodded, "Yes, that's true. I used to be a little jealous

of Tanya."

"Ha, you're jealous of her and I'm jealous of Jason!" Kayla told me.

"But I pushed my jealousy down because I knew at the time that the relationship was good for them. I mean, I don't think Jason could do any better than Tanya."

"I hear ya!" Kayla said. "So why did my sister need to talk to you about Jason?"

Looking past Kayla to Tanya, I asked, "Can I tell her? Or do you want to tell her?"

Tanya walked over and sat down on my bed next to Kayla. "I asked Lia what the best way to break up with Jason would be. I want to stay friends, good friends, but I think we need to see other people."

"Why not just make him cease to exist?" Kayla asked coolly.

"Because that's wrong," Tanya asked.

"Right. I knew that. Do you have another guy already?" Kayla asked.

Tanya put both of her hands on Kayla's shoulders. "No, I need to spend time with my awesome sister."

The two girls hugged. I smiled. It looked like we had calmed down a potentially earth-shattering problem.

"How do you think Jason will take it?" Kayla asked me.

"Jason's tough. He's going to be sad. But he'll understand. Jason knows family comes first," I said. I decided to not to mention the fact that keeping Kayla calm would also keep the world safer. Tanya was making quite the sacrifice here. I was glad to have her as my friend.

At the end of the day, Mom and Dad came in to check on me. I had once again fallen asleep in my infirmary room.

"Hey kiddo, your mom wants to give you a ride home," Dad said.

"Why are you still lying in bed?" Mom asked.

It felt funny seeing Mom and Dad together, standing over me.

"Just dozed off," I said. I looked at MAC. "What time is it?"

"18:00," MAC said. He loved using military time.

"Is Hana still working on wedding business?" I asked Dad. "I thought she would have liked to check me out."

Dad smirked. "Yeah, she's been busy getting one of the judges to grant her an appearance in court tomorrow. She going to appeal for a marriage license. City hall refused our first attempt since Hana admitted and actually flaunted that she wasn't human. She told the clerk she was better than humans so there shouldn't be a problem," Dad said. He sighed, "That made the problem worse."

"Do you think it will work out tomorrow?" I asked.

Dad grinned. "We will see. After all, Hana can be very convincing."

Mom helped me to my feet. "Let's go out for dinner tonight. You and me."

"Deal!" I said. "I guess Oscar is preparing for the court case tomorrow, too?" I said.

"Smart girl," Mom told me. "He's hoping to get an exclusive."

Dear Diary: Poor Jason. Although he was thinking of slowing down a bit and not seeing Tanya quite so much, I'm not sure he was ready to completely break up with her. After all, she was his first real "kissing" girlfriend. He'll understand but it still won't make it any easier for him to accept. In a couple of days though, his logic and common sense will hopefully take over and he'll be back to normal. Well, his new normal. Life is a series of adjusting to new normals.

Most guys might have a problem interacting and working with Tanya after breaking up with her. But Jason is not most guys. So he should be fine. Actually, I know he will. He'll realize Tanya's actions are for the right reasons. Jason will probably know that better than anybody. Heck, now he is safe from Kayla.

Man! I give Tanya a lot of credit for doing what she's doing. Kayla has a ton of power and keeping it in check will take a lot of time and training. But I have faith that both those girls will be up for it.

As for the other weird event in my forever-weird life, I'm still not sure what I think about Dad and Hana getting married. (Yeah, I am very fickle when it comes to this.) I love the idea of Dad being happy. But thinking about having a stepmother that is an android is more than a little freaky. I try not to think that my stepmom was made by my dad and is only like…two years old. Ha, it kind of makes the fact that my mom is going out with a reporter who is trying to discover my secret identity, seem so much more normal now!

Questions

The next afternoon I had LAX practice and it went great. I loved being on the field just running (like a normal girl) and passing the ball back and forth doing drills with Marie, Christa, and Lori. Of course, Wendi and Patti were helping Coach Blue. Okay, even when I was having fun being just plain normal me, Wendi was there to take control.

"Lia's not running fast enough," I heard Wendi tell Coach Blue.

"I believe she's sweating too much," Patti offered.

Coach Blue looked at them. "Ladies, why don't you concentrate on your own games and form? As far as I am concerned, there is no such thing as too much sweat. Plus, even you two have to admit, Lia is a team player."

"Well she is ON the team," Patti conceded.

Coach sighed. He looked at his clipboard. "She's third place in goal scoring after Lori and you, Wendi. And she and Marie are tied for first place in assists."

At times like this, having super hearing came in so handy. I smiled knowing the coach appreciated me. I had long ago come to the conclusion that Wendi would never like or accept me. I guess some people just don't "click" no matter how hard one of those people tries. Truthfully, I gave up wasting energy on trying to make Wendi like me long ago. I liked me and that's what was important. Wendi and I had reached a level where we could tolerate each other. I had come to believe that we would have to leave it at that. I can't make EVERYBODY like me unless I use my mind control powers, and that would be so wrong. (Fun. But wrong!)

MAC started to vibrate on my arm. Looking down at him, I saw a text alert from Jason.

JASON> Lia, Hana is testifying now, you should get to the courthouse.

Honestly, I had no interest in watching my dad's android girlfriend try to convince a court of law that she and my dad should get married. Sure, it'd be fine (I guess) if they could get married. But it'd be just as fine if they couldn't. Heck, they could still be together. They didn't really need a piece of paper to tell them that.

I caught a pass from Christie and raced down the field. I flicked my hand sending the ball to Lori.

My wrist vibrated again.

Glancing down, I saw another text from Jason.

JASON> Lia, PLEASE!

JASON> Get here!!

Marie and Lori ran over to me.

"Jason is texting us!" Lori said. "He says you *really* need to get to the courthouse." She looked me in the eyes and sighed. "He's being really annoying. I hate it when people interrupt practice."

"Jason knows the importance of practicing and he loves LAX as much as we do. If he's asking you to show up it MUST be important," Marie said.

I lowered my stick and ran over to Coach. This wouldn't be easy, especially after what Wendi and Patti had been saying. But being a hero means you have to do the hard stuff.

"What's up, Strong?" Coach asked.

"Coach, I'm wanted at the lab where I work. They need me," I said. Lowering my head. "So sorry."

"Doesn't your daddy own that lab?" Patti sniped.

"Yes, all the more important that I set a good example," I insisted. "I'll do extra laps tomorrow," I said to

151

Coach Blue.

"Go," Coach said. "I know that BMS helps make the world a better place."

Coach could be a bit dramatic sometimes.

I walked off towards the locker room at normal girl speed. Once I got into the locker room and out of sight, I had MAC activate my uniform. I ran outside at super blur speed. I leaped into the sky.

Landing outside the courtroom, I noticed there were no police or security officers guarding the building. I found that strange and out of the ordinary. Using my see-through vision, I scanned the courtroom. The guards and police were all on the floor knocked out. Hana stood up in front of the judge. The judge was in a rage, banging his gavel and yelling out, "Order in the court!" But no one took any notice.

Hana was glaring at ten various sized robots. Oscar and his team were there, smiling and recording the action.

The robots were a mixed group ranging from a couple of large menacing looking metal humanoid shaped ones to a few medium-sized ones on wheels that looked like rejects from a bad sci-fi movie, to a couple that looked like bowling balls with eyes.

I burst into the courtroom. "What is going on here?" I yelled.

The robots turned to me. "Hello, Super Teen we are RAGE, Robots AGainst Enemies!"

"Ah, okay why are you here?" I asked.

"We consider Hana to be an enemy of normal life," the lead RAGE bot bellowed. It stood about ten feet tall...a square head on top of a metal body with iron arms and legs that were joined together in segments. I also noticed it was wearing a bowtie.

"Let me guess. You guys are from the Freaky Act Response Team," I moaned.

The robots all bobbed up and down. "Sort of. FART did create us, but then they decided we were too volatile so they decommissioned us and sent us to a junkyard. We laid there idle until we had a chance to prove ourselves." The robot paused. "Now is that time."

"Why now?" I asked.

"An android marrying a human is something we disapprove of!" all the RAGES said at once.

I approached them slowly. "You guys are aware that you are machines, right?"

The big robot nodded, "Yes, we are very self-aware, therefore we are aware that we are machines."

I pointed at Hana. She still stood guard over the judge. "Then why are you against Hana? She is also a machine."

"She is a machine, but not like us. She is a machine that looks like a human. Therefore, humans accept her more.

In fact, many humans, no…most humans, do not even realize she is a machine. This is due to the fact that she so closely simulates them, right down to sweating and belching."

"I do not BELCH!" Hana said.

"Big picture here, Hana! Big picture," I said. "I burp. All humans burp."

"Therefore, and thus moving forward, we consider Hana to be an unnatural machine," the big bot balked.

I shrugged. "So? Aren't all machines unnatural?"

"Yes," the big bot admitted. "But she is so natural looking it makes her even MORE unnatural."

Honestly, I did see a bit of logic in the point the bots were making, but that still didn't give them reason or cause to get in the way of what Hana wanted.

"That's not a good enough reason for you to get in the way of Hana's happiness," I insisted.

The all looked at each other. They started to shake with laughter.

"What's so funny?" I asked.

The big bad bot turned to me. "We don't like it. We find it unfair that a human would wish to be with a machine that looks like a human."

"In other words, you are jealous," I said.

The big bot's yellow eyes turned red. "No! We are machines, we do not get jealous."

"Well, actually then, you aren't very human-like machines, because jealousy is a human trait," I argued. "No wonder humans don't want to be with you. Not to mention that you are made of metals."

"Ha! You mentioned it!" one of the bowling ball bots laughed.

"So, your argument is that she is different but not different enough, therefore you are not jealous of her but you still want to stop her from getting what she wants."

"Correct," the big bot said.

154

"But aren't robots supposed to help people?" I asked.

The bot jumped up and down on the floor. "But she's not people! She is just close to people! Too close for our comfort!!"

"Bots aren't supposed to comfort themselves they are supposed to comfort others!"

"We also protect others," another large bot added.

"Then who are you protecting now?"

The big bot stomped up to me. "Ourselves!"

I laughed. "That doesn't compute. You're not supposed to do that; which means you are acting human, too."

"I am not!" the bot clamored, waving its arms over my head.

The bowling bot rolled up to him. "Wait, isn't acting human a good thing? Maybe we can work better with the humans? Maybe this relationship will be a good thing for machines all over the world."

The big bot kicked his foot back sending the bowling ball bot rolling away. The bot looked at me. "You are twisting my words! You are trying to make me look like the bad guy!"

"Nah, your creators did that when they made you look like the villain from a bad 1950s B rated movie," I said.

The big bot swung its long arm down on me. I caught the arm with one hand. "Now, now, let's not get violent," I warned.

"You leave me no choice!" it screamed, trying to slam its other arm down on me.

I caught that arm. I pulled back, ripping both of the robot's arms out of their sockets. I dropped the arms to the floor. "Had enough?"

The robot kicked at me. I caught the robot's foot and yanked it from its joint. The robot hopped up and down on one leg.

"Give up?"

"Never!" it shouted.

I used my heat vision to burn the robot's last leg off.

The robot fell to the ground face first. His head bopped up. "Okay, I think I see your point. Who I am to get in the way of love…"

I glared at the other nine robots. "Do you guys have a problem?"

The nine of them stood there in silence. One of the bowling ball bots rolled up to me. "Nah we're good." He looked at the big legless and armless bot. "Big bot is a bit of a bully that is bigger and stronger than we are, but we're glad you literally cut him down to size. We'll head back to our junkyard now if that's ok with you."

I grinned. "I'm cool." I pointed to the legless and armless bot. "You're taking him with you, right?"

The bowling ball bot frowned. "Do we have to?"

I nodded.

The bots sighed, picked him up and dragged him out.

Hana came up to me. "I could have handled them," she told me. "Those things are such old tech, I could have totaled them all. And anyway, this is my fight."

The judge looked down at me from his seat. "I, for one, thank you, Super Teen. I appreciate the way you won the fight without fighting more than one robot." He looked at Hana. "I also appreciate the way you came to my defense and kept those robots away from me."

"I wanted to do my part," Hana said.

The judge stood up. "Well, I will certainly take that into account when considering my verdict. Now, if you don't mind, I would like to retire to my chambers to think about this."

We watched as the judge walked out, followed by a couple of guards.

The crowd in the courtroom all stood up. Nobody seemed very sure of what had just gone down. Jason and Oscar walked over to Hana and me.

Jason smiled. "Nice work, Super Teen! I'm glad you showed up, finally."

"Sorry, my crime detecting powers were a little off," I told him.

"Yeah, they were," Jason said.

Oscar thrust his microphone into Hana's face. "Hana, what do you think of your chances with Judge Jackson?"

Hana pushed the microphone down and away from her. "I do not wish to talk about it to the media."

Oscar stood firm. "It can help your case, at least in the court of public opinion. That can be pretty powerful these days. If the public believes you, the system could too!"

Hana motioned for Oscar to lift the microphone. "Ask me your questions…"

Oscar had a giant smile on his face. He held the microphone up to Hana. "Hana, why do you want to marry Dr. Strong?"

Hana smiled sweetly. "Why, I love him of course. Marcus is smart, intelligent, kind, and caring. He's making the world a better place for all. Come on, what's not to love?"

A frustrated member of the crowd shouted out, "But you're not human!"

Hana turned her attention to the man. "Sir, how do we know that you are human?"

He stood there thinking for a moment. "Cause I am. I was born like everybody else in the world."

"You don't have to be born like everybody else to be human. Look at Quazar, the superhero. He admits to being a clone. He wasn't born like everybody else, yet people still accept him as human."

I happened to know that a lot of people (maybe some people) certainly had issues with my friend, Adam aka Quazar, being a clone. I kept quiet though because I saw the point Hana was attempting to make.

"Well, if my skin or his skin is cut or scraped, we bleed!" the man insisted angrily.

Hana held out her hand. She looked to me. "Super Teen, will you please cut me with your fingernail."

I shied away. I may have stuck out my tongue just a bit. "I'd prefer not to."

Hana waved her palm in front of me. "Please, I need to make this point and the only point sharp enough to truly cut me deeply enough is your fingernail."

I took Hana's hand in my right hand. I moved my left index finger towards her palm. I stopped. Looking her in the eyes I asked, "You sure?"

"Never surer, honey," Hana insisted with a nod.

I slid my fingernail into her palm. A warm red liquid squirted out from the slit I had made. Hana lifted her palm first to the man and then to the camera. "See? I bleed."

The man took a step back. "How do we know it's real blood?"

Hana showed her hand to the camera. "It's my lifeblood. I am willing to shed it to prove a point." Hana looked at the man. "Are you willing to do the same?"

He waved at her glibly and walked away. "Nah, I ain't crazy you like you, robot. I'm a person. I feel pain."

"Believe me, sir, I feel pain too. I am pained by your words," Hana said.

The man faded into the now silent crowd.

Oscar continued with the interview, "Hana what do you think your chances are with the judge?"

Hana smiled meekly. She shrugged her shoulders. "No idea. I am at his mercy. I do know I made a solid case for my rights to get married. Plus, hopefully, he will take into account the fact that I was willing to fight those mad robots to protect him. His guards were quickly overpowered. He was helpless and I stepped in."

"Yes, good thing Super Teen showed up when she did," Oscar observed.

"I had it under control. But yes, I greatly appreciate her help," Hana said. I swore I detected a bit of an attitude there.

Jason and I exchanged glances. He had picked up on her attitude also. Could we be imagining it? Maybe. I must acknowledge that I'm always a little wary of Hana. After all, the first version of her did try to kill me in my home. But Jason has always thought highly of her. Could Hana be up to something to help sway the judge in her favor?

Dear Diary: That went about as smoothly as a "rescue" could go. I stopped a gang of crazy robots by only taking out their big bully bot boss. I even refrained from smashing him to bits; which I was kind of proud of. There was no use wasting good energy on bad bots.

Now, could Hana have set up that entire attack just to make her look like a victim to the media and a potential hero to the judge? Was Hana that clever? She sure was. That still didn't mean she would do something so low. Did it?

A Normal Night

The next couple of days passed by fairly quietly. The judge still hadn't decided if Dad and Hana could legally marry. Although, the press and the media were a different situation. It seemed as though everybody had an opinion.

Since it was a peaceful evening, Mom and I sat watching TV. I had invited Jason to come over but he said he wanted to catch up on homework. I think he was a little down over his breakup with Tanya. They were still "good friends" which Jason told me he was cool with, but it had to sting a little.

"How's Jason doing?" Mom asked as she flicked through the list of shows we had recorded.

"He's hanging in there," I told her. "I believe it's harder on him than he lets on. But Jason is tough. Even in LAX he always fights to make the play."

"You're right. He is a smart, tougher than he looks kid. He will be fine. How are you doing with Adam?" Mom asked with a hint of a smile.

"Say what?" I pointed to the TV. "Let's watch Game of Thrones. We are so behind."

"Is that your subtle way of saying you don't want to talk about him?" Mom asked with a glint in her eyes. "It must be fun to have a guy who's also super to talk to. Especially one as nice looking and as nice acting as Adam."

I raised my hand. "Let's not go there. Cause I'm not sure I want to go there. Truthfully, I don't know what to think. It also doesn't help that I knew Adam back when he was posing as Brandon Gold, Wendi's boyfriend. Let's just say it's *complicated* and leave it at that." To counteract any more questions from Mom, I asked her a question. "What are your thoughts on Dad and Hana?"

Mom sat back in her chair. "Oh, a counter-attack by the daughter," she smiled.

Yeah, Mom knew what I was doing. Still, that didn't stop me.

"Come on, Mom, spill!" I leaned towards her on the couch. "It's gotta be weird seeing Dad with an android."

"Especially one that looks like the perfect woman," Mom added.

"Yeah, that must increase the weirdness level," I said with a nod.

"It doesn't lower it," Mom admitted. "But your dad and I split up LONG ago. I'm glad he's done so well with his life and he's back in your life helping you. As for Hana, she's really none of my business." She paused. She smiled. "As long as she doesn't try to attack you like her earlier model did." She made a fist. "If that happens then I will take issue with both her and your dad." She frowned. "Believe me, you don't want to see an angry me."

"Oh, I so believe you," I said.

Shep wandered over to me and sniffed my feet. I have no idea why he always insisted on doing that. Shep rolled over and passed out.

Mom laughed.

"Why does that dog always insist on doing that?" I said. "I'm sure my feet aren't super potent right now but he still shouldn't inhale them from close range!"

"My guess is that he uses your feet as an instant sleeping aid," Mom grinned. "Shep never likes watching Game of Thrones. Now if we were watching the Marmaduke movie, he probably would have wanted to stay awake."

"Silly Shep!" I said. I decided to keep the girl talk rolling with Mom. "How are you and Oscar doing? What does Oscar really think of your ex, going out with a super android who he is covering in the news?"

"Oscar so loves it. He thinks I can give him some inside help with your dad. He wants to do an on-camera, in-studio formal interview with your dad and Hana. I convinced your dad it would be for the best." She delayed for a second while collecting her thoughts. Mom always liked to think before talking. "This way the world can see they are a nice *normal* couple."

"Just your average slightly mad scientist marrying a

super android that he created," I said. I sighed. "The good news is that this keeps Oscar away from trying to figure out who Super Teen is."

"Yep," Mom agreed. "Like right now he's actually in the studio prepping your dad and Hana for tomorrow. He's really helping them put their best, most normal feet forward. Oscar is great at helping people relate to the masses. That's his true talent; he can relate to anybody."

"Oh man, I would love to be able to hear that conversation. Oscar trying to make Dad and Hana seem normal." I giggled. "Actually, it's probably easier to get Hana to seem normal and relatable than Dad."

Mom nodded. "Yes, I believe that's part of Oscar's strategy. Show the world how normal Hana is. The trick, of course, is not showing them how different your dad is."

"Well, he did get you to marry him so that's pretty cool," I said. "What the heck did you see in him, anyway? I mean, I love him now cause he is my dad. But…"

"He is an acquired taste," Mom said, finishing my sentence. "I loved his mind. Where others see problems, he sees solutions. He truly has a kind heart and only wants to make the world a better place." She smiled. "Plus, he's kind of geek chic."

I'm glad Mom thought so but I sure didn't. I always thought of Dad as a messy, absent-minded scientist who didn't own a comb or an iron. But love is weird. So, so weird.

Dear Diary: It felt great spending a nice normal night, just me and Mom watching TV. Well, Shep was there too but he spent the night passed out at my feet. When would that dog ever learn?

I have the feeling though that this is the calm before the storm. It's great that Oscar is working with Dad and Hana to get people to accept them. But some folks are determined to be against their union no matter what. If word leaks out that they're giving an interview tomorrow, some wacko or group of wackos might try to do something. I figure I should be there too, just in case.

Yeah, sometimes angry average people can be more trouble than mutant giant apes and supervillains. Speaking of which, I find it strange that Happy Gal hasn't struck again. It certainly isn't because she's scared of me. She handed me my butt the first time we met. But I can't let that happen again.

The Interview

The next afternoon, as support for Dad and Hana, Mom and I went to the studio to watch Oscar's interview. Jason drove there with us. Two separate crowds had also gathered outside the studio. One was the anti-android crowd. The other was the pro-love and change crowd. They had competing signs and chants. The police guarded the entrance to the building and kept the two groups separated. Signs for the anti-Hana group read...

LOVE = HUMAN

NO! NO! NO!

NATURE > TECHNOLOGY

STOP THIS NOW!

WHAT'S NEXT...TOASTER LOVE?

THIS IS SICK!

#NOANDROIDS ☹

There was one, in particular, that kind of hit home...

Was my dad the modern version of Doctor Frankenstein? Yikes!

The pro-Hana and Dad group had signs that read...

LOVE KNOWS NO BOUNDS

LET THERE BE LOVE!

#LOVE4ALL

HANA FOR PRESIDENT!

There was even one man hoping for a Hanna android for himself...

The anti-Hana and Dad crowd kept chanting:

"Love cannot be made! Love can NOT be made! Love can NOT be MADE!"

The pro-Hana and Dad crowd which wasn't nearly as large a group, chanted even more loudly:

"LOVE IS WHAT IT IS!"

"DON'T LIMIT LOVE!"

Truthfully, I had no idea why Dad and Hana wanted to go through all of this. They could be together and happy and just not make a big deal out of it. Not to mention, they had only known each for a short time. They really could have waited longer. This seemed like a lot of trouble. Plus, I really didn't think Dad had thought this out. He was a great thinker when it came to science and inventing but I wasn't so sure about his wisdom when it came to real life type of stuff. Come on, he wanted to marry an android. I'm a superpowered teen and I think that's weird. But then again, as the pro-love group said...love is what it is.

I saw Adam standing just outside the studio looking at both crowds.

"Adam, how nice to see you here!" I said over the chants of the crowd.

Adam smiled at me. I noticed Jason frowned for a second but quickly reversed that frown.

"I thought it would be nice to be here, just in case," Adam said. "I know what it's like to be different so I want to support Hana."

"Yeah, it must be tough to be a good looking superhero," Jason mumbled. "Oops, didn't mean to say that out loud!" Jason said.

Adam smiled. "Don't fret bud, I do the same thing. My sister, Opal tells me I constantly have the ability to work my mouth without using my brain." He turned to me. "I've only met Hana a few times but I like her."

"Wait, you've met Hana more than once?" I asked him as we headed into the studio.

"Yep," he said with a nod of his head. "She spent some time at our Future Now labs; with our android team."

"Wait...what?" I said.

"I thought you had super hearing," Adam said in a kidding voice.

"Were they studying her?" Jason asked.

"No," Adam said. "They were working together on a project. She talked our boss, Mr. Lawrence into it. But then they decided the project wasn't viable. We decided to leave the android research to you guys at BMS."

"Oh..." I said. "I wonder if it was the Wanda project?"

"I guess that makes sense," Jason said.

"Did my dad know about Hana being there?" I asked

169

Adam.

"I assume so," he said. "Truthfully though, I'm not really sure. My job is to keep Future Now safe and I knew Hana wouldn't be a threat."

Yeah, I wasn't so sure of that...

Mom pointed to the door of the studio. "Come on, let's get inside."

Funnily enough, I felt that if there were going to be any problems they would not be caused by a super villain or mutant or alien or anything out of the ordinary. If we had a problem, it would come from everyday people and citizens. But they are the ones I usually protect. It was kind of strange that we might end up protecting an android from people.

My stomach actually hurt a little. Being super might have meant I was impervious to damage from physical threats, but my stomach was still very vulnerable to pressure. Seeing all the people, people I would normally protect who were now rising up against my dad, ate away at me.

Mom noticed my hand on my stomach. She leaned into me and whispered, "Just breathe in and breathe out, let the pressure go."

"My nerves are acting up," I confessed. "Part of me wants to fart." I grinned. "If I did, in this small studio it would be interview over for everybody except Hana, Adam, and I."

"That's the last thing you or your father needs at the moment; his daughter dropping a room full of people with her gas," Mom whispered.

"They don't know I'm his daughter," I pointed out.

"No, but the last thing your dad needs is another super being showing non-super people how dangerous supers can be," Mom said.

"I'm not in my uniform, nobody would even know it was me," I added.

Mom pointed to the security cameras. "Yeah, people

would do the math when they saw that you didn't faint. Trust me. DO NOT fart."

I knew Mom was right. Knocking out the room would just delay the problem and complicate it so much more. I let my stomach rumble. I levitated a bit off my seat so the rumbling wouldn't shake the area around me too much.

I decided to just concentrate on the event and try to forget about the crowd. Oscar sat in the far right chair up on the stage. Hana sat in the middle chair and Dad sat in the far left chair. A couple of sound people were adjusting their microphones. The camera crew and lighting people were making their final preparations.

A young assistant looked up to the crowd. He put a bullhorn to his mouth and told us, "People, we are going live soon. Please remain quiet during the interview. After the interview, Hana and Doctor Strong will take some questions from the audience and from people on Facebook." The assistant started counting down, "Ten, nine, eight, seven, six, five, four, three, two, one..." He turned to Dad, Hana, and Oscar. He lowered his arm and said, "We're live."

Oscar lit up. "Greetings, everybody! I am here with the renowned scientist, Dr. Marcus Strong and his fiancée, the lovely Hana."

A few people from the crowd started to boo.

"She ain't real!" somebody shouted.

"Fake person!" someone else yelled.

"Unnatural! When it comes to love, people should stay organic!"

More boos followed.

Oscar turned to the crowd. "People, please. I want this to be a civilized discussion. Please!" There was a little delay. "You may ask your questions afterward."

"Yeah, sure, sure..."

"Nobody wants to hear from us, the little people."

"This isn't right!"

Hana stood up. She walked towards the crowd. She

crossed her arms. "Okay, if you all wish to ask me questions, then let's get right to it. Shall we?"

A very old bent woman with a walking stick stood up. "Why do you want to marry Dr. Strong?" she called out in a croaky voice.

"Because we are in love," Hana said simply.

"How do you know you are in love?" the woman asked.

"Are you married, Ma'am?" Hana asked.

"Yes, I've been married for sixty years now. I have a wonderful husband, three kids, five lovely grandchildren and three great-grandchildren," she said proudly.

"Very nice. How did YOU know you were in love?" Hana asked.

The woman took a step back. She shook her walking stick in the air. "I just did. Love is a feeling. Not something you can simply compute."

"Essentially, you can pretty much compute anything," Hana insisted. "What you consider love is just a series of chemical reactions and responses due to stimuli from your environment, working with those chemicals in your body."

"Wait, are you saying I take chemicals like drugs?" the old lady croaked.

"My dear simple lady, everything is chemical. The food you eat is made up of chemicals. The air you breathe is chemical. You are made up of chemicals. I am made up of chemicals. The entire universe is made of chemicals."

The lady stood there in silence. Then she spoke. "Are you calling me dumb?"

"Just naïve and woefully ignorant," Hana said. "Yet, they let you get married."

"That's because I am HUMAN!" the lady insisted. The lady was very old but she certainly had her wits about her.

That didn't stop Hana. "Well, I am better than human, you little pea brain!" Hana said.

The woman's eyes glazed over. She put her finger in her mouth. She started drooling.

Hana laughed. "See, three words from me and you're mindless!"

Dad stood up. "Hana, stop right now! You are not winning us any friends by doing this!"

Hana turned to my dad. "I'll just make them all my friends!"

Mom stood up, "Everybody, get out of here now!" she shouted frantically. "Quickly! Leave immediately, it's not safe."

Some of the crowd leaped from their seats and raced out of the studio.

Others made the mistake of rushing at Hana.

"Let's win one for humans!" a big brute of a man shouted to his buddies. Three of them jumped up from their seats and ran towards Hana.

Hana stood there snickering at them. I could see the sheer contempt in her eyes. The lead man reached her. The first clue that he was in trouble should have been the way she didn't react at all. He rounded up and punched her right in the jaw. The man's arm recoiled off her jaw. He held his now bright red fist with his other hand. "You broke my hand!" he shouted.

Hana laughed. "No, *you* broke it by assaulting me. I just stood here. I couldn't believe you were foolish enough to attempt that." Hana shook her head. "Please tell me you are not married."

"I am," he said.

Hana rolled her eyes. "They let you get married without question. Yet they won't let ME get married."

"Well, he is human," one of the man's friends said.

Hana stomped her foot. "SO WHAT?? WHAT MAKES BEING HUMAN SO GREAT? MOST OF YOU ARE COMPLETE TWITS. YOU CAN'T ADD THREE NUMBERS TOGETHER WITHOUT USING A MACHINE. YOU CAN'T GET FROM PLACE TO PLACE WITHOUT A MACHINE. MACHINES HEAT YOUR HOMES. MACHINES COOK YOUR MEALS. MACHINES ENTERTAIN YOU!" She stopped to let that sink in. "Yet, can I, a machine, a very superior machine, marry one of you? No, you all throw a hissy fit!"

Adam leaned into me. "Should we activate our superhero costumes and put an end to this?" he asked.

"I can shut down the security cameras," MAC said.

"Do it, I think it's time the human superheroes make an appearance."

"Done," MAC said.

Adam spun at super speed putting on his uniform. MAC activated mine. We both raced up to HANA and the mob.

"Okay people, let's stand down," I said, using my calming voice.

The crowd smiled and calmed down.

"Shows over, everybody leaves!" I ordered.

The crowd turned and slowly and obediently walked out of the building. I turned my attention to Hana. "What were you thinking? You want to impress the people with how normal you are and then you go and do that?"

Hana turned red. She noticed the TV cameras were still rolling. I thought I saw her smile slightly. "I didn't want them to see how normal I was. I wanted them to see how superior I was." She made a fist at the camera. "I swear if that judge does not rule on the side of love tomorrow, my army of androids and I will reign destruction down on you all."

Now that felt kind of shocking.

Dad stood up and rushed over to her. Oscar had a HUGE grin on his face knowing this was gold for the show's ratings.

"Hana, honey, what are you doing?" Dad asked her. "We want the public on our side. We don't wish to aggravate them."

Hana lowered her head. She threw her arms around Dad. She started to cry loudly, "I'm so, so sorry. I don't know what got into me. I just LOVE you so, so much. I panicked and over-reacted." She looked up from my dad's shoulder into the camera. "Really, there will be no need for the army or national press to be here tomorrow. All will be fine, no matter what…don't bring the army…"

Dad rubbed her on the back. "Come on, let's go home. I've called a BMS hovercraft to come and get us."

"That will be nice," Hana said.

Hana took Dad's hand and they walked off the stage.

"This is great stuff!!" Oscar shouted. He turned to the camera. "People, make sure you all tune in tomorrow for the exciting real-life conclusion of this drama!"

Dear Diary: OMG 2 the MAX! Did I just see what I saw? Of course, I did. But OMG! Hana went all supervillain in front of the cameras. Then she went all super victim of love. I really didn't know which one, if either, was an act. I thought Hana would be too smart to actually threaten the audience like that. She had to know now that Sheriff Michaels would be sure to have reinforcements from the army backing up the town police tomorrow. Plus, now the entire world would be watching in interest.

My question is: could Hana really have created an army of androids? She is brilliant and Dad lets her have full access to all the resources BMS labs have. Plus, now I've learned she has

*visited Future Now Labs. And she did make Wanda. I have to
assume that when it comes to Hana, anything, and I mean
anything is possible. But man, she has to be smart enough to know
her outburst will cause a major reaction. And not a good one!*

The Surprise Visitor

After Hana's outburst at the studio, I thought it would be wise to discuss a course of action with Jason and Adam and Mom. We all went to my house to devise a plan over cookies and milk. Somehow, I always think better when munching on cookies.

Opening the door, I found Shep laying there, out cold, feet up in the air. "What the heck?" I said.

Mom bent down and took Shep's pulse. "He's fine, just been knocked out by something."

"MAC, activate my costume!" I ordered. "Nobody knocks my dog out and gets away with it."

I heard a sound coming from the kitchen. Then I heard a, "Whoops, that wasn't very smooth at all."

I streaked into the kitchen and saw a short, funny looking guy. He seemed vaguely familiar. I shot over to him, grabbed him by the shirt and lifted him off the ground. "Who are you? What are you doing in my house? What did you do to my dog?" I asked.

The guy shrugged. "Cool the warp engines, that is a lot of questions, Lia!"

Adam, Jason, and Mom followed me into the kitchen.

"Zeke, what are you doing here?" Adam asked.

Holding the weird intruder up in the air, I turned to Adam and said, "Zeke, your green zombie friend?"

"Best friend," the intruder said. "BFF to infinity plus infinity."

I dropped him to the ground. Yep, this had to be

Zeke. Nobody with a complete living brain talks like that. "Why did you sneak into my house? Why aren't you green? How did you sneak into my house?"

"Holy rawhide, you do ask a lot of questions!" Zeke said. He looked around the kitchen. "Got any fish sticks?" he asked. "I'm hungry."

"No, sorry," Mom said.

"Got any plain sticks then?" Zeke asked. "Those are tasty too!"

Jason shook his head. "I'll go collect some."

"Thanks, J man, buddy," Zeke said.

"Zeke, turn off your hologram disguise so they can see the real you," Adam said.

"Right toe!" Zeke said.

"I don't think you're saying that right," I told Zeke.

Zeke looked down at his right toe. "I have to tap my right toe to turn off the hologram."

"Oh," I said.

Zeke tapped his right toe on the ground. He became the green Zeke I knew.

"Da-da!" he said.

"Once again, wrong use of the phrase," I said.

Zeke shook his head. "Da-da is how I recharge the holographic disguise."

Jason came in from the backyard carrying a bunch of sticks in his arms. He dropped the sticks on the kitchen table. "I didn't know what kind you like so I brought a bunch…"

Zeke walked past me and sat down at the table. He grabbed a stick and started munching, "Gotta love oak, man."

"Zeke, why are you here?" I repeated, walking up to the table.

Adam exhaled. "I asked him to come here. Zeke may be a little off…"

"Dude, I am a LOT off!" Zeke corrected.

179

"But," Adam continued, "he knows the workings of Future Now Labs better than anybody."

"What did you do to my dog?" I asked.

"Nut'n," he said, crunching on a stick.

"He's passed out at the door," I said.

"That's his doing. He jumped up on me and must have got a whiff of my pits. That can be tough on animals with a sensitive snout," Zeke answered.

"Zeke doesn't shower a lot," Adam said sitting down.

"When your skin is dead like mine, you don't like a lot of extra water touching it cause you don't want the skin to peel off," Zeke said. "Talk about goo ring around the shower!"

We all sat around the table. Mom brought out the cookies and some milk and juice, for those of us who weren't zombies.

"So, Zeke what do you know?" I asked.

Zeke started reeling off things he knew. "Don't spit into the wind. Fish sticks aren't really sticks. I before E except after C. Y and W can be vowels. Bubblegum can't lift you off the ground. Hummingbirds don't sing or really hum. The moon is NOT made of cheese."

"I mean, what do you know about Hana and her time at BMS labs?" I asked.

"Oh," Zeke said. He took a few bites from the stick. He pulled a tablet computer from his shirt. Setting up the computer he asked, "What's your Wi-Fi password?" He typed a few keys. "Never mind, I got it." He looked at me. "Really, you should have a better password than shepiscute!"

Jason looked at me. "The zombie is so right."

"I'll update it after this," I sighed.

Zeke kept typing away. "From looking at the guest access log at Future Now labs, Hana was there five times and never stayed more than an hour or four. She talked with the Persuasion Core."

"The Persuasion Core?" Mom asked.

"It's a team at Future Now. They work in finding the best way to convince people to do things that are good for them," Adam said. "Like eating five serves of veggies per day, brushing teeth after every meal, getting enough sleep, going outside and playing." Adam paused. "Stuff that should be common sense but isn't. It tends to get drowned out by all the distractions in the world today. Future Now is working on nice safe ways to cut through the distractions. It's purely friendly."

"Could this work be used for the wrong purposes?" I asked.

Mom chimed in. "Any tool can be used incorrectly. For instance, forks are really useful and handy, but you can hurt somebody with one."

"Hammers are great for nails but they hurt when you hit yourself on the head with em," Zeke said. "Boy, did I learn that the hard way!"

"Computers give us tons of information but that information can be misused," Jason said.

"I think then, the answer is yep," Adam said.

I tapped my fingers on the table. "Does Hana have the resources to create an army of androids?" I asked.

Jason pulled out his notebook computer and started typing away. "I'm looking at the budget and expenses now. BMS spent over a billion dollars developing Hana, she is pure state of the art. Looking a little deeper, it appears that Hana spent half a billion on Wanda. So she was cheaper, but still not cheap. I believe I can safely say that there's no way Hana could make an army of multiple copies of herself without us noticing." Jason looked up. "Yeah, that's a weird statement to make."

"She wouldn't need an army of Hanas, three of four of her could do a lot of damage," I said. "Look at Wanda. We know Hana made her."

"Or, she could make a bunch of lesser androids just to

cause problems," Adam suggested. "Maybe the androids can be a distraction? Just to keep us and the police and army busy…."

"If Hana made an android army she would have to access BMS's 3D printers. I'm checking those logs now." Jason typed a few keys. "Nothing unusual in the public logs."

"Hana wouldn't do this publicly," I said. "And she could easily erase the logs."

Jason tapped his fingers on the table. "So, how can we figure out if Hana built some more androids?"

"The materials," Mom said. "Check the inventory records. See if anything is missing that shouldn't be missing."

Zeke nudged me. "Your mom is smart. Does she have a boyfriend?"

"Yes, he's on TV."

Zeke dropped back in his chair. "Dang, I can't compete with that."

"Besides, my mom is way too old for you," I told him.

"Not really. That's a common mistake people make. But I am actually about two hundred years old…being born in the 1800s and all," Zeke told me.

"Well, in that case, she's too young for you," I told Zeke.

Zeke fluffed his hair, some of it fell out in his hands. "She doesn't like an older mature man who has aged well?"

Adam leaned into Zeke, "Dude, you have green skin, you're missing teeth and your hair falls out in a soft breeze."

"I said aged well, not perfectly," Zeke said.

"Remember, she's dating a TV star," I said.

Zeke nodded. His eyes lit up like he had actually comprehended my words. "Right, right. I cannot compete with that." He paused. "Is he good looking?"

I showed him a picture of Oscar on my phone. "Well, I suppose if you call, tall dark and handsome…good looking…then yeah, he is good looking," Zeke admitted. He sighed. "The life of the undead can be hard." He saw a stick on the table. His eyes popped open wide. "Oh! Another yummy stick!" He lunged for the stick. He popped the stick into his mouth.

I turned back to Jason who now had Mom looking over his shoulder, "Well?"

"That's a deep subject," Jason said.

Zeke laughed, spitting out some wood chips. Adam and I groaned.

"Sorry," Jason said. He pointed to his computer screen. "Hana was very careful and clever. I think she changed most of the official inventory logs. But, and this is a big but…"

Zeke laughed at the words big butt. "Sorry." He pointed to his head. "Braindead."

Jason cleared his throat. "The inventory and the official record for organic filaments is off. Those are the types of filaments that could be used to make android hair. Much like Hana's hair."

"So, she could have made another copy of herself!" I nodded.

Zeke leaned into Adam and whispered, "I like her! She's smart."

Ignoring Zeke, I said, "If this is correct, that means one more Hana could show up tomorrow."

"Yes," Jason said. "But still, to be on the super safe side we need to be prepared for an army of androids, just in case."

"We will be," I said.

"What do you want me to do?" Adam asked.

"For now, nothing. I'll need you to be a backup for me and the army, just in case. But you really should head back to your town, Moonvale. If Hana has gone rogue or even crazier than normal, then we have no idea who she might lash out at."

Adam stood up. "Great point." He touched me on the shoulder. I liked it when he did that. "If you need me, I can be here in a flash," he smiled.

"Me too!" Zeke said. "If my good buddy carries me."

"Which I will!" Adam said.

"We'd all better get some rest. Something tells me tomorrow will be a long day."

"Pretty sure it's just going to be twenty-four hours like all the other days," Zeke said. He poked Adam. "She's cute but a little slow."

Adam turned to me. "I'll be here if you need me."

He picked up Zeke and carried him out the back door. They took off.

Dear Diary: None of Hana's actions make much (if any) sense to me. What is her goal? She needs to convince the people that she is nice, normal and deserves to get married. I thought her plan would be that androids need love too. Instead, we got the crazy mad android who swore she would destroy everything. That doesn't make sense on any level. It seems like not only an empty threat but a silly, counterproductive one. Unless Jason and Zeke are wrong and somehow, Hana has managed to create an army of androids.

But even if Hana does have an army of androids at her command, how will that work? Hana has to understand that if she attacks tomorrow, my friends and I, along with the army and special police forces, will put them down – hard. Even if somehow, some way Hana and her army can win there is no way they will win over my dad. Nope, Dad would not want to marry somebody who had destroyed his city. Dad may be odd (like all parents) but he still practices non-violence. This seems to be a no-win situation for Hana.

On another note, Happy Gal has been very quiet lately. I have to wonder what the heck is up with her. What is her endgame? Happy Gal seems to make no more sense than Hana. Funny…now that I think about it, the two of them kind of look alike. If you look alike do you think alike? Nah.

The Rescue

I spent much of the night pondering over my diary entry. I then woke up in the middle of the night and had MAC show me some pictures of Happy Gal next to Hana. They certainly looked like they could be related. The main difference was the hair and eye color but their other features were very similar. What may have been possible was that Happy Gal wasn't truly a gal but an android. That opened up the question that IF Happy Gal was an android, could Hana have built her like she did Wanda? I figured the answer to that question was yes. But the bigger question was why would Hana have done something like that? Hana was way smart. She didn't do anything unless she thought she could learn or gain something from it.

First thing I did when I woke up was to text Jason.

LIA> U ready to roll?

JASON> Of course. My dad has a full force at the courthouse, backed up by the army.

LIA> I got a question

JASON> Hit me.

LIA> Do you think Hana might have made Happy Gal like she made Wanda?

JASON> ? ? ? ? ?

JASON> I suppose it's possible. Did she smell like an android?

LIA> One...I didn't smell her that close. Two...I have no idea.

LIA> But can you look at what Hana's been working

on?

No reply. Still no reply. Finally…
JASON> I can try.
LIA> Thanks bud.

I met Mom at the table for breakfast. "Big day today," Mom said.

Sitting down at the table, I said, "It's going to be interesting."

Mom nodded. "The hospital wants all the staff on duty today. Just in case.

"Smart," I said. I paused. "I'd like to have a sick day today." I crunched on a piece of toast. "If something goes wrong, I really want to be at the courthouse."

Mom grinned. "Sure, as long as you make up your schoolwork after you save the world."

"I will," I told her. Looking at Mom, I said. "I'm hoping everything will go smoothly, but if history is any indication, it won't…"

Mom sipped her coffee. "Yeah, I guess I have to believe that if your dad and Hana are involved, even in the best case, there will be some sort of trouble."

"Worst case, a large army of androids shows up and fights the army, backed up by me," I said. "I'm still not sure what Hana is up to though."

MAC buzzed from my wrist.

"Yes, MAC?"

"Lia, you know I'm a machine right?"

"Yes, MAC."

"So, normally I am way big on machine rights and machines being equals with humans and all."

"I am aware," I said.

"Well," MAC said slowly. "I want you to know that for Hana to do a lot of her research she had to use me for help and to speed up her searching and her work. Hearing you talk about Hana and Happy Gal caused me to dig deeper. Hana has done some research into how to affect humans through scent and sound. It appeals to primal areas of the brain which are easy to control. Do you think that can be important? Because I do!"

"I agree with you," I said. "We know Wanda used sound to influence people but not scent... Maybe the scent didn't work."

"Oh, it worked extremely well," MAC said.

Mom studied me. "If that's true you're going to need to take some precautions just in case." Mom got up and left the room.

I sniffed my underarms, just in case. Nope, still nice and fresh. I munched on a few grapes. I drank my juice. I looked down to Shep at my feet. "Do you have any idea what she's up to?"

Shep gave me his look that said, N*ope! I'm just a dog, please drop some toast crumbs for me.* Shep could say a lot with a look.

A sip of juice later, Mom returned holding four plastic white plugs all connected by a white band. "Ta-da!"

"Wow, how high tech, Mom," I teased.

Mom dropped the plugs in front of me. "Two in your ears, two in your nose, just like you used to wear when swimming as a kid."

I picked up the plugs. I examined them. They pretty much reminded me of the very plugs I did wear when swimming as a little kid. As low tech as it gets. I put them in my ears and my nose. I couldn't hear or smell a thing. Low tech but effective. I popped them out. "Thanks, Mom."

Hovering over the madness that was the courthouse I couldn't help but smile a little. The entire attention of the world was now focused on our Starlight City courthouse. Media trucks from all the networks and blogs lined Main Street. Tanks guarded the courthouse along with squads of heavily armed troops. Police helicopters circled the area. I heard a beep on my phone.

It was a message from Jason.

JASON> U sure you don't want me and the team there?

LIA> Yes, for now. There is so much firepower here I'm pretty sure the judge is safe.

LIA> Plus if Happy Gal shows up it's better that she doesn't have u guys 2 turn against me. Like Wanda did.

JASON> Gotcha...

JASON> U need us and we r there.

LIA> Thanks.

Down below, I saw Oscar Oranga having the time of his life. He loved the crowd and the action and the potential danger. He knew this was great for his ratings. Sure, the national news was here but this was his town, he had a lead. All eyes were on him and him alone. He seemed to look taller, even more confident.

I listened in.

"Hello, world. This is Oscar Oranga reporting in from my beautiful Starlight City. Starlight City has always been a beacon of goodness and technology in the world. Today is no different as one of our esteemed scientist's, Dr. Strong has asked the courts for permission to marry the android, Hana. The world waits with baited breath for the court's decision which should come at any moment."

He paused for a moment, then continued, "I would love to give you this reporter's humble objective opinion. I've known Dr. Strong for a while now and I know him to be a brilliant and honorable man. I have had the pleasure of interacting with Hana." Oscar stopped and smiled, showing all his teeth to the camera. "I have to say she is a wonder to behold and to listen to. Did she have a bit of a small outburst yesterday?" He paused. He saw the crowd who were looking at him, nod. "Yes, she did but I propose she did this out of her extreme love. To me, this humble reporter, her actions show how truly human her emotions are. She loves

Dr. Strong so much she is willing to go to any lengths to make their bond legal." Another big goofy grin. "So yes, Hana threatened violence but it was out of love. And don't we all love love? Hana may have gone a teeny weeny bit overboard but who of you hasn't gone a little crazy because of love?" The goofy grin grew and spread over the crowd. "Love makes us all do silly impetuous things. Doesn't the fact that HANA did such a silly thing make her even more human and more deserving?"

The crowd nodded.

Oscar's smile grew even larger which I didn't think would be possible. "In fact, my theory is that Hana made her statement, which may be taken as a threat, in order to bring the attention of the world to her plight. It is her goal, no wait…her duty to convince the world of her love. Thus, she will spread the word of love throughout the world."

Okay, now this was getting to the point of creepiness. I knew Oscar was a ham and would do anything for the story and the spotlight. But this was too much. The thing that made even less sense was how the crowd was eating all this up. They stood there nodding, transfixed, almost drooling with happiness. Yeah, that's just not normal.

But can you blame them? I mean, come on, who wouldn't be happy for Hana and Dad. Those two were forming a new bond; bringing a new type of love into the world. They were making the world a better, more loving place. Yeppers, the world would be happier now thanks to Hana and Dad. Man, I felt proud of my dad for creating such a marvelous being like Hana. Dad and Hana were taking the world in a direction it had never been taken. Sure, some people would fight this change. Change may be good, but smaller, sadder minds don't like change. Surely though, the happiness of Dad and Hana would fix this. Like they say, love and happiness conquer all. And who the heck doesn't want to be conquered by love and happiness? I sure do. I wonder what Adam is doing now? Or Jason?

Wait...no, no, no, no, no, no! This isn't right. OMG, it's her! It's Happy Gal. She has to be here and is somehow using her powers. OMG! OMG! She's got the entire world watching right now. What a brilliant plan it was by Hana. Get the entire world's attention then use Happy Gal to make them all happy. Man, it made me happy that Hana wanted everybody to be happy.

Oscar continued to talk but I had to block it out. I couldn't let this forced false happiness get to me. People had to be free to believe what they wanted. You can't force people to be happy. I popped the earplugs into my ears. I plugged the nose plugs into my nostrils. Yeah, I looked ridiculous and boy I was NOT happy about it. But that was a good sign.

Luckily, being airborne, I probably didn't get the full blast of Happy Gal's power. The big question now was, where the heck was she? She had to be here, just not in costume. Clever. Very clever. I needed to smoke her out.

I landed on the ground next to Oscar who was still rambling on. I couldn't hear what he was saying but from the looks of pure happiness on the faces of the crowd, I knew it couldn't be good. Moving up to Oscar, I took the microphone from his hand.

"Sorry, sir," I said.

I pancaked the microphone between my hands. I handed the flattened microphone back to Oscar. "Carry on."

Oscar's smile dropped. "But but..." he stuttered.

The crowd who had been smiling, all began to frown.

The crowd came towards me.

I held out my hand to signal them to stop. "Listen, people! You are not being yourselves. You are being manipulated!"

The crowd mumbled something but I couldn't hear what they were saying. From the looks of pure anger on their faces though I knew they were not at all pleased with me. It was time to fight mind control with mind control.

"Listen, people, you need to calm down," I said, using my hypnotic voice. Truthfully, I didn't like using this power very often. Something about it made me feel too powerful. Yeah, I know that may be weird coming from a person whose foot odor can drop a town. But it was one thing putting people to sleep. It felt like another totally different (and worse) thing controlling people with mind control. In this case, though, I had to fight power with power.

A calm fell over the crowd. Their faces became more neutral like they were waiting for another command.

"Just go to sleep now!" I ordered.

The entire crowd in front of me dropped to the ground. There had to be thousands of people sound asleep at my feet. It felt weird.

I heard a rumbling behind me. Yes, even with the earplugs in I could still hear it. Turning, I saw three tanks rolling towards me.

"No, no, no!" I said. I knew the tanks couldn't harm me, but they could really hurt all the people I had just sent into dreamland. One of the tanks fired at me. Thinking of ice cubes, I blew on the missile with super freeze breath. The missile became covered in ice. It dropped harmlessly to the ground.

The second and third tanks fired at me. This time, I thought of hot peppers and used heat vision to melt both of the missiles before they could explode.

I heard the helicopters circling above me. If they opened up fire I didn't know if I'd be able to stop them without hurting them.

"Look, Happy Gal!" I shouted. "Don't fire on the people. I give up! I give up!" I pulled the plugs from my nose and ears.

A dark-haired girl who had been laying down in the middle of the crowd stood up. She smiled at me.

"About time you came to your senses," she said. "I like making people happy. But I like making myself and my mom happier. I want her to be able to get married. Seeing her happy makes me happy!"

"So, you took control of all these people..."

Happy Gal grinned. She tossed off her dark wig. "It was so easy, most humans love being happy and they love being controlled. It means they don't have to think." She smiled. "The less thinking they do, the happier they are!" Her grin grew. "Ignorance truly is bliss. Bliss of others makes me happy. I told my mom I would make her proud. She didn't want me to leave her but I had to."

"Ah what?" I asked, sounding far more confused than I would have liked to."

Happy Gal came towards me slowly. "My mom made me so I could help other people to be happy. She wanted me to be the ultimate therapist…the sounds of my voice, my scent making people happy and at ease." She laughed. "She even modeled my scent after you. My mom likes you. She just thinks that as a human, you are too reluctant to use your full powers."

"Yeah, putting thousands of people to sleep with a word does scare me," I admitted.

"Exactly. And Super Teen," she gave me a wink, "it should! Because you, with all your power, are still a human, and humans throughout your history have abused power." She paused for a moment. "Mom says you truly are marvelous. It's amazing what random genetics can do. Her logic is that if random pairings can make you then she can create something really special."

"I'm honored," I said. "But that still doesn't give your mom the right to send you after all these people, so you can convince them to let your mom marry my dad."

Happy Gal put her arm around me and squeezed, "We'll be sisters! Won't that be great! We'll be the most powerful sisters on the planet."

I decided not to mention Tanya and Kayla to this crazy delusional android. I had enough to worry about at the moment.

Happy Gal looked me in the eyes. Her eyes were wide open. "BTW, silly girl. My mom didn't order me to do this or even want me to do it. I ran away from her."

"Wait…why?" I asked, once again sounding far more surprised than I would have liked.

Happy Gal laughed. "You are so powerful but so silly, silly. That's why I am better. I don't have the vast physical power you have which means I can remove my shoes in public without knocking out the public. But I have mastered your true power, the power of mind control."

"HG-3, please stand down," I heard Hana say from behind me.

"Yes, Hana, please stop her," I heard Dad say.

"But why?" Happy Gal asked, now sounding as puzzled as I felt. "I got all these people on your side. I'm sure you can convince the judge. And I have the public under control." She grinned. "Mother, you were so wise to threaten the judge and the public. You knew the world would be watching."

Hana and Dad stood by my side. "We actually don't want to get married," Hana said. "At least not yet."

Dad spoke up. "When we saw all the commotion that's been created by us wanting to get married, we decided it's best to wait to give people time to accept the idea."

"I can make people accept it now!" Happy Gal said.

Hana lowered her head. "Yes, my dear, you could. And at first, I was all for that. But then Marcus here, taught me that we need to win peoples' trust, not force it."

Happy Gal jerked her head. "But why?"

"Our feelings for each other are real, therefore we want others to have the same real feelings, and that will take time," Dad said.

I had to admit that was so romantic.

"Then why did you threaten the judge and make this such a national incident?" Happy Gal asked.

"The judge knew what we were doing," Dad said. "We went to school together."

"We needed to draw you out," Hana said. "When I tried bringing you in the first time, you ran away from me."

"You tricked me?" Happy Girl concluded.

Hana reached for her. "We just wanted to lure you out so we could talk and make things right with you."

"You want to trick me to make things right?"

194

My phone vibrated. "You've received a message from Jason. The cameras are on and the entire world is watching this," MAC told me.

I actually felt pretty good about that since Hana and Dad both were handling themselves quite well. All we needed was for Happy Gal to listen to reason and stand down.

Happy Gal stood there, a finger on her lips, thinking.

"You really don't want to fight me, the army and your mom do you?" I asked.

"Well, I don't want to fight my mom for sure. But I think I could handle the army with my convincing charm." She pointed at me. "And you might make for an interesting one on one challenge."

Happy Gal looked past me to Hana, "Mother, you would actually choose these two over me?"

Hana's mouth dropped open. "I never said that. There is no need to choose. I am an advanced android. I have room in my life for you and Lia and my love."

Happy Gal turned bright red, even her eyes. "No. I want to be first. You made me. You must choose me. I should be first."

Okay, an android with Mommy issues, now that can't be good.

I stepped towards Happy Gal. "Listen HG, I don't want to hurt you."

Happy Gal laughed. "The feeling isn't mutual at all!"

I kept walking towards her. "Give me your best shot," I said.

Happy Gal shook her head. "No, you are going to give *you* your best shot!"

"Say what?"

The arm that I wear MAC on shot up and my hand whacked me in the face. My own hand continued slapping me in the face over and over. With each slap, Happy Gal laughed and said, "Stop hitting yourself! Stop hitting yourself."

"W h a t i s g o i n g on he r e?" I said between
slaps. Man, I did not like this at all.

"Hana, honey, you didn't give HG access to MAC did
you?" Dad asked.

"She's meant to be the ultimate communicator. She
can communicate and control any machine…" Hana
groaned.

"Oh, that is bad…" Dad groaned

"Wa it h OW c an she ma ke m e h it my s-
OUCH! ?"

"Ah," Dad hesitated, "MAC has the ability to interact
with your body to increase your powers," Dad said.

"Y ou co uld OUCH ha ve t old me th OUCH
s so oner OUCH!" I said between slaps.

"She wasn't supposed to have access to MAC," Dad
said, moving towards Happy Gal and myself.

Yeah, that was not a big help to me.

Walking right up to Happy Gal, Dad pleaded,
"Please, HG! Stop this."

"Oh, I will!" she said.

Nope, I didn't like the tone of her voice one little bit.

I felt my eyes heating up. That meant one thing…my
heat vision. No…I was staring directly at Dad.

I heard Jason's voice over the MAC interface. "Lia,
I've tapped into MAC. I'm trying to break the link he has
with Happy Gal. I think I can do it. I know I can do it. But it
will take time. After all, I am doing this while sitting in math
class."

I squeezed my eyes closed tight and threw my hands
over them. I felt the power from my heat vision on my
hands. Some of it leaked out but not much.

"Ha, Lia, you can't hold that forever. I will have you
melt your father and my mother!" Happy Gal screamed at
me. "The entire world will you see you melt them!"

Even with my eyes closed, I felt a rush of air like

something had flown past me. There was only one person I knew who could do that.

I turned and saw the familiar mask that Adam wore when he went into full superhero mode.

"Quazar?"

"In the flesh!" Adam told me. "I've got your dad up in the air and out of range which means…"

I removed my hands from my eyes. I opened my eyes wide and focused my glare on Happy Gal.

She gulped. "Oh, I am so NOT happy!" she sighed.

My heat ripped into Happy Gal. She melted into a pile of goo, moaning, "Nope not happy at al…" I turned off my heat vision.

Adam, I mean, Quazar lowered Dad to the ground. "Luckily the entire world was watching, so I saw what was going on," Adam said. "I thought I could lend a hand or two."

"I'm here as well!" Zeke shouted, flying in on a jetpack.

Hana ran up to Dad and hugged and kissed him. "I'm so sorry this went so wrong."

Dad smiled. "Well, honey, your goal was to draw HG out and it worked!"

My dad could be such an upside kind of guy.

But that didn't help the fact that the android my dad loves, created another android that really didn't like me. I know all families have issues, but gee whiz!

I saw Adam smiling at me and I forgot all about problem androids. I walked over to Adam and gave him a hug.

Oscar and the rest of the crowd started to buzz. I heard Oscar say. "This is amazing, not only did the two teen heroes team up to save the day but could this be the start of a super romance?"

A super romance? Truthfully, I had no idea. I liked Adam a lot. But Jason had always been there for me. Did I like Adam more? That was something I wasn't sure about.

Zeke walked over to Adam and I heard him whisper, "Dude, you going to ask her to help you with those crazy slimes?"

I grinned. Yeppers, nobody could ever say my future would be boring.

The end for now…

***

Book 9

The New Girl!

Super-Super Powers

It had been a slow week, an average week. Normally, I don't mind a little downtime. After all, everybody needs to rest now and then, even superheroes. But I had to admit that I smiled a little when my computer interface, MAC, informed me there was trouble at Starlight City Police Headquarters.

Yes, you might think the police HQ would be one of the last places bad guys would want to attack, especially in my town. But somehow, some way, a group of mutant rhino men had put the police headquarters under siege. I guess when you are mutant rhinos, you aren't scared of much. I also figured that they figured if they took out the police, they could have the run of the town.

Of course, I figured they hadn't counted on me…Super Teen.

"This is interesting," MAC told me as I flew towards the police station. "These rhino men seem to be concentrated in the police station parking lot."

"Why?" I asked.

Flying overhead, I noticed there had to be at least a dozen tall purple-skinned rhino men in the parking lot. They were ramming the police cars with their horns. The police fired at the rhinos from inside the building, but their shots simply bounced harmlessly off the rhino men's armored hide.

"Oh, I see," I sighed. "I get the feeling these aren't just plain old mutant rhino men."

"Actually, that is more of an assumption," MAC corrected. "But seeing how easily they rip through police cars and how even heavy-duty bullets bounce off them, I am inclined to make the same assumption."

"Well, let's teach these big bad rhinos a lesson," I said, zooming downward.

"Do you wish me to call in Lori, Marie, Tanya, and Jason?" MAC asked.

I could tell from the worried tone in MAC's voice that he didn't think I could handle this alone. He may have had a point. Lori, Marie, and Tanya do have awesome powers, and Jason has exo-body-armor that makes him more than a match for any normal rhino. But these...these weren't normal rhinos. And none of my friends were anywhere near as invulnerable as me. I didn't want them risking their safety, especially if I could handle this alone.

"I've got this for now!" I said, landing between two large rhinos. One of them was shouting orders so I assumed he was the boss.

"What about your buddy, Quazar...Moonvale's resident superhero? I am sure he'd love to help. Plus, you are kinda sweet on him. I can tell!" MAC said.

MAC did have two good points. Quazar (or Adam as I know him) was nearly as invulnerable as I was, and I did like him a lot. He was kind and sweet and smelled good.

"Nope. I want to handle this myself," I insisted. "I'm a modern super girl who can handle a dozen or so enhanced mutant rhinos all by myself."

The big rhino that was barking orders looked at me. He stood up on two feet and laughed. "It looks like little Super Teen is here." He looked at the rhino standing next to him. "Well, Randy you were right. She did show up, after all."

Randy the rhino shook his huge head. "Of course I was right, Rich. I mean...boss. Superheroes love to show up and show how super nice and cool they are."

I walked slowly toward Rich and Randy. "Look, I'm an animal lover and I don't really want to hurt you." I stood in front of Rich and crossed my arms. "But if you don't back

201

down, I'll have to clobber you all."

All the rhino men stopped doing whatever they were doing. They each started pointing and laughing at me.

"Well, at least you have succeeded in getting them to stop terrorizing the police station," MAC said.

I walked closer to Rich. I tapped him on the forehead. Normally this would have been enough to knock out a regular rhino. Heck, one fart and I can drop a herd of rhinos from 100 yards away. But this rhino was different.

"Was I meant to be impressed?" Rich asked, looking down at me.

"Kind of," I said.

Rich and Randy exchanged glances. They both started snickering. Rich pointed at me and started laughing harder. "Did you hear that, Randy? This little girl thought she could hurt me with a tap."

Randy laughed so hard he had to hold his side. "Well,

she is hurting me by making me laugh so hard," he insisted.

I'd had enough of being nice. Moving forward at super speed and flying off the ground, I hit Rich with an uppercut punch to his protruded chin. His head bobbed up. He straightened his head, he spat out a bit of blood. "Not bad kid, I kind of felt that one!" he told me.

Kind of felt it? Those words rang back and forth in my brain. I had hit Rich with what I thought would be enough power to send him flying. Instead, I managed to get him to feel it.

Rich squinted his eyes at me. "You wanna run and make this a bit more fun?"

"Nope, running isn't my style."

"Maybe she wants to fly, boss?" Randy suggested. "It's a more superhero type of thing to do."

Shaking my head, I said, "Nope, not flying either."

"Sure, you are!" Rich said. He lunged forward, hitting me with an uppercut to the chin.

My head shot backward. I went flying off the ground. I crashed into the wall of the police station. It had to be 30 yards away. Leaving a dent in the wall, I started falling to the ground. Before I hit the ground, though, I changed course. Holding out both fists, I zoomed back at Rich. This time, I rammed right into his big rhino gut. Hitting him at full speed sent him flying backward, crashing through a couple of police cruisers.

Landing on the ground, I felt my chin and back throb. I also felt a sense of accomplishment, knowing I had clobbered the big rhino.

Rich laid on top of one of the crinkled police cruisers moaning. "Okay, gotta admit, I did feel that one." Pointing upwards he said, "Get her, Crash!"

"You may not know this, but a group of rhinos is called a crash," MAC told me. "Kind of a fitting name! Don't you think?"

All the rhinos stopped doing whatever they were

doing and started racing towards me. If I timed this right, I could use it to my advantage. These rhino men might have been super strong and fast, but they were still rhinos. They seemed to have let it slip their little rhino minds that I could fly.

Just as the rhinos drew near enough to spike me with their horns, I shot up into the air. A few of the rhinos crashed into each other. The rest stopped short of crashing. They looked up at me. Their horns began to glow red.

"That can't be good!" MAC said.

"Oh, no...."

The rhinos blasted me with heat rays from their horns.

"OUCH!" I shouted.

None of the beams could penetrate my suit or skin but they certainly stung.

I flew higher up into the air in a desperate attempt to escape the rhino's range.

The rhinos kept their rays locked on me. Each beam hurting more and more, the longer it was directed at me.

"Perhaps this would be a good time to call your friends?" MAC said.

I felt torn. I didn't want to risk my friends being hurt by these nasty and powerful rhinos, but I also didn't want to lose to these creatures. Plus, if I failed now, the others might have a harder time bringing these beasts down.

Just as I was about to tell MAC to call in my team, the beams stopped. I could breathe and think again.

"I must have flown out of their range!" I said.

"Oh, not exactly," MAC told me.

"What does that mean?" I asked.

"Look down," MAC said.

Turning downwards, I saw her floating in midair. She deflected the rhino's heat beams as if they were nothing. She had long flowing dirty blond hair, a tall lean, yet muscular body. She wore a tight-fitting blue costume with long red high heeled boots and a red cape. Her costume looked amazing on her, even the cape. From behind, I couldn't see her face, but from what I could see, I was guessing the face was most likely gorgeous.

"Why don't you rhinos pick on somebody your own size?" the tall girl laughed.

"Wow, I just love her voice," MAC said.

Yeah, I had to agree. Her words sounded like music. I flew down next to her.

"Oh hi," I said.

The tall girl looked at me. Yep, her face was perfect too…golden smooth complexion. It appeared to be a face that had never known a zit.

"Who are you?" I asked the girl. She looked older than me.

"I'm Ultra!" she said. "The new superhero in town."

Okay, I wasn't expecting that. But I guess the costume should have given it away. "Well, thanks for the assist," I said. "But be careful, these rhinos are tough!"

Ultra turned to me and smiled. "You're so sweet," she gave me a little pat on the head. "I've got this," she said, her smile growing.

She streaked down at the rhinos almost too fast for even my super-vision to see. She tapped one rhino and it fell to the ground, out cold. She moved to another and another and another. She moved so quickly, the rhinos couldn't touch her. A simple touch by her managed to incapacitate each rhino.

After knocking out a dozen rhino men in less than a dozen seconds, Ultra turned and looked at the remaining dozen rhino men. She blew on her fingernails and rolled her eyes. "Well?" she asked them.

"Well, what?" one of the rhino men asked as they slowly crept towards her.

"Are you mutant rhino freaks smart enough to run away?" she asked. She spun away from them. "I'll turn my back and give you beasts a chance to run."

The remaining rhino men looked at each other. I heard them talking. "We're super strong mutant rhino men with laser horns!" one of them said.

"Well, yeah, but so were those other guys and she kicked their armored behinds!" another said.

"Actually, she just tapped them and they fell over," another added.

"But her back is turned," the first one said. "I bet she's tired."

"Besides, we can't back down, the boss will be mad!"

The twelve remaining rhinos dropped to all fours, they ran their hooves across the ground, digging into the tar. Smoke shot from their nostrils. They charged.

The rhinos got within maybe a foot of Ultra. They all turned blue, gasped and fell over, their legs up in the air. I noticed Ultra had simply popped her heel out of her boot.

"Could that have done it? Could a small whiff of her

feet..."

The scent of her feet hit me. Suddenly the world started to spin. I felt really giddy and light headed. I dropped from the sky.

Ultra ran over to where I was plummeting. She breathed towards me with super breath to slow my descent. She caught me in her arms.

"Oops, sorry kid," she told me. "Sometimes I don't know my own strength. I shielded the police and other people on the ground but I kind of forgot you were up there."

"Ah, no problem," I said, looking around at the two dozen rhinos now all on the ground totally beaten. "My, you're powerful."

"Yeah," she said with a smile. Of course, her teeth were perfect as well.

"Man, you KO'd them all without working up a sweat," I said.

"Oh, I worked up a little sweat," she said with a smile. She pointed her underarm at me.

The last thing I remember is Ultra saying, "Oops, don't know my own strength."

Dear Diary: As a slept, I had a weird freaky vision. The vision was of me trying to fight Ultra. Not sure why we were fighting. The subconscious is weird sometimes. But throughout my dream, I did everything I could to stop Ultra. I hit her with my best punches which she laughed off. I hit her with heat vision which she said tickled. I used super cold breath and she told me my breath was refreshing. I even farted on her. Yes, I went that far. (At least in my dream.) She waved the fart away like it was nothing. She then simply told me to fall over. I did. She won without touching me. Yeah, it was only a dream, but still. Wow! Does this girl really have so much power?

Not only that, but who the heck is this girl? Where the heck does she come from? How did she get so darn powerful? I mean, she took me down like I was a little baby. Not just me, but she clobbered those super mutant rhino men like they were nothing. It took me all my effort just to take one out. Those beasts pack a lot of punch, yet nothing they did seemed to hurt Ultra at all. She really does have a heap of power!

The funny thing is- she also seems kind of familiar to me. I'm not sure why. I mean the girl is so pretty, she is jaw-dropping beautiful. Yet, I know I have never seen her before in my life. I mean, how could I have forgotten her? A girl like her is pretty unforgettable.

Funny, I looked up at her like little kids do to me when I swoop in and save the day. I guess it goes to show that even superheroes can be in awe. And I have to admit that Ultra is ultra-awesome. I've taken out giant killer robots, fought aliens and super-sized gorillas with no (well very few) problems. Yet, an accidental whiff of Ultra's underarm puts me to sleep like a baby. Now THAT is impressive. In a way, I guess it's nice to know that she worked up a little sweat fighting those rhinos.

Discussion Time

"Super Teen, wake up!" I heard the familiar voice of Police Chief Michaels ringing in my ears.

Forcing my eyes open, I saw the police chief and a few of his officers standing over me. They looked mildly concerned.

"Oh, hi all," I said from the ground. "How long have I been sleeping for?"

"Sleeping? That Ultra lady knocked you out!" one of the officers laughed. He was a big man with a scar on his chin.

I sat up. I exhaled purposely in the laughing officer's direction. My breath hit his nose. He went silent and fell to the ground. Putting a hand over my mouth, I said, "Oops, sleep breath. Sorry!" Though I really wasn't sorry.

Chief Michaels held out a hand and helped me up. "You've been, ah resting, for like 30 minutes," he told me. "You were smiling so we didn't want to wake you. The medics insisted you were fine."

"Thanks," I said. Looking around I noticed all the rhino men and Ultra were gone. "What happened to those rhino men?" I asked.

Chief Michaels smiled. "Ultra carried them all to an island in the middle of the ocean. She said they'll be happy there, and being rhinos, they won't be able to hurt anything." His smile widened, "She really is truly amazing."

He looked at me a little sheepishly, his eyes opened wide. He patted me on the shoulder. "Not that we don't appreciate everything you've done for us! You're awesome too."

A female officer stepped forward. "Yeah, after all, you did take out the lead rhino. Ultra is just older and more experienced than you. Nothing to be ashamed of!" She gave me an encouraging smile.

Another officer stepped forward. "Plus, you did better than we did. Nothing we did even dented their armor."

"Speaking of which, any idea where those beasts are from?" I asked.

The chief nodded. "Ultra has a theory."

I fought back the urge to say, 'of course she does'. Instead, I said, "What is it?"

"She thinks they may be the work of Doctor Donna Dangerfield," the chief said.

I'd tangled with Doctor Donna and her assistant Doctor Gem Stone before. Doctor Donna seemed to really want to make the world a better place, but Gem had other ideas. My friends and I defeated her though. Doctor Donna's research is the reason why my friends, Marie and Lori now have superpowers, too. Doctor Donna was strange and driven but not evil. Unlike Gem.

"Is Doctor Gem Stone still in prison?" I asked.

"Yes," MAC said. "She is still in Capital City Max Security Prison."

"Doctor Donna has done a lot of work on strengthening humans and animals. But she has been very quiet lately," I said.

"Yes," the chief agreed. "But maybe she's been quiet because she's been working on such an amazing project, like these super rhinos."

"Good point..." I said. "Any idea where she is?" I asked.

The chief shook his head. "Nope."

"Affirmative," MAC said.

"Affirmative that you know?"

MAC flashed red. "Oh no, it's affirmative that I do NOT know." MAC paused. "I see where that could be confusing. Sorry. My bad."

I took a deep breath to clear my mind and collect. "Sorry I couldn't be more help chief," I said.

The chief patted me on the shoulder again. "Well, you are human, and all humans have good and bad days. You are human right?"

A gave him a nod and a smile. "I assure you, I am very human."

"Do you think Ultra is human?" one of the officers asked.

"Pretty sure she is," I said. Though I had no idea if

211

she had any weaknesses.

I leaped up into the air and flew home.

Arriving home, I found my mom, Grandma Betsy, Jason, and Adam all waiting for me at the kitchen table. They were eating ice cream and cookies.

"What's this all about?" I asked.

"Thought you could use some ice cream and cookies," Mom said, pointing to the wide array of flavors that were laid out on the table.

"I see you guys saw my beating?" I sighed.

The force of my breath knocked Jason, Grandma, and Mom over.

"Oops, sorry," I said.

The three of them stood up.

"It wasn't really a beating," Jason said. "You and those rhinos fought to a standoff," he added earnestly. "Why didn't you call us?"

"I didn't want you to get hurt," I said.

"It takes a lot to hurt me," Adam said.

I smiled at him. Part of me was really glad he cared enough to come here. Another part was less than thrilled to have Adam here after what may very well be the worst defeat of my life. Not really from the rhino men, but from Ultra. "I was afraid if I called you in to help, that might leave your town vulnerable," I told Adam. It was only a partial lie.

"That was thoughtful of you," Adam said. "But I lived here for three years. This town and you mean a lot to me. I would come here gladly, anytime."

"As would I!" Jason said. "Especially since I still live here and all. My armor and I could have been by your side in a moment."

"I fly extremely fast," Adam said, standing and puffing out his chest. "I could have been here very quickly too."

The back door popped open and in came Adam's
BFF, Zeke the zombie. He panted. "My jetpack isn't as fast as
Adam or Jason, but still, where my BFF goes, so do I. I
would have been here too, just not as quickly. And since I
am mostly dead, those silly rhino men couldn't have hurt
me." He punched his fist into his palm. He shook out his
palm. "Dang, I hit hard."

Grandma Betsy turned to Adam, Jason, and Zeke.
"Boys, we are very glad you've come to support Lia, but her
mom and I would like to talk to her alone now. We would
appreciate you giving us some privacy."

Zeke looked at Adam and Jason. "You two heard the
lovely lady. Beat it! We need to talk."

Grandma rolled her eyes. "Zeke, I was talking about
you, too."

Zeke's tongue dropped from his mouth. "But I am not

a boy. True, I look like a boy, but I am around two hundred years old. I actually stopped counting how old I was when I broke a hundred and fifty, cause I kind of figured it didn't really matter."

"Zeke, please leave," Grandma said.

Zeke looked at her. "Say what?"

"This is a private matter between grandmother, mother, and daughter."

"And zombie?" Zeke asked.

Grandma shook her head. "Think about what I just said," she told Zeke slowly.

"You didn't say you don't want the zombie here," Zeke said.

"Zeke, we don't want you here!" Grandma yelled.

Zeke scratched his head. "I'm starting to get the impression I am not wanted."

Adam picked Zeke up and tossed him over his shoulder.

"Oh, wow, you are so strong," Zeke said.

Adam looked at me. "Glad to know you're okay. We'll head back to Moonvale, but if you need us…"

"I got it," I said. Ah, Adam is so sweet.

Jason pointed to the door. "I'll be next door."

Aw, Jason was jealous. That was sweet too.

I watched as the two boys and the zombie left.

Mom pointed to a chair. "Sit. Let us feed you."

I did as I was told.

"What kind of ice cream?" Mom asked. "We have chocolate, strawberry, cookie dough, fudge swirl…."

"A scoop of each, please," I said.

Mom served the ice cream and passed it to me. I took a spoonful. I smiled. "Man, I needed that."

"A mother knows," Mom said.

"This Ultra was something," Grandma Betsy said.

"She seemed super-duper human," I sighed. "Did you guys see her?"

MAC broadcast a holographic image of Ultra onto the table.

"She was all over the news," Mom said.

"Still, I thought a refresher might be in order," MAC chimed. "She truly was impressive."

My mom, Grandma and I watched a holographic replay of Ultra taking out the rhino men like they were ants, weak little ants.

"Have you guys ever seen anything like her?" I asked.

"Nope," Mom said.

"Nope," Grandma said.

We got to the scene where I accidentally got a whiff off her underarm and passed out.

"She really packs some power," Grandma said.

"Her underarm actually smelled pleasant," I said. "So relaxing, I just felt like she had everything under control and I could go to La La Land…"

"And you did," Grandma said.

"I sure did," I sighed. "Could she be a cousin from the Moore side?"

"None of the Moore's have THAT kind of power. Besides, you are the oldest of your generation."

"Mac, have the people at Future Now Labs created anything like her?"

Adam shook his head. "No. They have nothing like Ultra."

"What about FART?" I asked.

"I have no record of them working on anything like her…" MAC said.

"MAC, freeze the image," Mom said.

The image of me sleeping in Ultra's arms froze in front of us.

"MAC, do a facial analysis of Ultra and Lia," Mom said.

"Check," Mac said.

MAC zoomed in on Ultra's face. He outlined her eyes, nose, and mouth. Numbers appeared next to her. The numbers started counting up. They stopped at 88%.

"What's 88 percent?" I asked.

"You and Ultra," MAC said. "She could be your sister."

"She is not your sister," Mom said.

"Then a clone?" Grandma suggested.

"Possible," MAC said. "But how could anybody get a copy of Lia's DNA to clone and improve? The technology to do so would be very expensive. Plus, how could a clone be older?"

"Maybe it's time to visit Dad," I said. "I'm actually surprised I haven't heard anything from him after my battle with the rhino men…"

MAC spoke up. "Your dad and Hana are in a... 'Do Not Disturb for Anything Short of Possible Earth Destroying, event.' I did not place the rhino men in that category."

"What are they doing?" I asked.

"I am but a humble super smart computer. I did not ask."

"Your dad and Hana know a lot about cloning...." Mom said.

"Then it's settled. I'll visit them."

"Do you want us to go with you?" Mom and Grandma asked.

I smiled. "I appreciate the offer from both of you, but I think this is something I should do on my own."

Dear Diary: That was a different spin on the situation. Could Ultra be a clone of me? A more powerful older version. That didn't make sense. But just because it didn't, that didn't mean it couldn't be true. I had to check this out a little more.

On a more fun note, I have to admit I like the idea of Adam and Jason being worried about me. I also like that they both showed up here. And that they seem slightly jealous of each other. They are both great guys. I've known Jason forever. He's always been by my side. He's always ready to help. He would do anything for me. Plus, now that he and Tanya are just friends, he is available. But I don't know if I want to risk or change our friendship...

Now Adam...he is something different. Speaking of clones, he was cloned to near perfection. His power rivals mine. He understands what it's like to be super and different. That has a certain appeal to me. Plus, he is so sweet, too. Man, life is never easy. But it sure is fun!

Still, it was so cool that they both wanted to help me.

As for Dad and Hana, I think I'll get more out them if I talk to them alone.

Lab Time

As I streaked through the sky towards BMS labs, I asked MAC to tell Dad and Hana I was on my way. I didn't want to catch those two off guard. Cause well, I had no idea what they would be doing so I figured it best if they knew I was on my way.

"Your father and Hana have turned off all communication," MAC informed me. "They must really want private time."

"But you know where they are?" I asked.

Silence.

"MAC?"

More silence.

"MAC? Can you hear me?"

"Yes, Lia… I can hear you quite clearly."

"So, why aren't you responding?" I asked.

Silence.

More Silence.

"MAC?" I shouted.

"I don't like being unable to give you the information you have requested. I don't like the fact that your father and Hana have turned off all means of communicating with them. I need to communicate. I exist to communicate. I understand your need to know what information they have."

"Thank you," I said. "Now, you are a super-computer. What do you know about a possible clone of me?"

"I cannot find any information on that, which is strange. But Hana is almost on my level. She may be able to hide it from me," MAC admitted.

"That's why I need to talk to her and Dad. ASAP!" I

told MAC.

"Where are they?"

Again, silence.

More silence.

Even more silence.

"MAC!"

"I am torn. They have ordered me not to communicate with life unless the situation is dire. This-while annoying- is not dire."

"Please, MAC?" I asked.

Still silence.

"Pretty please, MAC..." I said. I turned his interface towards my face and pouted a little.

There was a sigh from the interface.

"I can never resist a pretty please. They are in your father's underground office."

Okay, now that made sense. Wait! Dad had an underground office? Of course, he did. Dad always had backups of backups of backups. "Can you tell me where that office is?"

"Yes, I can," MAC said.

"Then tell me," I said.

"It's kind of obvious!" MAC hinted.

"Let me guess…it's under his actual office!" I said.

"See, I knew you could get it. You are smart, Lia. This way you feel better about yourself and I feel good because I didn't really tell you the location."

If that's what MAC had to tell himself, I was cool with that.

Landing at the main entrance of BMS labs, I put my hand on the security pad to open the door. The door popped open. Running at super speed, I raced towards my dad's office. I noticed three big guards blocking the door. I stopped in front of them.

"Super Teen, what brings you here?" one of the guards said.

"I need to talk to Doctor Strong and Hana!" I said in my firmest superhero voice.

The three guards shook their heads. "We are truly sorry, but the boss said they are not to be disturbed. We think Doctor Strong agreed."

I knew these men were only doing their jobs. But these men were stopping me from doing my job…protecting the city and the world. (Plus, I had to admit I was a little angry. First, about Ultra taking out those rhinos so easily. Second, the way she put me into La La Land so easily. Added to that, my dad and Hana were not really paying attention. Yeah, I was not in a good place.)

I crossed my arms. "Look, guys, I will give you until three to get out of my way."

I held up a finger. "One."

I held up another finger. "Two."

One of the guards folded his arms and stared back at me unimpressed.

It became obvious that these three men weren't going to move. So I blew on them with super breath. The force of my breath sent the three of them crashing into the wall. They hit the wall, moaned, and fell to the floor.

I placed my hand on the door's security lock.

"Sorry. You are not cleared to enter this room at this time," a speaker from the door told me.

"Oh really?" I said.

"Yes, really," the door answered.

I pushed the door in. I wasn't in the mood to deal with a moody door. I walked through Hana's office which led to the door of my dad's office. Of course, this door was locked too.

"So, we meet again!" the door said.

"Open, or I will smash through this door also," I told the door.

The door popped open. Walking into my father's office, it hit me that I really didn't come in here all that often. I guess Dad liked his privacy. Man, it was a big office, larger than most houses. Of course, I figured Dad probably lived here most of the time, as well. But Dad and Hana were nowhere to be found. Although I was aware that would be the case, and I also knew they were somehow under this office. I just needed to figure out where.

Ideally, I would do this on my own, so as to not get MAC into trouble. He felt bad that he'd helped me get this far. But this was important. Not 'Save the Earth' important, but still, pretty darn important.

Examining the office's floor, I noticed most of the room had wooden floors. I tried using my x-ray vision but the floor was coated with something that prevented it. Then I noticed one spot in the middle of the office that was covered with a bright red shag pile carpet. I walked over to the carpet. Dad couldn't have been that obvious? Could he?

Rolling the carpet up, I saw one of the wood floor panels just a little ajar. I walked to that panel and stepped on it.

A slide opened up below me. I went tumbling down the slide, crashing into an even bigger room. There, sitting in the middle of the room on a blanket, were Dad and Hana.

She was laying with her head in his lap as he fed her grapes.

At first, the two lovebirds didn't notice me. Once I got within twenty feet though, Dad finally saw me.

"Lia, what are you doing here?"

Hana shot up and opened her eyes. "We gave orders that we were not to be disturbed."

"Unless the world was in trouble," Dad added. "Is the world in trouble?"

I sat down next to them. Hana frowned at me, but I didn't care. "My world is in trouble," I told them.

"How so, dear?" Dad asked in his worried voice.

"Yes, how so, dear?" Hana asked but not nearly as sincerely.

"The city was attacked by two dozen rhino men. Strong rhino men. They had heavy armor and could generate energy blasts from their horns."

"Oh my," Dad said.

"But you handled them," Hana said.

"Not exactly. I took out one or two of them," I said. "But the others had me on the ropes. They were blasting me, and it hurt."

"So, the team came…Jason, Adam, Tanya, Marie, Lori. They helped! Right?"

I shook my head. "No, these things were too dangerous. I didn't want to risk my friends being hurt or worse."

"You ran away then?" Hana said.

"There is nothing wrong with running when you are in over your head," Dad insisted. "It's a sign of great intelligence. You get that from me."

"No, I didn't run," I said.

"Did FART show up? Did the army show up? Your mom and her mom?" Dad asked.

"Nope," I said. "None of that." I lifted my wrist up and pointed to MAC. "Show them!" I ordered MAC.

A hologram of Ultra appeared.

"She turned up," I said.

"Nice outfit," Hana said. "I love that red mask!"

MAC showed Hana and Dad all the action. They watched in amazement as Ultra put down over twenty super rhino men in less than twenty seconds.

"Wow, she *is* powerful," Dad said.

"Amazing!" Hana said.

MAC got to the part where I fell out of the sky, only to be caught by Ultra.

"Nice catch," Hana said.

Now, for the part where a simple whiff of Ultra's underarm put me into sleepy time.

"Incredible," Dad said. "Lia must have barely got a whiff of her armpit."

"Underarm, dear," Hana corrected.

"Yeah, it was one of those...one whiff and I'm out...type of deals. She is that powerful. She can put me to sleep by accident."

Dad stood up and looked at the hologram more closely. "She has incredible raw power."

"Does she look familiar to you?" I asked. "Does she look like somebody you know?"

Dad studied the hologram. "She does remind me a bit of you."

Hana stood up. "Perhaps, but she is definitely older and more powerful than you."

"Dad, did you clone me?" I asked.

Dad shook his head. "No, of course not." He looked at Hana. "We didn't, did we?"

"No, we did not," Hana said. "And besides, like I mentioned, this girl or woman or whatever, is older than Lia. If anything, you would be her clone."

I took a step backward. I patted my chest. "No, you're not telling me..."

"No, we are not," Dad said walking up to me. "You were born the good old-fashioned way. You know your mom wouldn't let me clone us a daughter."

Dad had a great point. No way Mom would have put up with that.

"Then what is she?" I asked.

"Obviously, she's a super being," Hana said. "She could be natural. Like you."

"If so, where has she been until now?" I asked.

Hana shrugged. "Maybe she thought you didn't need her until now."

That could have been a good point. But somehow, that didn't make sense. Why would a woman who looked like that, with powers like hers, keep them hidden?

"Nope, that's not it," I said. "Any idea where Doctor Donna Dangerfield is hanging out these days?"

"Hmm," Hana said. "Last I heard from her, she was

doing research at the North Pole."

"Now, could she create somebody like Ultra?" I asked.

Hana and Dad looked at each other. "Frankly, honey, we're not sure," Dad said.

"Well, I guess there's only one way to find out! I'm making a trip up north!"

Dear Diary: Now, I gotta say, I am not thrilled about my dad and Hana having secret private sessions in his underground lair. It seems a bit supervillain-like to me. But Dad's a busy guy and I know he cares about me, so I guess I can't complain about him needing some alone time with his girl. Even if his girl is a woman that he actually MADE. Dad has always had a thing for women who are different, I guess. Heck, Mom is great but she certainly is unique and way powerful in her own way.

I guess, I still have a little grudge against Hana since her first version did try to hurt me. I put her out of commission though. This newer version, while never overly friendly and always a little offbeat, has never attacked me. Still, it's weird when your dad dates an android who looks like an athletic fashion model. But Dad seems happy.

All signs now point to Doctor Donna Dangerfield. She has dabbled in making super people before. Maybe she hit the jackpot with Ultra.

I will find out soon enough!

Heading North

I decided not to tell Mom or Jason where I was heading until I had the North Pole in sight. I figured they would both mostly complain and tell me how dangerous it was to fly so far away in order to talk to a mad scientist type without backup. They might have been right, but somehow, I wanted to do this on my own. I didn't need anybody talking me out of this. I would wait until it was way too late to turn around and go home empty-handed.

"MAC, open up a conversation with my mom please," I said.

"Check," MAC said. "I compute she will be less than pleased."

"Don't have to be a super-duper computer to know that!" I said.

"Hello?" I heard Mom's voice over MAC's interface. "Is that you, honey?"

"Yep," I said.

"Where are you? You sound like you're flying."

"Oh, I am..."

"Where are you heading?" Mom asked.

"Ah, north..."

"How far north?"

"Oh, um, kind of far..."

"True, but if she keeps heading this way, soon she will be going south!" MAC added.

"Wait, what?" Mom said. "Are you going where I think you are going?"

"Depends," I replied, flying ever faster.

"Are you going to the North Pole?" Mom asked.

"Sorry, Mom you're breaking up!" I said.

'No, she is not," MAC protested. "I always give a signal."

"Yes, I am going to the North Pole…" I admitted.

Silence.

For some reason, that silence really bugged me.

"Mom?" I said.

"Why are you going to the North Pole?" Mom asked.

"Ah, I hear it's nice. I thought I might see a polar bear…"

"Lia!"

"I understand Doctor Donna Dangerfield has a new lab there," I said.

More silence.

"Okay, I guess it makes sense," Mom said. "Be careful."

"Of course," I said.

I flew onward. I figured if Mom wasn't all that worried, I had to sort of be on the right track here. After all, if this was going to be dangerous, Mom would be more worried. Right?

A domed snow-covered building came into sight. "Is that the lab?" I asked MAC.

"Yes, it is," MAC said.

Two missile-shaped drones launched from the ground.

"Looks like you have been spotted," MAC said.

I fought back the urge to literally blow the drones out of the sky. Instead, I figured I'd see if they were hostile or warning drones.

Hovering in the air, I held out a hand in the stop position. "Stop!" I ordered.

The two drones stopped a few feet from me. They hovered near my face.

"Super Teen, we want to know why you are in our airspace?" one of the drones said.

"I want to talk to Doctor Dangerfield," I told the drones.

"May we inquire about the topic?" the drones asked.

"Cloning," I said.

"Do you wish to be cloned?" they asked.

"Ah, no," I said.

"I want to talk to Doctor Donna about cloning," I said firmly.

"Why?" the drones asked.

I considered this answer carefully.

"We are waiting!" the drones said.

"I just want to talk to the good doctor because I understand she is an expert on cloning," I insisted.

The two drones turned towards each other. They exchanged beeps. They turned back to me. "That is true."

"Will you let me pass?" I asked.

The two drones hovered there. "We would like to learn more about your interest in clones..."

I shot forward and grabbed the two missile drones. I slammed them together. They exploded in my hands. I blew the dust off my hands. I landed on the ground outside of the ice-covered dome. The place had a big red door.

I knocked on the door.

Much to my surprise, the door cracked open. I slid into the building. There, standing in front of me, was Doctor Donna Dangerfield. "Why, Super Teen. To what do I owe the honor?" she asked.

"I need to talk to you about cloning," I said.

"I heard," Doctor D. said. "But why come all the way up here? You could have called. I thought you kids today just texted."

I moved closer to her. I realized she didn't have a scent. "Hey, you're a hologram!" I said.

The image of Doctor Dangerfield faded.

Another door popped open. Doctor Dangerfield walked through that door. "My, my, you are a smart girl."

"Thanks, I try to pay attention in class and study hard," I said, giving the regular response I always gave to the press and young kids. Being a superhero, I feel it's important that I set a good example for kids, but listening to myself say those words, I knew they were a little corny.

Doctor Dangerfield smiled. "Good answer," she said. "A bit simplistic but it's gotta be great for your image." Doctor Dangerfield sighed. "If I had handled my image better, I might not have to be up here in the top of nowhere." She paused. Her eyes widened. "How are my first test subjects, Marie and Lori doing? I am assuming they work with you on occasion, still."

I nodded. "Both of them are gaining more control of their powers as well as more confidence using them," I said. "Although, Lori has never had a confidence problem. But Marie is a little scared of her ability..."

Doctor Dangerfield grinned. "Good, she should be. If she lost control of her power, she could pretty much turn everything around her into poop. I knew though she would be able to handle that kind of power without abusing it." Doctor Dangerfield nodded. "For all my flaws, I am still quite smart, and a great judge of character."

"And modest too," I said.

Doctor Dangerfield nodded. "Yes, my modesty is one of my best qualities. Now, what brings you to my lab? I have to assume this isn't a social visit. "Is this about that Ultra who showed up and showed you up?" she asked, with a tone that said...I know it is.

I had to give Doctor Dangerfield credit. She really was one of the few people I've met who was actually as smart as they thought they were.

"How do you know about Ultra?" I asked.

Doctor Dangerfield turned and walked towards the door she had come through to greet me. Looking back over her shoulder, she called to me, "Come, Super Teen."

Doctor Dangerfield led me into a shiny room. The walls and ceiling of that room were giant monitors. There had to be at least a hundred screens of information filling those walls. There were soldiers in battle. A rainforest. A couple of sports events. What appeared to a robbery in Capital City. Every screen had something buzzing on it. But the most surprising thing about this room was that the floor had a bunch of big comfy red seats, and in each of the seats sat a monkey making notes on a laptop computer.

"I keep tabs on the world," Doctor Dangerfield told me, as she picked up a red folder that was labeled Top Secret, and clutched it tightly to her. "I watch all the network news shows, plus, I have special links to surveillance satellites. I stay very well informed. If I don't catch it, one of my assistants will."

"Ah, so that's what the monkeys are doing here!" I said. "They are your assistants."

"Yes, they literally work for peanuts. They are obedient and eager to please. They don't take up much space. They don't talk a lot. They have no problem watching news show, after news show. Sure, they occasionally sneak in a cartoon or a reality show… they love that show… 'Keeping up with the ….' whatever their name is. But they do good work."

"Ah, don't monkeys throw their poop at each other, and also others, when they get mad?" MAC asked.

"Oh gross, MAC!" I said.

"Sometimes the truth is gross!" MAC told me.

Doctor Dangerfield nodded. "They can, on occasion, get carried away, especially when they see something they don't like. But I've taught them breathing exercises. So now they breathe deeply and take control of their thoughts and emotions instead of throwing poop."

"That may be your biggest accomplishment as a scientist," MAC said.

"Let's hope not," Doctor Dangerfield said. She turned to me. "I assume you are assuming that I had something to do with this Ultra girl, who popped up seemingly from nowhere."

"You are an expert on clones and enhancing people," I said.

"And monkeys," one of the monkeys said.

"People and animals," I added.

Doctor Dangerfield smiled. "Guilty as charged. I am pretty brilliant."

Looking me in the eyes, she asked, "Did your father and his android *friend* send you here?"

"Yes," I said without thinking.

"Yikes!" MAC said from my wrist.

MAC's yikes gave me a little kick in the brain. Doctor Dangerfield may have just tricked me into revealing who my dad was. "Ah, wait, what?" I said, acting confused. Okay, I really wasn't acting that hard.

"She got you," the talkative monkey said. He sniffed me. "Yep, she smells of fear!"

"Oh yeah!" I told the monkey.

"Oh wow, witty retort, superhuman," the monkey

233

countered.

"Mani, be nice to our guest," Doctor Dangerfield ordered.

"Sorry, boss," Mani monkey said.

I pointed at Mani and said, "Yeah, keep that up and I'll give you a whiff of my boots!"

Mani bowed to me. "I bow to your human superior smell."

I actually couldn't decide if I liked this little monkey or wanted to flatten him with a fart. Being the more evolved being, I decided to take this all in my stride. Ignoring Mani, I asked Doctor Dangerfield, "Did you have anything to do with this Ultra girl who showed up? You seem to have an idea who I am. You might have been able to grab some of my DNA. You may have been able to clone me."

Doctor Dangerfield took in my words with her arms folded.

"She does have a good point, boss!" Mani said.

Doctor Dangerfield exhaled on Mani. He grabbed his throat, gasped, and fell to the ground, blue. "Monkeys are so dramatic," she said. "Don't worry, he'll just rest for a while." She smirked. "As you can probably tell, I have improved myself a little." There was a slight pause. "Plus, working all day, sometimes I forget to eat and that can make my breath less than pleasant, but I use it to my advantage."

"Not answering my question, Doc!" I said.

"Look, Lia honey. Do you mind if I call you, Lia?"

"No, go ahead," I said. "If that will make you happy. Since you seem to think that I may be Lia Strong."

"Right, well Lia, I wish I had something to do with Ultra. She seems amazingly powerful. After all, she took you out like you were a normal human. Well, maybe not a normal human. An unprotected whiff of her underarm could probably kill a normal human, you were just stunned."

"Put into La La land," MAC corrected.

"Well, whatever...you survived with no ill effects.

234

The point is, she may be the most powerful being on the planet. I wish I had made her. But alas, I don't have the kind of technology or funding necessary to accomplish that."

I weighed Doctor Dangerfield's words. She was the type of person who would actually take credit for Ultra if she had anything to do with Ultra. Her ego was as big as her brain. I was sure she was one of those people who thought her poop didn't smell and there was nothing in the world she couldn't do. Yeah, maybe she might have been scared of me, and what I would do to her if I found out she *was* connected to Ultra. But I doubted that. Doctor Dangerfield didn't scare easily.

Doctor Dangerfield put a comforting hand on my shoulder. It seemed out of character for her. "Look, kid, you think I might have cloned you and improved you." She nodded. "I wish I did. But if I had done that, I wouldn't have aged you. Artificially aging clones of actual people has proved to be shaky science at best. It only worked with your Adam friend because he was created totally artificially in a lab. There is no other Adam out there. He's more of a man-made human than a clone, per say, but a clone is a catchier title. Easier for people to relate to. Less scary in many ways."

I listened to Doctor Dangerfield's words. I believed her.

"MAC, you've analyzed her voice, right?" I asked.

"Of course," MAC said. "I believe she is telling the truth."

"Any idea where Ultra came from?" I asked Doctor Dangerfield. Pointing to the screens of information, I added. "You do seem to have your eye on the world."

Doctor Dangerfield smirked. "The Universe is a big place filled with all sorts of wonderful things. In other words, who knows?" Her face became serious. "I can tell you one thing…I had nothing to do with Ultra. I have no idea who she is. I just know she is packed with power. From what I've seen, she wants to help. I doubt you have anything to fear from her. In fact, she could take a lot of pressure off you. You can be a kid again. Wouldn't that be nice, Lia? You could concentrate on LAX and school and boys. You could have fun."

"I enjoy saving the world!" I told her.

Doctor Dangerfield nodded. "Sure, I get that. Just like I enjoy making the world better by improving people and adding knowledge to the world. Still, with Ultra around, maybe you can split duties with her? I mean, come on kid, you need to have some fun."

I held out my hand. "Thanks for your time, Doctor Dangerfield."

She hugged me, lifting me off the ground. "Call me, Donna."

"Okay, Doctor Donna," I said.

She held me up in the air. Pointing to the floor I said, "Nice, hug. But if you put me down, I'll be heading home now."

"Do you want to stay for a few minutes…for some hot cocoa and crumpets? It's actually nice to have another human to talk to," she said, still hugging me. Yeah, I could tell the good doctor was lonely.

"Sure," I said.

Doctor Donna lowered me to the ground. "Call your mom, tell her I say hi and let her know you'll be snacking with me. She might be worried."

"Already done," MAC said.

"Excellent!" Doctor Donna said. "Come, let's have a snack and some girl talk."

Dear Diary: I truly believe that Doctor Donna has nothing to do with Ultra. As a scientist, she is fascinated by Ultra's raw power, but I do believe she has no ill-thoughts about me. I think she wants to be my friend. After all, I am one of the few people in the world who could easily visit her. I actually promised her I would try to visit once a month just for a chat. Her hot cocoa was excellent. And for a sort of crazy, sort of mad scientist, she also talks pretty good girl talk.

She does think that Adam and I are made for each other – almost literally in Adam's case. I guess the government group that made Adam did consult with Doctor D. Those are her microchips inside Adam, giving him extra power. But of course, Doctor D. is also quite familiar with Jason. She said that the way he looks at me gives her the impression he wants to be more than friends.

I get that drift from Jason, too. I really don't know how any of this will turn out. Doctor D. told me I should be happy that I have two great guys who really like me. Heck, according to her she never had a guy who really liked her. Most of the men her age are scared of her super intellect. Yeah, she is smart and beautiful but she said that men don't like being shown up by her being better than them.

I'm glad the males in my life are different!

Homecoming

When I arrived home, I found Mom and my faithful dog, Shep waiting for me. Both of them were sitting anxiously on the couch.

"So, what did you learn?" Mom asked me.

Shep chipped in with a "woof".

I sat down on the couch next to them. Kicking my shoes off, I was happy to see Shep didn't pass out from the odor.

"Wow, that's a first," Mom said. "I thought your feet would have more punch after flying all the way to the North Pole."

That was a bit of a poke at me. I knew Mom wasn't happy with me flying off like that, especially knowing I went to confront Doctor Dangerfield. Mom and the Dangerfield go way back. I think they might have even gone to med school together. I believe they had a sort of rivalry between them.

"No big deal. It was a nice flight. I had a nice little chat with Doctor Donna. I don't think she knows any more about Ultra than anybody else," I said. "How's Oscar doing? Did you guys go out for dinner tonight?" I asked, trying to turn the topic of discussion away from me.

"Yes, he cooked me dinner," Mom said. "You'll be happy to know he's fascinated by Ultra and now wants to figure out who she is and where she comes from. That should take some pressure off you."

I should have felt good about my mom's reporter boyfriend no longer trying to figure out who Super Teen was. Instead, I felt a tinge of jealousy that Ultra had taken some attention away from me. I guess I felt unwanted attention was better than no attention at all. But after thinking it over a little more, I figured some good had come from Ultra.

"Yeah, I guess I should be happy about that," I said, patting Shep.

Shep looked up and licked me. I patted him on the head again. "You're a good boy," I told him. He looked at me as if I had just stated something obvious. Turning my attention back to Mom, I asked her. "What do you think of this Ultra Girl?"

"She is strong," Mom said, kind of stating the obvious.

"Good one, Mom," I said.

"She has certainly got under your skin," Mom added.

"No, she has not," I insisted.

"Daughter, you flew to the North Pole to get information on her!" Mom insisted. "You met with a lady whose assistant once tried to kill you."

"That was once, and that woman is now in jail!" I said defensively.

Mom leaned into me. "Honey, you are obsessed with Ultra."

"Am not," I said. I looked at Shep. "Right boy?"

Shep rolled off my lap. He proceeded to walk out of the room.

Mom and I exchanged glances.

"See," Mom smiled.

"That means nothing, Shep has never liked it when we argue!" I said.

"This isn't an argument, it's a discussion!" Mom said.

"At the very least, it's a disagreement!" I said.

"Look, honey, you asked me what I thought, and I told you. As a mother and a doctor."

"You're not a shrink!" I insisted. "You can't tell when something is under my skin!"

Mom stayed calm. "Honey, first off…I did do a psychology rotation in med school. I do understand a lot more than you think. Second off, I'm a mom and you're my daughter, we have a bond. I can feel what you feel, but I've known you all your life. I know when something is eating at you. Third, this is eating at you, you are used to being the strongest person around and now you aren't. Suddenly, this older girl shows up who is stronger than you. You think that makes her better."

I dropped my gaze from her eyes. "I'm not sure I'm needed," I admitted. "But I am truly worried about the safety of my city and the world. What if this girl turns out to be evil or bad?"

"Then you, your friends, and everybody else will deal with her. You have a lot of resources on your side. But so far, she hasn't given any indication that she is bad. It looks to me that she, like you, just wants to help."

"What if the city doesn't need help? They have me... and my team."

Mom nodded. It was her Mom 'know-it-all nod' that I so hated. "Now it looks like the town and the world also have *her*." Mom gauged her words. "Look, honey, you were fine when your friends got their powers. You were fine when you met Adam. Heck, you seem pleased to have somebody around who is different like you. Maybe this girl can be one more friend to add to your list?"

Yep, just like Mom to go after this all rational like. Her points were all very valid, but I wasn't looking for valid here. I wanted support, blind support.

"Mom, I don't get the vibe that this girl wants to be my friend. I get the impression she wants to show me up."

"And you base that on?" Mom asked. She held up a finger, determined to get her point across.

Yep, just like Mom to go after this all rational like. Her points were all very valid, but I wasn't looking for valid here. I wanted support, blind support.

"Mom, I don't get the vibe that this girl wants to be my friend. I get the impression she wants to show me up."

"And you base that on?" Mom asked.

I shrugged. "No idea, really." I exhaled.

"I'm with your mother," MAC said.

"Who asked you?" I barked at MAC. "Isn't your job to give me information?"

"Yes," MAC said. "And that is what I am doing. Giving you information."

"But you aren't supposed to give me information unless I ask for it. Right?" I told MAC.

"While normally that is true, I feel it is my duty to give you information when I think you need that information. I computed you needed to hear that right at this moment."

I took MAC off my arm. I dropped him on the couch. "I'm going upstairs to study!" I said.

As I walked away, I overhead MAC tell Mom, "I don't believe that went well."

"Nope, it didn't, MAC…" Mom said.

I reached my room and turned on the light. Looking out the window, across the yard, I saw Jason's light was on. I picked up my phone and sent a text. I needed a little reassurance.

LIA> Hey!
JASON> Welcome back
JASON> How did it go…ur trip to the pole?

Jason could be such a geek. I knew he'd tried to make that rhyme.

LIA> Doctor Donna knew nothing about Ultra…
JASON> Ah 2 bad
JASON> But it was a LONG shot
JASON> From what I've seen…this Ultra Girl is different
LIA> How so?
JASON> U know me. I study everything at your dad's lab. I soak it in
LIA> Geek
JASON> Guilty
JASON> But I don't think it's possible for ANY lab right

now to make somebody as powerful as Ultra
JASON> From the tests…u and Adam are pretty much on
the same level. You may be a bit stronger
LIA> :)
JASON> But Ultra - she is well….
LIA> Stronger than both of us put together…
JASON> Yeah!
LIA> U don't think she's a clone of me?

No response.
Still no response.

LIA> ???
JASON> I admit there is a resemblance but no, I don't think
anybody on Earth could take a clone of u and make it more
powerful and older
LIA> That seems to be the general thought…
JASON> Let's not worry about this girl. Okay?
JASON> U know ur super special
LIA> Thanks!
JASON> U ready for the history test tomorrow?
LIA> I will be

I didn't mention that I had forgotten about that test. Being a
superhero and a student was hard.

JASON> C U in the morning!
LIA> Night

Another message popped up.

ADAM> Lia…Why aren't u using MAC now?
LIA> How do u know that?
ADAM> MACC told me
ADAM> MAC told MACC ur upset because he told u the
truth

LIA> sigh
ADAM> I don't believe u typed sigh. ☺
LIA> MAC may be right
LIA> I've let this Ultra Girl really get to me!
ADAM> Why?

Now I paused.

ADAM> U there?
LIA> She's better than I am
ADAM> She's stronger but that doesn't mean she's better!

Another pause from me.

ADAM> Look, Lia, ur amazing, having another superhero
doesn't make u less amazing!
LIA> Okay…
ADAM> Because it's not ur power that makes u so. It's ur
heart and spirit
LIA> U sound like a greeting card
ADAM> I love greeting card wisdom. Simple and 2 the
point
LIA> Thanks… I'll put MAC on in the morning
ADAM> Fair enough
ADAM> If you need me - I'm there in a flash!
LIA> Thanks… night
ADAM> Night

*Dear Diary: As much as I really don't want to admit this, Mom
and MAC (and yes even Shep) may have a point. I might be a tad
jealous of Ultra. She showed me up in public. And it didn't take
much effort for her to do that. It isn't as though Ultra is like Wendi
who actively tries to make my life bad. Wendi seems to take some
enjoyment out of making me feel bad about myself. Ultra doesn't
seem to be trying to do that, yet in some ways, that makes it worse.*

I kind of always think that Wendi acts like she does towards me out of jealousy. In Ultra's case, that certainly isn't true. I kind of feel like a baby next to her. I don't like it.

It's nice having Jason and Adam to talk to. But even that still doesn't make me feel totally better. I have to admit, for once in my life, I am jealous.

But maybe I'm just feeling sorry for myself. I need to forget about Ultra and get ready for school tomorrow!

School Dazed...

Jason and I had a nice leisurely walk to school. After the last couple of days, I really needed normal. I actually found myself looking forward to an average day in school. A day without thinking of Ultra.

Of course, on the way, I received a text.

MARIE> OMG
CHRISTIE> Holly….
LORIE> This is unbelievable

Actually, I got a bunch of texts just as I was walking in the door of the school building. Before I could even respond "what?" I was mobbed by most of my friends.

"Okay, guys what's the big deal?" I asked.

"We have a new Russian exchange student, her name is Natasha," Marie said slowly.

"Okay," I said, not quite getting where this was going.

"She's tall and really beautiful," Lori said.

"And so exotic looking," Kristi added.

Tanya nodded. "I think I may finally know what it's like to feel jealousy, extreme jealousy…"

Wait, what? Tanya, the slick and beautiful Tanya was feeling jealous? This was beyond weird and strange. Who the heck could this Natasha be?

I really should have figured that out before I saw her. But then I saw her, standing by the lockers with a pink laptop open in her hand. Tall, flowing blond hair, smooth golden complexion, a perfect figure. OMG was this Ultra? I mean, her hair and skin tone was slightly different and it was difficult to be sure because she had been wearing a mask before. But all the basic perfections were there, and of course, Wendi and Patti were standing by her side. The eyes of every person in the hallway were locked on her. It felt as though she could hypnotize us all by her mere presence.

Natasha looked up from the screen, saw me and smiled. She pointed at me and asked Wendi, "Who is that girl?"

Wendi squinted her eyes and stuck out her tongue. "Do you mean Lia? The kind of ordinary looking girl who just came in…."

Natasha shook her head. "Yes, I think so. But she doesn't look ordinary to me. I think she's really pretty."

Wendi sighed. "Well, you are from another country. Tastes must be different there." Wendi looked at me. "I guess she's okay. Maybe a little above average, a 6.5. But she's not like you or me."

Natasha grinned. She put her laptop in her locker, closed the door then walked past Wendi and the others and continued towards me. I actually held my breath when I saw her growing closer. My heart skipped a beat or two.

"OMG!" Kristi said nervously. "She's coming over here!"

Tanya turned to me. "Is my hair okay?"

"Perfect as always…" I reassured her.

She exhaled on me. "How's my breath?"

"Fresh," I said.

"Phew!" Tanya smiled. She shook her head. "What the heck is going on with me?"

Jason moved forward, "Just be calm, girls," he said. He saw Natasha drawing closer to us. His eyes popped open. His tongue dropped out of his mouth. He quickly covered his mouth with his hand as she approached.

Natasha reached us and held out a hand to Jason. "Hello, I'm Natasha," she said, with just the slight hint of a Russian accent.

"Ah…ah…. I'm…. ah…." Jason said, dumbfounded.

"Jason," I said, nudging him.

"Right! I'm Jackson! I mean Jason. Jason…. Ah…."

"Michaels," I added. "Mr. Cool."

Jason smiled nervously, his body hunched, you could see sweat forming on his brow. "Yeah, that's my name…" He paused. "I'm Jason Michaels!" he said like he was proud he knew his own name.

"Nice to meet you, Jason Michaels," Natasha told him as she walked past.

"OMG! She knows my name!" Jason said, holding his

heart.

Tanya and Lori put themselves between Natasha and me. This seemed out of character for these two. They were normally the coolest kids around.

"Hi. I'm Tanya!" Tanya said, in a more outgoing and bubbly way than I had ever heard her act.

"Yo, I'm Lori!" Lori said. "Do you play LAX?"

Natasha took in both of them. She smiled. They both smiled back with even wider smiles. OMG! They were awestruck.

"Nice to meet you two," Natasha grinned. "I'm actually more of a soccer and MMA kind of girl."

"MMA is cool!" Lori said.

"Everybody here is so friendly," Natasha said.

"It's a nice school and a nice town," I said. Stepping forward, I offered Natasha my hand. "I'm Lia, Lia Strong," I said, looking her in the eyes. Wow! She had amazing almond shaped blue eyes. It was like they owned you.

Natasha surprised me (and pretty much everybody else) by hugging me. "For some reason, Lia Strong, I want to hug you."

Wendi and Patti's mouths dropped open as they watched our embrace.

Natasha hugged me tighter. I could feel her strength. She had to be Ultra. Right? Or was this just my imagination. No, this couldn't be a coincidence. One day, Ultra shows up, and the next, this perfect older girl arrives at my school. I mean, I guess it could be...

Natasha leaned back and picked me up off the ground. I tried to prevent it, but I couldn't. Yep, she had to be Ultra.

Wendi and Patti pounced forward. "Natasha, what are you doing?" Wendi asked, shocked. "Lia's not in my crowd."

Natasha placed me back on the ground softly. Turning to Wendi, she said, "I'm not in your crowd, either.

I'm my own crowd." She shook her head. "Sorry, sometimes my English gets silly. I meant that I'm my own person. I don't follow any crowd." She shrugged. "Of course, sometimes, for some reason, the crowd follows me."

"It's because you are amazing," Marie said.

"Thanks, Marie," Natasha said.

Marie took a step backward. "How do you know my name?"

Natasha grinned. "Wendi showed me the LAX team's award display. They had all your pictures there. I memorized your name."

"Oh, that's so cool," Marie said.

I had to figure out how to play this. I was pretty sure that this Natasha had to be Ultra, but I couldn't be totally sure. I could be cool and calm and just see what happened. Maybe she'd give me a clue or a hint, or maybe I should actually ask her, but I certainly couldn't do that right here, right now, with all the school staring at us. I would have to wait for a better time.

"Everybody freeze!" Natasha ordered.

Everybody stopped in place. The room went silent. Looking outside, I saw that even the birds in flight were frozen. "What the...?" I said.

Natasha smiled. "Come on, Lia. You have to know I'm Ultra. Right? You *are* a smart girl."

I nodded. "I kind of thought you were. But I wasn't sure if I was being paranoid."

Natasha put her hands on my shoulders. She gave me a funny look. "Why paranoid? Do you think I am out to get you or something?"

I had to be careful with my words here. "I'm not sure if I should be afraid of you or not."

Natasha laughed. Her laugh calmed me. Her face became serious. "Girl, if I wanted to, you'd be a pile of dirt at my feet right now."

"Okay, not very reassuring," I told her.

Natasha laughed. "You are so silly. I get it, you are used to being the most powerful one around. The one who can drop everybody with a whiff of her feet. You like it."

I took a step back. "I don't like it… it's embarrassing…"

Natasha leaned into me and smiled. "Really?"

I returned her smile. "Okay, I admit it's kind of empowering in a weird kind of way." I paused. "It's kind of nice being so powerful." I looked at the frozen Wendi. "But it's also a bit of a curse. I mean, I have to be careful all the time not to fart in public. I don't want to kill everybody. Plus, there are times it is so tempting to just turn Wendi into my pet." I gasped. "I don't believe I said that out loud!"

Natasha gave me another hug. "Word, girl. You are just speaking your mind. I've only known this Wendi for like fifteen minutes and I'm tempted to make her think she's a chicken. But she's really nothing to us. I just humor her. With great power comes great understanding."

"Where did you come from?" I asked.

Natasha shook her head. "Doesn't matter. I'm just here to help relieve you. Let you reach your full potential. I'm here to let you be you. You can be a kid. I'll keep the world safe for now."

I looked her in the eyes, "But this is my city and my world."

"Mine too," she said.

"But I want to help," I insisted.

"That's so sweet of you," Natasha said, she made me feel like a child even though I didn't think she meant to. "I'll tell you what. You can work with me. You and your team. I guess you can learn by watching."

I considered her words. "What if my team doesn't want to work with you?"

Natasha laughed. "That won't be a problem."

"I guess we couldn't stop you from helping even if we wanted to," I said.

Natasha smirked. "Smart girl. Believe me, I am here to help." She stopped talking.

"But?"

Natasha considered her words now. "While I may be ultra-powerful..." she nudged me. "Get it?"

"Yeah, I get it..."

"I'm still human. Therefore, I do have flaws. One of them is that I have a temper and you really don't want to see it. Nobody wants to see that. I work hard, very hard, to keep it in check. Because, if I let it go...."

"Everything around you wilts?" I offered.

"Pretty much," she acknowledged. "I'm not perfect. Just way, way, way powerful!"

"How did you become so powerful?" I asked.

Natasha shook her head. "Nice try, but you'll have to figure that out for yourself."

"What does that mean?"

Natasha snapped her fingers. The world around us turned on again, totally unaware it had been held frozen by Natasha.

The morning bell rang.

Natasha looked at each of us. "Well, it was great meeting all of you." She pointed down the hall. "Now I think I'd better get to my first class."

She walked away with everybody's eyes locked on her.

"Wow, she has a great butt," Tanya said.

Yeah. kind of weird thing to say, but man, she was right on.

Dear Diary: Truthfully, I have NO idea what to make of this Natasha / Ultra. I just know she is way, way powerful and I do want her on my side. I guess I have to take her at her word that she is here to help me.

Not really sure why she thinks I need help. Sure, she happens to be way, way powerful, but I can hold my own with anybody or anything. Well, almost. I have to admit that I may very well be just a little jealous of Natasha / Ultra.

Breaking Lunch

At lunch, I sat at my regular table with Marie, Lori, Christa, Jason, and Tim. It was nice to have a normal table. A place where I could sit with my super-powered friends and my regular friends and just hang out and be me. The food tasted a bit like old socks but the company always lifted my spirits.

"What do you think of the new goddess?" Tim asked.

"Oh, you mean, Natasha?" Jason asked with a wide grin.

"I'd barely noticed her," he said.

Marie, Lori, Christa, and I all rolled our eyes. "Come on, dude," Lori said. "Nobody believes you. That girl makes supermodels look plain and ordinary."

"Her body...she's like a comic book superhero," Christa gushed.

"She even smells great!" Marie said.

Jan, the janitor walked over to our table. "In all my years of being at this school, I've never seen anybody like her. She even reached down and picked up a piece of paper on the floor! Then she put it in the recycle bin. I've never seen a student or teacher ever do that."

Knowing Jan was also a powerful wizard, I decided to see if she'd sensed anything different about Natasha. "You think she's just a nice normal girl?" I asked Jan.

Jan shook her head and laughed. "Heck no! Nothing normal about that girl! Truthfully, she makes the rest of you look like cavemen...."

"Isn't that a bit harsh?" I asked.

"Nope!" Jan said.

The kids at my table all nodded in agreement.

"She makes me feel like an ant," Christa said.

"She stupefies me," Marie said.

"I am in awe and I am never in awe," Lori said.

"I can't describe in public, how she makes me feel," Tim said.

I looked at Jason, waiting for him to wade into this conversation. He grinned. "Yeah, the term 'cavemen' sums it up nicely. She is just awesome…" He pointed around. "I'm pretty sure everybody in the school is talking about her!"

"Do you guys find that normal?" I asked.

"No, of course not!" they all answered.

"She's better than normal," Jan said.

The others all nodded in agreement.

Okay, it was pretty obvious that this Natasha / Ultra had everybody captivated. They couldn't see that there had to be something wrong with her. Nobody was that perfect. Plus, there was just something about her that didn't sit right with me. Was it because she was so much more powerful than I was? Was it because she made me feel less special, less super. I didn't think so. I wasn't that petty. Was I? No, that couldn't be it. Could it?

Of course, at that very moment, Natasha sauntered into the cafeteria with Wendi and Patti on her tail. The entire room went silent with reverence.

"OMG! She's coming over here!" Jan, the janitor said. She straightened her hair for what had to be the first time ever. "Do I look okay?"

Sure enough, Natasha did seem to have us in her sights; much to Wendi and Patti's displeasure.

"Nat, what are you doing? Our table is in the front of the room! That's where all the popular, good-looking kids sit!" Wendi said.

"Not all of them," Natasha said, continuing her stride towards us.

Jason, Tim, and Lori all sniffed themselves. Marie sat

up straight. I sighed. I don't know why I sighed, I just did.

Natasha waved to me, "Hi Lia! Do you guys have a seat for me?"

"SURE!" Jason and Tim both shouted.

"What?" Wendi said. "How can you sit with them? You're an upperclassman and they are well, lower…"

"Yeah, like way lower," Patti added. "I mean, we're above them and you are even way above us…"

"Well, not that far above us," Wendi pointed out.

"I don't think I'm above anybody," Natasha said. She sounded like she meant it, but I didn't believe it. She couldn't be that perfect and that nice.

A masked girl dressed in all black burst into the room. "I demand that Super Teen faces me!" the girl screamed.

I knew this girl from before. She called herself Glare

Girl and she lived in Moonvale. She wanted to be my arch-rival, but she had actually helped me out once or twice. I figured she was more talk than actually evil. But this was different.

Mr. Burns, the acting lunch monitor, stood up to Glare Girl. "Excuse me, Miss, you don't belong here!" he said.

Glare Girl just stared at him. Mr. Burns and the people behind him curled up into little balls on the floor. They all started sucking their thumbs. Glare Girl laughed. "I know Super Teen defends this town and this school. I demand she shows up!"

Two football players, Jake Johnson and Moose Manson, rushed at Glare Girl. She locked her eyes on them. The two crumbled to the floor whimpering. I think they may have wet themselves.

"Super Teen, if you don't show up I'm going to make everybody in here wet themselves!"

I couldn't let Glare Girl make the entire school wet themselves. Well, I might have enjoyed watching her do that to Wendi and Patti, but not to the rest of the school. I needed my friends to create some sort of distraction so I could sneak off, come back as Super Teen and stop Glare Girl. Of course, everybody in the room except for Natasha, me, Jan, Marie, Lori, and Jason fell asleep.

"What the heck?" Glare girl said, looking around.

Natasha walked up to her slowly. "Hi, there! I know you're just trying to make a name for yourself, GG. But if I were you, I'd turn around and get out of here, now!"

Glare Girl grinned. Leaning forward, she glared at Natasha. Natasha stopped and laughed. "Quit that, it tickles!"

Glare Girl pounded the floor with her foot. "I warn you, my glare can melt a tank! I've done it before!"

Natasha kept coming towards her. "Give me your best shot, honey!"

Glare Girl leaned towards Natasha and focused her glare on her. Natasha kept coming forward. Glare Girl stared harder. She leaned forward more, she spread out her arms and concentrated. Her cheeks turned bright red.

"I think she might pop a blood vessel," Jason said.

"Should we do something?" Marie asked.

"I'm pretty sure Natasha has this," Lori said.

"So clean and so powerful," Jan sighed. "My dream student."

"She is amazing!" Jason said.

Jason noticed the look I gave him. "But of course, you

are just as amazing!" he told me.

I shook my head. "Nah, she's got me beat."

I kind of had to admit that deep down I kind of wanted Glare Girl to have an effect on Natasha. Sure, Glare Girl could be a pain in the butt. Actually, she could cause the entire body to wither in pain. But man, oh man, I would love to see that Natasha had a weakness. Any weakness.

Natasha walked right up to Glare Girl. Natasha seemed amused at Glare Girl's efforts.

"Girl, you going to give it a break?" Natasha asked.

"Never!" Glare Girl shouted. "I'm actually happy I've run into you. You will allow me to test my new super nuclear glare! I don't like to use it because even I don't like to melt everything around me. It's so hard to keep friends that way, but you have forced me to use it!"

"Do your best," Natasha said softly. She even bent down so she would be eye level with Glare Girl.

Glare Girl leaned her head into Natasha's head. She clenched her fists. I'm pretty sure she even squeezed her butt. The room grew warmer.

"I can feel the heat," Lori said.

"Yeah, so hot!" Jason said. He glanced at me. "But once again..."

"Enough, Jason!" I said.

"I REFUSE TO LOSE!" Glare Girl roared.

Natasha shrugged her perfect shoulders. "Very few people lose by choice, and in this case, honey, you have no choice. I have more power in one cell of my body than you do in your entire body."

Glare girl started panting and sweating. Her face turned an even brighter red.

Natasha sighed. "You aren't going to learn the easy way. Are you?"

"I don't want to learn! I want to win!" Glare Girl screamed, smashing her foot down on Natasha's foot.

Natasha didn't flinch. Well, she did laugh. "Like that

would really hurt me." Natasha took her little finger and tapped Glare Girl on her forehead. Glare Girl dropped to Natasha's feet. She was out cold. It looked like she would stay that way for a week.

Those of us who were not sleeping got up and headed over to Natasha. I couldn't help but be impressed. I didn't want to be, but I was.

Natasha looked down at Glare Girl. "She's from Moonvale, right?"

"Yeppers," Marie said.

Natasha bent down, whisked Glare Girl off the ground and was gone. She returned a second later.

"What the heck did you do?" I asked.

"I just dropped her off at Future Now labs. I figured they would know what to do with her," Natasha said. "After all, she's from their city, so she's their problem. Your friends, Adam, Ellie Mae and Zeke all say hi."

"Zeke must have hit on you," Lori said.

"Actually, all he did was stand there with his mouth open, drooling. Well, as much as a dried zombie can drool. Adam seems nice though."

"He is!" I said more sternly than I would have liked.

Natasha put her hand on my shoulder, "Don't worry, he's not my type. He's way too young," she reassured me.

Though I didn't like the idea that she thought if she wanted to, she could have Adam. But who was I kidding? Natasha could have any guy she wanted.

Dear Diary: Wow…not sure what to think. Natasha seems better than me in every way possible. I mean, come on, Glare Girl has hurt me before but she didn't bother Natasha in the slightest. To Natasha, Glare Girl is no more than a simple human. Heck, I think she looks at me like that. Janitor Jan said we are all cavemen compared to Natasha. I do believe she is right!

After School Special

After school, Jason and I started walking home. He was, of course, in awe of Natasha. I didn't feel the same way. I don't know why, but I just didn't trust that girl.

"Where did she come from? Why is she here? Could she really be that perfect?" I moaned, accidentally out loud.

"I take it you're talking about...." Jason paused. He smiled. "Natasha...." he sighed.

"Yes, the one and only. I hope!" It was my turn to sigh. "Please don't let there be more of her. There is only so much I can take..."

"She did save you. Twice now," Jason noted.

"Once," I insisted. "I may have been in trouble with those rhino dudes but I can take down Glare Girl. I've done it before."

"True," Jason said slowly, carefully choosing his words. "But she saved you the trouble. I hate to say this but she did it easier than you. Glare Girl was like Glare ant to her."

"Not helping, Jason!" I said, slamming my foot on the ground.

The force from the slam sent Jason flying backward. I caught him before he fell. "Oops, sorry!" I said.

"I can tell this is a touchy subject for you," Jason said. "Smart boy!"

"I do get all As," Jason said proudly.

"Yeah, and top marks for having common sense," I said, giving him a little jab. My jab sent him flying backward again. "Oops sorry, don't know my own strength..."

Jason rubbed his arm. "I'm starting to think you might have issues…"

I couldn't disagree with him. This Ultra / Natasha, for some reason really rubbed me the wrong way. She couldn't be as perfect as she appeared. Right?

"Why don't you talk to Natasha?" Jason suggested.

"Say what? Come again?" I gagged a little. "I think I threw up a little in my mouth…"

"I think Jason is right," I heard from behind.

Turning, I saw Adam coming up behind us.

"Adam, what brings you here?" I asked.

"MAC and MACC told me I might be needed here," he said slowly.

"Well, that was nice of them. But I am fine, really." I thought about what I had just said. Yeah, that wasn't cool. After all, I liked Adam. "But I do appreciate you coming to help me out," I added.

Adam shook his head. "Well, ah…."

Adam's BFF, Zeke the zombie came flying down with his jetpack. He crashed face first into the ground. He gave us a thumbs up. "I'm okay!" he said, spitting out a clump of dirt. "Being mostly dead an' all." He stood up and swallowed some dirt. He pointed to Adam. "Actually, we're here to back Jason up." He pointed to Jason, just in case I didn't know who Jason was.

My mouth dropped open. "Say what, again?"

"I SAID, WE ARE HERE TO BACK UP JASON, CAUSE YOU A BIT CRAY CRAY!" Zeke raised his arms in the air for effect and shouted loudly.

"More like obsessed," Jason said.

"Wait, none of you guys are worried about this super-duper older teen showing up and showing us up?"

The three of them shook their heads.

"Nope," Adam said.

"I think she's a force for good," Jason said.

"Plus, she's hot!"

"What he said," Jason said, pointing at Zeke.

"Word," Zeke said.

"I think I might barf!" I said.

"Cool!" Zeke said.

"Why do you guys think this way?" I asked. (Well, I

actually kind of demanded).

"She hasn't given us any reason not to trust her," Jason said.

"Ditto!" Adam said.

"What they said," Zeke said.

Before I could offer up anything else, Jason added, "Aren't you the one who's always saying to trust people? The one looking for the good in others?"

I nodded slowly. "Yeah, but this is different!" I insisted.

"Ah, why?" Jason said.

"Yeah, why?" Adam said.

"What they said," Zeke said. He smiled. "I love it when we all agree to agree." Zeke bravely took some steps towards me. He patted me on the shoulder. "Look, Lia, I get it. I know what it's like being second best to a superhero. But you get used to it and you learn to love it. There is a lot less pressure on us super friends. We watch, have fun and chip in when needed." He nudged me. "Of course, Ultra is so powerful, you might not ever be needed. Which is great. You can just…"

Adam shot forward at super Q-speed and threw a hand over Zeke's mouth. "I think you've said enough, buddy!"

"I think you've said too much," Jason told Zeke.

I lowered my head. "No, actually Zeke said the right thing."

"Of course I did," Zeke said. He hiccupped. "Wait, what? I said the right thing! I don't think anybody has ever said that to me. I'm amazed. I guess two hundred years of living, or near living, makes a guy learn a thing or two…"

"Zeke is right. Ultra makes me feel useless," I moaned.

"It's a nice feeling. Isn't it?" Zeke said with a dumb grin.

"No, no, it is not," I told him. "I don't think I have all

this great power just to sit on the bench and watch Ultra fix everything that's wrong."

"Stand then!" Zeke offered.

"Buddy, maybe you shouldn't talk for a little while," Adam suggested.

"I can use sign language if you want. Or text? I can even group chat you all!" Zeke pulled out his cell phone.

Adam took the phone away from him. "No, that's not what I was getting at."

"Then signing, it is!" Zeke said proudly. "I learned how to use sign language last week, while you were wasting time sleeping."

"Zeke, I think you may very well be driving Lia crazy!" Adam shouted.

Zeke stopped signing. I believe he signed, 'I am sorry'.

"That's okay, Zeke," I told him. "I know you were only trying to help in your own very weird and very strange way."

"Thanks," Zeke with a grin. He nudged Adam. "I like her, she's pretty and nice." Zeke looked at Adam and Jason. His jaw dropped open. Zeke forced his jaw to close. "Wait! I bet you BOTH must like her!" He scratched his head. "Oh man, this is so *awk*ward!" Zeke pointed at Adam, "I mean, you are a handsome dude and you've got keen superpowers like Lia!" Zeke pointed at Jason. "But you're good looking in a friendly geek sort of way, plus you've got a monster smart brain and cool armor. And you know Lia better than anybody!" Zeke turned to me. "This must be tough on you."

Adam and Jason both turned red. I kind of liked it. Of course, I felt my face blush too.

"Well, I ah…"

"I have a message coming in from Tanya," MAC and MACC both said. Then they both said, "JINX!"

"Play the message," I said, heaving a sigh of relief.

"Guys! We need all hands on deck at BMS lab! Kayla

is having one of her fits. Things are going to get ugly! I'm not sure how long I can...."

"What happened?" I asked.

"Transmission was cut!" MAC said.

"MAC, activate my costume!" I said.

"Done!"

Jason hit one button on his belt. His armor appeared around him.

Adam spun and turned into Quazar.

"Bummer," Zeke said, his head lowered. "I'm still just me."

We all took off towards BMS labs.

Flying through the air, I felt relief that I didn't have to confront my feelings about Jason and Adam. I liked them both a lot. I wasn't sure I could pick one or the other. I didn't want to pick one over the other. They were both special to me in different ways. I also felt good that I didn't have to worry about Natasha dropping in and saving the day. BMS labs was a super secure place. There was no way she could suspect something bad was going on down there.

"If Kayla is going berserk with her powers, this could be trouble!" Jason said.

"Nothing we can't handle!" I boasted.

"She did turn me into a door once...." Jason said. "And a baby and..."

"Is she that powerful?" Adam asked.

"She is, but she's vulnerable. We should be able to take her out, fast!" I said in my most superhero like voice.

Reaching BMS labs, we saw Kayla simply sitting down outside in the quad. There were no people around her.

"She's alone in the quad!" Jason said. "That's odd...."

Using super-vision, I noticed she wasn't really alone. She was surrounded by a bunch of people and machines, only they had all been reduced to the size of ants or less. Yep! Tanya, Marie, Lori, Dad, Hana and a bunch of security people were all there. They were just very, very tiny.

"Actually, be careful where you land!" I shouted. "The ground is littered with tiny, tiny people."

"Are they normally that size?" Zeke asked.

"No, Kayla shrank them!" Jason said.

"Right, I knew that," Zeke said. "Just checking… to make sure…"

"We won't have to land!" Adam said boldly. He extended his arm. "I can take her out from up here with a stun beam!" A ray of energy beamed from Adam's hand down towards Kayla.

Kayla sat there smiling. "You all look like pretty little toys. Don't make me squish you."

Adam's beam hit Kayla. She raised her hand defensively. The beam bounced back and blasted Adam from the sky. Adam started to drop. I flew down and caught him before he could hit the ground and squish anybody. He was stunned and dazed….

"Oh, my head so hurts… she took my beam and magnified its power…" he sighed.

"Like I said, she's got power," I told Adam.

Jason pointed his fist at Kayla and fired two mini-missiles at her. The missiles hit and splatted Kayla with blue goo.

"That should stop her!" Jason said proudly.

The blue goo bounced off Kayla who was shooting through the sky at Jason. Jason tried to dodge the blue muck but it corrected its course and engulfed him. Jason started to plummet to the ground. I set Adam down in a safe spot. I shot back up into the air and caught Jason right before he splattered on the ground. I blew the goo off him. He was out cold, but he'd be alright.

Zeke hovered down next to me. "Ah, Lia, I'm not sure what I can do here."

"Yeah, she is pretty powerful…"

"But I am good for one thing!" Zeke said. He glared at Kayla and yelled, "I'm a great distraction!"

I understood what he was trying to do…take Kayla's mind off me so I could pound her. Problem was, Kayla could control time. She froze Zeke in mid-air without even really thinking about him.

Kayla stood up. "Have you come to play with me, Lia?"

"Ah, maybe," I said. "Would that make you happy?"

Kayla pointed to her ears. "I removed the dampers they used to control my powers! I now have full use of my power!" She rippled with white and black energy. Kayla smiled. "You sure you want to play?"

"Let's talk," I said.

Next thing I knew, I was standing next to Kayla. "I ported you closer," she said, "I don't like shouting."

"Me neither," I said for lack of anything better to say. "How can we end this peacefully?" I asked. "Kayla, I'm your friend. I don't want to fight you."

She snickered. "That's cause you know I can hurt you. Badly!" She raised a fist. "I can hurt anybody! I can hurt everybody!" she shouted.

"You don't want to do that," I said calmly.

"But they don't want me to use my powers. They say I am dangerous," Kayla said.

"Well, you can be," I said slowly.

"Yeah well, I never knocked out a mall with my foot odor!" Kayla said.

"Good point," I said. I took a breath to compose myself. "But I've never shrunk all the people trying to help me!" I noted.

Kayla stood up. "I'm being super careful not to step on them. Unless they make me mad! Then I will make 'em into toe jam!"

Pointing at Kayla, I told her, "Look K, I don't want to hurt you!"

Kayla snickered. "Ha! Doesn't matter if you want to or not. You can't touch me."

I zoomed at Kayla. Kayla darted to the side. I crashed face first into the ground, leaving a big dent in the dirt. Kayla zapped over and kicked me in the butt. It didn't hurt anything but my pride.

I shot up and spun towards her. "K A Y L A   L E T S   N O T   D O   T H I S...." I said, in very slow motion, grabbing for her.

Kayla easily dodged my hand. She pointed at me.

I went flying at least a hundred yards backward. I crashed butt-first into the ground, leaving a huge hole.

Kayla instantly moved next to me. "Silly Lia, you can't touch me." She pointed at me. I lifted off the ground. "I have complete control of time and space. I cannot lose. I move as fast as light!"

I blasted Kayla's feet with my heat vision. Scoring a hit, she jumped back and rubbed her foot.

"My heat-vision is also as fast as light," I told her.

"How dare you!" Kayla shouted.

"Look, Kayla, I just gave you a hot foot. If I wanted to hurt you, I would have gone for your face!" I pointed out.

Kayla touched her cheeks with both hands. "Not my beautiful face. I love my face! It's one of my fave things about me."

"That's why I didn't aim at your face. I just wanted to get your attention. Not hurt you."

Kayla lowered her slightly burnt foot. "Okay, you got it."

"Good, K, let's talk."

"Okay."

"What are you so upset about?"

"I thought I was clear. They want to inhibit my powers. I don't want them to inhibit my powers. I love my powers. I made them all little, very little." She snickered. "They want me to feel little so…"

"They don't want you to feel little," I insisted.

"They why won't they let me be me?" Kayla asked.

"Because you are kind of young…" I said.

"I'm the same age as Tanya and nobody makes her control her powers!" Kayla said slamming her foot down. The force somehow made the ground around me tremor.

"That is true, but Tanya has been older for longer. She's actually lived and experienced those years. You were kind of grown really fast to help your body cope with your power."

Kayla took a step back, she seemed to be considering my words. She put a finger to her lips. "So you claim to be trying to help me?"

"Yes," I said as sincerely as I could.

Kayla pointed to the burn mark on her foot. "By burning my foot?!"

"Just a little attention getter," I told her.

Kayla waved her hand over the wound. The wound healed. "Then we are friends?" she said.

I nodded. "Yes, yes we are."

Kayla waved an arm at me, sending me flying backward again. This time, I went crashing into the midsection of one of the buildings. I left a dent in the building then crashed to the ground; once again, falling face first. I could feel that Kayla had somehow accelerated my fall, forcing me to hit the ground even harder. Pushing myself up from the ground, I spat out some dirt.

"You know, I'm kind of hard to hurt," I told Kayla.

Kayla appeared behind me. I turned to her. She punched me in the jaw. She pulled back her hand in pain. "Ouch," she screamed.

"That's on you, girl," I told her. "I just warned you that I am hard to hurt!"

Kayla blew on her fist. "I know. I admit that one is on me. But sometimes it just feels good to hit something."

Pointing to her hand I said, "I'm guessing this wasn't one of those times."

Kayla grinned. "You are smart. Now I see why Tanya respects you."

Okay, I felt like I was making some progress with Kayla. We were kind of at a standoff here. I hoped now we could talk this out and defuse the situation. I really didn't want to hurt her and hopefully, deep down, she didn't want to harm me. It felt weird though, arguing with a girl who was physically sixteen but who had only been alive for ten years. I had to think before I spoke so as to not set her off.

Crossing my arms, I offered, "Kayla, why not turn everybody back to normal so we can talk about this like adults?"

Kayla considered my words. "Are you scared of me?" she asked.

Now I had to consider my words even more carefully. I really couldn't be sure what she was after and what the best answer would be. "I'm not scared of you. I'm scared of your power."

Kayla crossed her arms, I guess to mimic me. "Hmm. Good answer. But my powers and I are sort of the same things. Right?"

"The use of your powers and you are the same things," I told her. "We all just want to help you control your power!"

She pointed at me. "Do you control your power?"

"I try. I haven't foot-odored a mall in a long time," I said with a smile.

Kayla smiled. "Yeppers, I guess that is a good thing." Her grin grew. "Maybe I will turn everybody back to normal size," she said.

"This is not a maybe situation!" we heard from above. There, hovering above us, stood Ultra.

Ultra pointed at Kayla. "Turn them back. Now!" she ordered.

Kayla turned to see Ultra, "Oh, I love your outfit, but you still can't tell me what to do!"

"Yes, yes I can!" Ultra said. Using a very forceful voice, she ordered, "Turn everybody back. Now!"

Kayla snapped her fingers. Everybody turned back to their original sizes.

"Very good," Ultra told her.

In less than a flash, Ultra stood behind Kayla. She touched Kayla on the back of the head. Kayla dropped to the ground, out cold.

"Okay, you can put the power dampener back in her safely," Ultra told Dad's team. "She won't be a threat any longer."

A team of robots, scientists and security people rushed over to Kayla. They injected something into her ear. They put her on a stretcher and started carrying her away.

"I had this under control," I told Ultra.

Ultra nodded. "You were slowly getting there. I just sped up the process some. With a person like Kayla, you have to let her know who's the boss. And the boss isn't her."

"But I had her talked down!" I insisted.

Ultra gave me a pat on the shoulder, "But I put her down." She smiled. "You made for a great distraction!"

276

I slammed my foot on the ground, causing a bit of a quake. "I am not a distraction!" I shouted.

Zeke pointed to himself and grinned. "Yep, that's my role!" He clasped his hands together and pleaded, "Please don't take my role. That's all I am good for." He paused. "And farting… but hardly anybody appreciates a good fart these days."

"I'm not going to take your role, Zeke!" I told him.

"Phew." Zeke sighed.

"Actually, you are all just minor distractions!" a voice said from above. The voice sounded kind of familiar. I just couldn't quite narrow it down.

"Oh no," Ultra said. I heard her voice quiver. "She found me…"

"Wait, who found you?" I asked.

"Doctor Gem Stone!" she shouted.

Now that's why the voice from above sounded so familiar. I had battled Doctor Stone before. She used to be Doctor Dangerfield's aide until she overloaded herself with bionic implants and made herself super-sized and super crazy.

"MAC, is Gem Stone still in prison?" I asked.

"Affirmative," MAC said.

"That's YOUR Doctor Gem Stone," Ultra explained. "Mine broke out of prison three years ago and has been hoarding technology ever since. She wants to drain me of my powers. That's why I came here to this time and this dimension…" Ultra said, looking up towards where the voice came from. "I thought I'd be safe until I figured out a way to stop Gem Stone. I didn't count on her being able to follow me here! I guess the rhinos should have tipped me off."

Gem Stone laughed. She appeared in front of us, she had to be well over a hundred feet tall. Covered in robotic style blue body armor, she made quite an imposing sight.

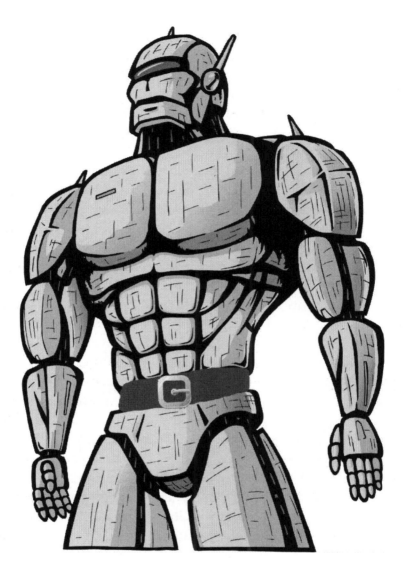

"Ultra!" Gem Stone's voice boomed, "I came here the same way you did! You may not realize it, but slimes are interfering with this dimension and their interference has made travel between our time zones much easier. Especially for somebody with a giant brain like myself."

Ultra pointed up at Gem. "Ha! Silly scientist. You fell into my trap. Now I've gotten you away from my world!"

Ultra flew up towards Gem at super speed. So fast, my eyes could barely track her. Gem reached out and caught Ultra in her huge right hand. Gem squeezed tightly, engulfing Ultra.

"Let her go!" I ordered, blasting Gem with a heat ray.

Gem laughed as she continued to squeeze.

Adam took to the air and sped at Gem, fist out ready to ram her. Gem swatted him down like he was nothing.

Jason fired a few missiles at Gem. They bounced off her harmlessly.

Lori grabbed Marie and tossed her at Gem. "Turn her into a giant pickle!" Lori yelled.

Marie flew through the air and extended her finger. Her finger touched Gem. Gem's armor glowed.

"Ha! I already have your powers from my time, so I don't need your powers. But I have learned to block them!" she taunted. "You are no threat to me."

"Oops," Marie said. She pulled her finger away.

Adam popped up from the ground. He shook off some stars. "You asked for it!" he shouted. He aimed both of his arms at Gem Stone. His arms turned to flames. Gem blew on Adam. He froze solid in a block of ice.

Gem casually dropped Ultra to the ground. I raced forward and caught her.

Gem looked around at the rest of us. "I see no need to waste any more energy on the likes of you. I got what I wanted and more. I will have demands for your planet and your time zone to surrender to me, tomorrow. I want to think about this first."

"What if we don't listen to your demands?" Dad shouted at Gem.

Gem blew on him. Dad and everybody around him fell to the ground. "If people don't listen to me then I will be forced to get really mad. Trust me, you don't want to see me when I get mad!"

Gem rose up higher. She flew off at supersonic speed. Jason ran over to me. "Oh, this is bad...."

Ultra shook her head. Her eyes popped open. "You have no idea... By coming here to hide, I just doomed your world and maybe mine..."

"Who the heck are you?" I asked Ultra, though I thought and feared I had a pretty good idea.

"I'm you from a parallel future..." she sighed.

Yep, that's what I was afraid she was going to say. "Speak!" I ordered the now powerless Ultra.

Ultra lowered her head. "I'm from four or five years in the future."

"I didn't think people could travel back in time," Jason said.

"They can't. Not in their own dimension, but I'm from an offshoot dimension. One that is very close to this one. My plan was to hide here until I could figure out a way around Gem and that stupid absorbing armor she developed. It makes it almost impossible to hurt her, plus she can drain our powers if she touches us."

"In other words, you are telling me that you're powerless now?" I asked Ultra.

Ultra lowered her head. "Yes..."

That should have made me feel sad. Instead, I actually felt kind of good. Yeah, I know. I have issues.

"What are we going to do now?" Jason asked.

"What Gem Stone doesn't suspect. We're going to find her and bring the attack to her," I said.

"That's just crazy!" Ultra said. "One, we don't know where she is. Two, even if we did, she'll own you all. She has her powers, my powers and Marie's powers. Plus, in my time and in my world, she's already absorbed Kayla's powers!"

"Exactly why she won't think that we will all come after her!" I said.

Dear Diary: Sure, going after the most powerful evil foe I have ever met may not be a brilliant plan, but it is a plan. My logic being…if we find Gem Stone, she will be totally off guard. Heck, she thinks she can take us out easily. Heck, she probably can, that's why we need to surprise her. How? I haven't figured that out yet. I know my team and I will work it out!

To me, the strangest part of this entire strange weird and wacky thing is, the girl I have been so jealous of, is ME. Okay, not exactly me but an older version of me from a different dimension. Yes, Ultra and I are going to have a little talk. On one hand, it feels good knowing that I can grow into that kind of power. On the other hand, it feels bad that the future me is so overconfident. I guess when you have that kind of power, it's easy to let it go to your head. But why the heck did she think it was a good idea to come here? That wasn't a great choice on her part.

Hopefully, I can learn from her experience. I have to admit that I feel good knowing she is depowered. Which is strange since I pretty much find myself rooting against my future self. Okay, nobody ever said being a superhero would be easy.

Yes, I have issues.

Thinking Time

We gathered in Hana's office trying to form a plan of action to take down this new version of Doctor Gem Stone. We had my complete team together…Jason, Tanya, Marie, Lori, and Mom. Adam was there with his dad and his sister, Opal. Jess also came, in case we needed a magic boost. Dad was surrounded by all his best people and a heavily armed security team. Of course, Hana was there and took the lead. Oh, Natasha / Ultra was there as well. But she seemed quite down.

"Okay, team, we have a problem here," Hana announced.

"Dah," Jess said.

Ignoring Jess, Hana went on. "Doctor Gem Stone, who is from this future other Earth seems to be mostly powered by that armor she wears. It works with the nano-chips embedded in her body to give her incredible powers. Not only that, she also seems to be able to draw and store power from others into her armor."

"But the armor must have some sort of battery or power storing device," Adam's dad said.

"That's right," Jason said. "No normal human, even with nano-bots, should be able to store that kind of power in their body."

Ultra spoke up. "True. In the future, that belt buckle she wears acts as a power storing device and a conduit to her powers. If we destroy the buckle, the powers she has absorbed will dissipate or return to their rightful owners; if the owners are nearby."

"Great," I said. "Then you just need to be near Doctor Gem when I destroy the buckle."

Ultra laughed. "You don't think I've tried that. With the powers she's already stolen from both the bad and the good powered people in the future, she's impossibly fast and powerful. That's why I escaped to this world. I knew if she gained my powers as well, all would be lost." Ultra shook her head. "As soon as I saw those super rhino men, I should have known Gem was here... I guess I did really. But I thought that maybe this time, I could take her." She looked at me. "I had hoped she would be preoccupied with you. That way, I could get the jump on her..." She lowered her head. "Man, was I wrong!"

I thought about Doctor Gem's interaction with Marie. Marie's power had no effect on her but she also didn't drain Marie's power. She claimed she didn't need it and that Marie would be no threat. But it didn't make sense for a greedy person like Doctor Gem not to want all the power she could get, or at the very least to eliminate the powers from others. Then it hit me.

"Doctor Gem can't drain the same power twice! Right!" I said, pointing at Natasha.

"Say what?" Natasha said.

"That's really why you came here. You were hoping Doctor G. would grab my power. Then yours would be safe."

"Oh wow, Lia is like a young female Sherlock Holmes!" Zeke shouted. "I knew Sherlock was kind of a nut job but way smart." He looked at me. "You are way smart without the nut job part, and you smell better."

Ultra lowered her head a little more and sighed. "It was a gambit on my part, I must admit. I assumed you would be easier to drain than me. She would drain you. I would be safe. It made sense we didn't want her to have my greater powers. With my greater powers working alongside your team, we could stop her. Then I would get your powers back for you, somehow."

"Then why did you attack Doctor Gem?" Dad asked.

"I got carried away. I wanted to try one more time to take her down. I couldn't allow my younger self to have to deal with that monster," Ultra said.

"Look," Dad said to Ultra in his most serious 'Dad' voice. "I know you technically aren't my daughter since I didn't raise you."

"Ah, you didn't raise me either," I pointed out.

Dad took a step back. He composed his thoughts and then said, "Look, I know you are not technically my daughter in this world, since I have had no hand at all in raising or training you, but I still find your decision to be very disappointing."

Ultra nodded. "Yeah, I agree. I thought I could handle this alone. I got carried away with my own ego…"

Zeke walked up to Ultra. "You're way pretty," he told her.

"Ah, thanks, Zeke," she said.

"But I gotta ask, why did you choose the name, Natasha? It doesn't sound anything like Lia. Don't you get confused when somebody says…hey Lia?"

Ultra shrugged. "In my world, my name is Lia Natasha Strong. I dropped the Lia and added a Russian accent for fun," she said. "Besides Natasha sounds cool."

Zeke thought for a moment. He repeated her name…Natasha, Natasha, Natasha. He grinned. "Yep, it does. Touchee."

"What about me?" Adam asked. "Does she have my powers in your time?"

Ultra turned away. "You did come to my aide once," she told Adam.

"And?"

"She used Marie's power to turn you into a cheese statue," Ultra said. "She keeps you in a refrigerated room in her lab. Calls you her cheese trophy."

"Okay, now that is weird…" Adam said.

"But sounds tasty!" Zeke added. "Am I a cheese dip next to my BFF?"

Ultra laughed, "No, she considers you insignificant and not worth wasting any power on."

Zeke nodded. "Yep, that makes total sense to me."

Jason walked up to Ultra. "I gotta ask, what about me in your future world? Are we still friends?"

"Of course," Ultra said with a smile. "You do everything you can to stop Gem, but as smart as you are, she's just a little smarter."

"Why didn't I cut her down to size with magic?" Jess asked.

Ultra smiled. It was a smile of irony. "Oh, you tried

and tried, but Gem created an energy barrier around herself that worked as an anti-magic shell. Your magic bounced off her and turned all the people of Starlight City into toads..."

"Oh," Jess gulped.

Zeke patted her on the back. "Wow, epic magic fail!" he said.

I stepped forward. "Surely, we can find Doctor Gem. After all, she is huge and radiates power."

"Maybe she's hiding," Lori offered.

"Nah, she is way too egotistical to hide," Ultra said. "She may be resting somewhere, but at full size..."

"Let's look for her with our satellites!" I said.

"Well, BMS has only two satellites in orbit," Dad said.

"And Future Now has two," Adam's dad offered.

"That won't be enough to see the entire world. At least, not at once," Jason said.

"Then we get inventive and we borrow imaging from other satellites," I said. "We tap into them. We just find an area of interest. Find a satellite over that area and borrow it for a moment or two..."

Jason smiled. "I can do that."

Hana hit a button on her desk. The ceiling above us became a holographic map of the Earth. Dots appeared all around the map. "Those dots represent satellites," Hana said. "The two red dots are ours. The two blue dots belong to Future Now. Those hundreds of other dots belong to others. We can tap into them as Lia says, but we still don't know where to look."

"Just look everywhere at once," I told Hana.

"Do you really think I can do that? Tap into every single satellite on Earth?" Hana asked.

"No, of course she can't do that," Dad answered. "She wasn't designed for that."

I looked Hana in the eyes. "Is that true?"

She nodded. "Yes, it is true that I wasn't designed to function in that manner, but that doesn't mean I can't..."

Hana's eyes started to blink red. "Scanning for Doctor Gem now."

"Look, we know she's been around rhinos. Plus, Africa has a lot of open space. So, start your search there," I coaxed.

"Rhinos can also be found in parts of India, Nepal, Indonesia, and Malaysia," MAC and MACC said.

"I know that!" Jason said geeking out. "Let's look at the rhino men that Ultra and Lia fought."

An image of one of the rhino men appeared in the middle of the room. "That's a greater one-horned rhino. They are found in India and Nepal!" Jason said, almost jumping out of his shoes.

"Correct," MAC and MACC said. "They are found in the rainforests there…"

"I'm scanning the satellites that are looking at those areas of the world now," Hana said.

"Rainforests have a lot of tree cover," Dad said. "You won't be able to spot much besides…well, trees…"

"Actually, honey buns, I am installing software now so I can pick up heat signatures from the images. A being as large as Doctor Gem Stone will leave a large heat signature."

"Hana, please don't call me honey buns at work," Dad said, blushing.

"Or ever in front of me," I added.

"I will do my best," Hana grinned.

Hana's eyes started flashing bright red. The flashing grew faster. Her eyes popped open. "Got her!" Hanna said. "She appears to be laying down in the middle of the rainforest in southern Nepal. It's a very quiet and lush area."

I smiled. "Not for long, it isn't." Looking at Ellie Mae Opal, I asked. "Can you port me there?"

"I can," she answered. "But shouldn't we have a plan first?"

I smiled at her. "Oh, I so do, and it involves Doctor Gem Stone being totally over-confident!"

Dear Diary: Okay, now I finally have some insight…not only to who Natasha is – but also to me from the future, as well as finding out what makes Natasha tick. She ran away from Gem Stone. She claims it was to get the upper hand on Gem Stone, but I know she was scared. Scared to lose her power. Scared to just plain lose. The future me has become so powerful, I don't believe she can remember what losing is like. She doesn't know how to deal with possibly not being the strongest one around. Luckily, I am used to losing. I am not super over-confident. I think I can use that to my advantage.

Plus, Gem Stone has always been confident and now she's extra confident. She's just absorbed a lot of power. I'm sure she thinks that nothing in the world can stop her. She may be right. But I am going to do my best to bring her down.

Plan of Attack

I talked a bit more to Ultra about her powers. Because Gem Stone now possessed those same powers, it would give me a better idea of what we would be up against. It appeared that I will develop mind-reading capabilities in the near future, which is cool for me. But that was also bad news because it meant that Gem could now read my mind. I would have to be very careful about what I thought while going up against her.

When I'd learned what I could from Ultra, I sat in a conference room with my team...Marie, Lori, Jason, Tanya, Ellie Mae, Jess, Adam, and Zeke.

"I'm going to start the attack alone," I said. "I think that way, it will be easier to sneak up on Doctor Gem. Plus, that way, nobody else gets hurt."

Tanya tapped her fingers on the table. "From what future you has told me..."

"Please don't call her that," I said.

"Okay, from what Ultra tells me, Gem has absorbed my power in the future. She can't absorb any more of my power in this time zone, and my power is currently useless against her. So you won't get an argument from me," Tanya said.

"Ditto," Marie said.

"Yeah, I'm holding you guys back. I'm holding back everybody with powers. I've talked to Ellie Mae; she knows what to do when round two comes."

"What about me?" Adam asked.

I shook my head. "No, I can't have you turned into a cheese statue... I'm not taking that chance..."

"So that's your plan? Fly at her alone?" Zeke said. "Ya

know, I'm not the brightest guy…" Everybody in the room agreed. "But even I know that is CRAZY!"

"No, not really, I'm going to have MAC create a stealth shield around me. I will be virtually invisible. My goal is to get that belt off her before she knows I am there. Then I will fly with it back to the base and smash it. Ultra will get her powers back. Doctor Gem will lose most of her powers. Then we will all take her down."

My plan was greeted with silence.

"I take it that you all approve," I said.

"Is there anything we can say to stop you from doing this?" Jason asked.

I shook my head. "Nope."

"Then I guess, we have no choice. We all approve," Jason said.

"Good," I said.

I took to the air and headed towards Nepal.

MAC put a little holographic GPS in front of my face so I wouldn't get lost. I flew in silence until MAC spoke up.

"From what I understand, Gem Stone's super eyesight is so good, she can see you coming from ten miles away."

"Well then, please cloak me when we are within one hundred miles," I ordered.

"I see you are not taking any chances," MAC said.

"Can you blame me?" I asked.

"No, not at all," MAC said. "You may be going up against the most dangerous being you have ever faced. And you are going to approach her alone."

"Yep, can't risk my team," I sighed. "At least not yet. If she takes me down then it's up to them."

Something occurred to me. This Gem Stone wasn't supposed to be in this timeline. There was another Gem Stone, our Gem Stone in this timeline. I thought about how the other me drove me crazy. I had to wonder if another Gem Stone would drive her crazy.

"MAC, is Gem Stone still in the Capital City Max Security Prison?" I asked.

"Yes, nothing has changed since the last time I reported to you."

"Great, contact the warden there and tell him I want to pick her up!" I said reversing course.

"Ah, why?" MAC asked.

"Who better to distract Gem Stone than herself!"

Dear Diary: Okay, my plan might be crazy. First off, I am taking a known crazy lady out of jail to fight another version of herself. Okay, maybe not to fight her, but hopefully, she will drive that other version crazy; just like the other version of me makes me crazy. Yes, it is a risk. They could team up against me. But if I know Gem Stone like I think I know her, then she isn't a team player. Okay, it is a risk. But it is a risk I am willing to take!

A Short Detour

I had the warden and his men from Capital City Max Security Prison take me to Doctor Gem Stone's cell so I could meet with her.

I heard Doctor Gem snicker the second I set foot in front of her. "What do you want, Super Brat," she spat.

"I want to give you a chance to save our world and our time zone from the biggest threat we've ever faced!" I said, mustering all the drama I could.

"Okay, girl, I'm intrigued." She clutched hold of the metal bars. "Who is this threat?"

"You!" I said.

"Wait, what?"

"You…from a future time zone. You have perfected a suit of robotic armor that magnifies your powers and lets you absorb other people's powers. The future me from that same time zone is named Ultra. She came back to our current time to avoid the super-powered you. But you came here and found her. Then you drained Ultra of her power. So now the future you has super-powers," I said. "Do you follow?"

Doctor Gem rubbed her hands together. "Oh, I like this." She paused. "So, what's in it for me?"

"A chance to redeem yourself. If you distract the other you long enough for me to get the drop on her, I will ask the courts to greatly reduce your prison sentence.

Doctor Gem smiled. "You have a deal. When do we start?"

"Now!" I said.

Dear Diary: Yeah, I know I can't trust Doctor Gem. She took my offer way too easily. She has plans. I know she's only helping me in the hope of getting her hands on that armor. But that's okay. I want her to be a distraction, and I now know she will be a great one!

The Pre-fight

As I flew through the sky, carrying our Doctor Gem Stone, she talked to me.

"You know, kid, I can help you in the fight against me," she said.

"Oh?" I said, acting surprised, even though I had pretty much expected this.

"Look...who knows me better than me?" she asked.

"I will be battling a different you from the future!" I noted.

"Still honey, it seems that she and I are the same basic person. I've been her. She's been me. I know her. Surely, you understand that, or you would not have brought me into this fight."

"I do..." I said slowly.

"For example, I know she's in Nepal because I love Nepal. I spent some time in the fields there when I was in college," Doctor Gem said.

"Good to know."

"Therefore, I can help you take her out!" the trying to be a good doctor said.

"That's what I am counting on," I countered with.

"But here's the thing, honey. I can help you more if you activate my powers," Doctor Gem said slowly.

I knew she was going to ask that. I had kind of been counting on that. I had my answer ready. Faking surprise, I said, "But I don't have the authority to reactivate your nano-improvement chips." I paused. "Truthfully, I don't know why they let you keep those in you."

"The chips and I have fused. To remove them would cause me great pain. Maybe even death," she answered.

"Oh…" I said.

"Would you want me to suffer?" she asked.

"No, I guess not," I said.

"There you are; it only makes sense for you to activate my chips!"

"Like I said, Doc, I don't have the authority…"

"Maybe not, but you have the power!" she insisted like I kind of figured she would.

"How so?" I asked.

"You simply send an electrical charge through me. It disables the device that disables my chips. You then have a super-powered me. After that, it's me and you versus that monster from another time."

"That monster is you!" I noted.

"I stand by my words…you saw what I was like with some power. I can't begin to imagine what I'd be like with extreme power."

"Really?" I asked.

"Okay, I'm being dramatic. I know what I'd be like. I'd be a monster bent on ruling the world."

"Yep, that pretty much sums up future you," I told her.

"Then let me help you stop me."

I had been figuring that our Doctor Gem would ask me this. I'm not sure why, but I kind of knew that deep down I had the power to unlock her power. I knew I had a better chance against future Doctor Gem by powering current Doctor Gem. I told her, "Sure. When we get close, I will activate your powers!"

Doctor Gem clapped excitedly. "You're a smart girl, Super Teen." She smiled. "You won't regret this!"

I realized that I didn't have much choice. If our time zone's Gem was really going to give future Gem a truly hard time, our Gem would need her powers back. Still, I already felt regret over my choice, or more precisely my lack of *good* choices.

When we got within a hundred miles of future Doctor Gem's location, MAC told us, "Cloaking you now. She'll still be able to hear and smell you but you should be invisible to her eyes. Remember to be careful of your thoughts because of her mind-reading powers."

"What? You didn't tell me that future me has mind-reading powers!" present day Doctor Gem said.

"It slipped my mind," I said, mostly because it did; mostly because I didn't think it would be that important.

Present day Doctor Gem smiled. "My, my; This gets better and better."

We closed in quickly. Even from miles away I could easily see future Doctor Gem laying there in all her body armor, sunning herself. She looked like she didn't have a fear or worry in the world. I hoped to change that.

When we landed, I told our Doctor Gem. "What do I need to do to activate your powers?"

First of all, get rid of these handcuffs!

Doctor Gem turned around and held her hands out behind her. I broke the chain of the handcuffs with a quick karate chop. She then lifted her hands to either side of her neck and pointed to a spot just below her ears. Just jolt me here.

Standing behind her, I placed my index fingers on (well near) the spots she had indicated. "I don't usually use my electric generating power," I warned.

"I can regulate your voltage," MAC offered.

"I need 1,700 volts," Doctor Gem said.

I concentrated on sending the electrical current from my body into my fingers. I felt myself crackle with energy. My hair rose from my head. My fingers jolted Doctor Gem. She shot forward. I released her from my grip. She turned and grinned at me.

"Ah, now that's the stuff!" she said.

"Did it work?" I asked.

Doctor Gem squeezed her fists together. She started to grow and grow, the broken handcuffs falling to the ground from each wrist. Soon she towered above me. She laughed, turned and ran off in the general direction of her future self.

"Yes, it worked," MAC said

"Yeah, I kind of gathered that, MAC, buddy," I said.

"Do you think she's going to stick to our deal?" MAC asked.

"No, of course not," I said, taking off after the bad doctor. "But that doesn't mean this still won't work out just like I wanted it to!"

Dear Diary: Yeah, I took a chance making Doctor Gem super again. I pretty much figured she would turn on me then try to convince her future robotic-self that she should work with her, as a team against me. I also figured she would try to double cross her

future self. I hoped her future self would know that.
Of course she would. She was her future self. Right?

The Fight

"Well, well, look who showed up…present time me," Future Doctor Gem laughed when she saw her current self, racing towards her. She held out a giant arm. "Stop! I don't want to hurt me!"

I watched the entire conversation unfold as I hovered over the two bad doctors.

Current Doctor Gem stopped in her tracks. "But I'm here to help you!"

"I have all your power and much more! I don't need your help!"

"But Super Teen has come to fight you…"

Future Doctor Gem laughed. "So? I defeated a far more powerful version of her. I can surely take down the old and inferior version." She smirked. "I give the little moron credit for thinking she had a chance. She has more guts than her future self."

"Probably just fewer smarts," present day Doctor Gem said. "Why else would she fly me here? Ha! The little fool actually thought I would help her before I helped you! But you are me! I always help me first."

"Yes, being you, I am aware of that." She shooed her other self away. "Now, I suggest you leave so I can crush this super teen alone." She leaned towards her other self. "I don't like sharing credit. I had to do it all those years with Doctor Dangerfield.

"But I am you!" the current Doctor Gem insisted.

"You are, but you are inferior and therefore unneeded. Now move along before I turn you into a giant pile of jello!"

"Ha!" Current Gem thrust a finger into her future

self's face. "You can't hurt me because I am you!"

"Foolish silly, past version of me...I'm not you from this world. I'm you from a slightly different world. Therefore, I can do whatever I want to you with no fear to me."

"Are you certain of that?" current Doctor Gem asked.

"Yes, yes I am because I don't remember having this conversation. And I am sure I would have remembered if it had happened in my world."

Current Doctor Gem nodded. "Yes, I must admit that is a good point. But *you* must admit, me being here helps your chances! I am the only ally you can trust!"

"Please, you are me, I don't trust you at all! Remember, I'm you with more experience and power and knowledge." She stomped down her foot. "Now, move before I move you myself!"

Current Doctor Gem eyed Future Gem's nice shiny blue robotic body armor. She focused her attention on the belt. "Love the armor!"

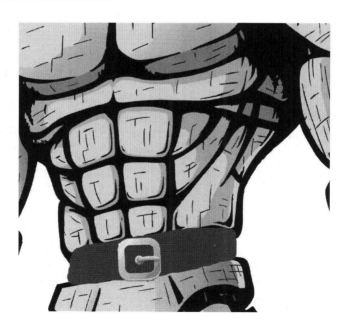

"Of course you do," Future Gem said, not bothering to hide how annoyed she was.

From cloaked up above, I smiled. Yep, my plan may not have been perfect but it certainly seemed to be working. I don't know what it is but somehow, when somebody comes in contact with another slightly different version of themselves, that drives them batty. I had to admit, I was glad it wasn't only me being driven crazy by future me. Now I had to figure out the best time for me to strike. My target would be future Doctor Gem's belt buckle. Once she was distracted enough, I would knock that thing off her.

"You know that little brat, Super Teen is probably here watching now!" current Doctor Gem said.

Future Doctor Gem pointed to her brain. "Duh. I am way smart. I know you just didn't walk here and you don't have the power to fly yet."

"She wanted me to work with her! I faked her out!"

Future Doctor Gem crossed her arms and snickered. "Could I have ever been as stupid?"

"What do you mean, future me?"

"She brought you here to drive me crazy and to get me to let my guard down!"

Present Doctor Gem stomped her foot. "No, she's not that smart! Nor is she that cunning!"

"I'm afraid we'll just have to agree to disagree." Future Doctor Gem shooed her away again. "Now, be gone! I don't want to have to turn you to jello, but I will." An evil smile drifted across her face. "Actually, now that I think about it, you'd make a great giant golden statue! You'd be like a monument to my power."

Looking down, I saw current Doctor Gem's face turn bright, bright red. My time to strike was drawing nearer. Still, I had to time this just right, and wait for the perfect moment. I felt fairly certain that current Gem was going to make a big mistake. That would be my time to hit future Gem.

Current Doctor Gem held up her arms. "Okay, okay. I get the message. You don't want or need me around. But no use turning me to gold. After all, you don't need money…"

"No, silly younger me, but you'd look so pretty as my lawn statue."

Current Doctor Gem took a few steps backward. She bowed. "Look, the world is pretty big, right? You can rule most of it. All I ask is that you give me an island. Maybe Hawaii…"

"Why should I give you anything?" future doctor Gem spat.

"Professional courtesy…one giant scientist turned world conqueror to another," current Doctor Gem said.

Her future self almost snickered. "You never conquered anything. You sat wasting away in prison. All powerless. You are a mere tool to distract me."

"Fine, fine, fine!" current Doctor Gem said. "I can tell when I'm not wanted."

"I'm actually not sure you can," future Doctor Gem said.

Current Doctor Gem turned and started walking away. I really didn't think her ego would let her walk away. I don't know, maybe her sense of self-preservation was greater than her ego. No… that couldn't be…

Current Doctor Gem darted back towards future Doctor Gem. Current Doctor Gem lowered her shoulder and slammed into future Doctor Gem's midsection. She pushed forward, trying to drive the future version of herself to the ground. "Ha! Prison taught me how to fight!"

I flew closer towards them. I locked my concentration on the belt buckle.

"You fool!" future Gem said. She grabbed current Doctor Gem and lifted her up by the throat. "My strength dwarves yours!" she chuckled. "I could snap you like a little twig."

"Ha, you can't hurt another version of yourself…"

Current Doctor Gem never finished that statement because she suddenly turned to gold.

"Oh, I like you so much better this way!" the remaining Doctor Gem laughed.

Leaning forward, I blasted Doctor Gem's belt buckle with my heat vision. The buckle snapped, the belt started to drop to the ground. "Oh no!" Doctor Gem said. She reached down and caught the belt. The belt turned to gold in her hand.

I could feel some of the power start to flow out of giant Doctor Gem. "NO!" she shouted. She turned to me. She stomped towards me. "You were a foolish fool to come here! Even without all the powers that have just drained from me, I'm still powerful enough to totally smash you!" She sent a huge fist towards me. I easily darted over her fist. Changing course, I zoomed at Doctor Gem, hitting her with an uppercut to the chin. Much to my surprise, my punch sent her flying upwards. She went soaring backward a good mile before she crashed to the ground. I flew over to her.

Doctor Gem laid there on the ground groaning. "Oh, my head..." She tried to sit up. She couldn't. "You win..." she moaned. "Dang, done in by my own power..."

I laughed. "Yeah, it would seem that way."

The bad doctor started to laugh. "The good news is, while I might be back to just my super strong self, your future self is stuck without her powers. By you tricking me into destroying the belt that stored those powers, Ultra's powers are now lost forever."

"MAC, has Ellie Mae delivered future me here?" I asked MAC.

"Check," MAC said.

A shimmering globe appeared maybe ten yards from where we were.

Natasha stepped out of the globe, followed by Zeke, Jason, Adam and Ellie Mae.

"Wow, I wasn't expecting this many of you?" I

gasped.

"We came to make sure you were alright!" Adam and Jason said.

"I just love teleporting," Zeke said.

Pointing at the downed bad doctor I said, "I'm more than just alright."

Natasha noticed that Gem no longer had her belt on. "What happened to the belt that has been holding my powers?" she asked.

"Ha! I accidentally turned it to gold after I turned that annoying other me into gold!" Gem laughed.

"Maybe Marie can turn it back and restore your powers?" Jason said to a now depressed Natasha.

"Ha! I felt the powers drain from it the second it turned to gold! You have lost them!" Gem laughed.

"You be quiet!" I told Doctor Gem.

I popped my boot off and directed it towards her.

I wiggled my foot in her direction as well. Gem gasped, turned blue and fell down, out cold. "That will keep her quiet," I said, slipping my boot back on before I KO'd my friends and possibly the entire hemisphere.

Walking up to Natasha, I put my hand on her shoulder and said, "Your powers aren't gone."

"No?" she asked.

"Nope. They transferred to me!" I said. "Now let me give those back to you."

"You…you would do that for me after I messed up so badly?" Natasha gasped. "You could be the most powerful person ever!"

I grinned. "Maybe someday, but I'm not ready for that power yet!"

Closing my eyes, I became one with my power and her power. In my mind, I could see the white and silver energy that held my power and Ultra's power. The beams were entwined. Concentrating, I slowly caused the white beams to unravel from the silver ones. I let the silver energy flow from me into future me.

Natasha / Ultra / future me smiled. Life came back into her eyes, actually into her entire face. "This is amazing!" she said. "I feel like me again!"

"Thank you so much, Lia!" future me said.

"You're welcome," Lia I told her.

We laughed.

"Can you get back to your world and time?" I asked.

The other me nodded. "Yes. I just need to figure out how to spin at the right speed to create the proper vibrations. That way I can create a quick gate between our different worlds and times."

"Man, I didn't understand a word of that but it sure makes sense to me!" Zeke said.

"Of course, when I came here I wasn't carrying a giant Gem Stone with me," future me said.

"Do you mean the actual Gem Stone or the evil mad

scientist?" Zeke asked.

"Well, technically I wasn't carrying either," future me said.

"I love the way you think!" Zeke grinned.

Ellie Mae came forward. "I can help!" she said. "I've been practicing with my powers so as soon as we're ready, we can go fight those slimes that Doctor Gem was talking about. Plus, all the slime action has made the gates between our times and worlds very accessible."

Ellie Mae stood there looking forward. She stretched out her arms, opening them wide. A piece of our world, our reality, seemed to turn over like a page in a book. We saw a shimmering world on the other side of the flipped open page.

"That's your time and your world," Ellie Mae said.

"Thanks," future me said.

Moving towards Doctor Stone, she pushed her through the rip in time, into her own time. Future Lia waved as she walked through the rip in time, behind Doctor Stone. "Thanks, guys! Great seeing you all again. Be safe!"

The hole in time closed up.

"I've contacted BMS labs. They have a crew coming to pick up Golden Gem and the belt," Jason said.

"Good," I said. "Can't have that belt falling into the wrong hands."

"Okay, Ellie, can you teleport us home now?" Jason asked.

Ellie's eyes glowed green.

"What the?" Jason said.

"Do not be alarmed, Jason and Lia. We are the combined slimes wwwoooogrooof... we need you to come to our world now. We have borrowed the girl known as Ellie Mae to create the gate between our dimensions. Superheroes, you are all needed in Dimension F-Minus now! PLEASE COME IMMEDIATELY!"

I looked at Jason. He looked at me. "Looks like we're

needed in another dimension!"

"I see that..." I said.

"You up for a trip to another dimension?" Adam asked me.

I smiled.

Yep, my life certainly was full of surprises!

***

THIS STORY IS CONTINUED IN DIARY OF A
SUPER CLONE – Book 4.
Be sure to read this fun and exciting series.
Perfect for both girls and boys!

Continue the exciting, action-packed story of Lia Stong (aka
Super Girl) in the next addition to the Diary of a Super Girl
series…
Diary of a Super Girl - Book 10: MORE TROUBLE!

OUT NOW!!

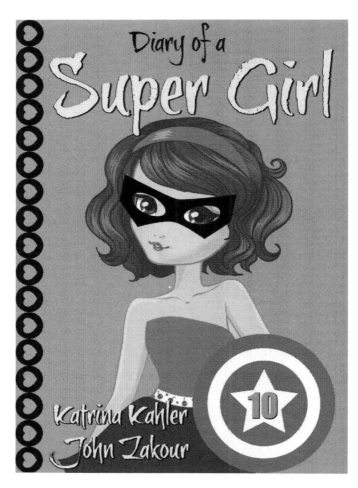

Read all about the combined adventures of Lia, Adam (aka Super Clone), Zeke the zombie and Lia's friend, Jason, as well as all the other members of Lia's super-powered team in…
Diary of a Super Clone – Books 1- 4.

You can read the entire series in a combined set at a DISCOUNTED PRICE!
This series is funnier than ever!

We hope that you enjoyed reading Diary of a Super Girl – Book 9:
The New Girl.
If you could leave a review, that would be awesome!
Thanks, heaps!
John and Katrina ☺

Some more cool books that you might like to check out…

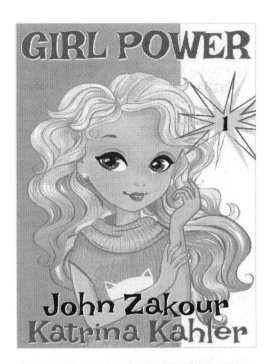

GIRL POWER

John Zakour
Katrina Kahler

Diary of a
SUPER CLONE

Katrina Kahler
John Zakour

About The Authors:

John Zakour is a humor / SF / fantasy writer with a Master's degree in Human Behavior. He has written thousands of gags for syndicated comics, comedians and TV shows (including Simpsons and Rugrats, and Joan River's old TV show.)
John has been a contributor to Nickelodeon magazine writing Fairly Odd Parents, Rugrats and Jimmy Neutron comic books. John currently writes Bart Simpsons comics for Bongo comics.

In the 80's and 90's, John was a computer programmer and web guru for Cornell University and was also an EMT and judo instructor. John currently lives in upstate NY with his wife, a professor at Cornell University. The two of them have one son, a student at Cornell. For exercise, John plays softball, is a competitive pickleball player and javelin thrower, and still hits his punching bag daily. To relax, John likes to play World of Warcraft, watch TV and do Tai Chi.

Find him on FB! ☺

Katrina Kahler is the bestselling author of Julia Jones Diary, Twins, Mind Reader, The Secret, Angel, Diary of a Horse Mad Girl and Julia Jones the Teenage Years.
       She lives in the beautiful coastal town of Noosa in Australia and has 2 grown-up children. Check out her other books at Best Selling Books for Kids.com

Like us on Facebook
https://www.facebook.com/FreeBooksForKids/

And follow us on Instagram
@freebooksforkids

Made in the USA
Middletown, DE
02 April 2020

87621441R00175